Starry Lake will have
on the next. A beautiful blend of romance, suspense,
recommend this great read!

— Lisa Elliott
Inspirational Speaker
and Award-Winning Author of *The Ben Ripple*
and *Dancing in the Rain*

L. D. Stauth's third book in the Campground Mysteries series, *Starry Lake* doesn't disappoint. L. D.'s writing style is down-to-earth, honest, and wonderfully addictive and I find each time I read her books, I have to stay tuned and read longer. Not only is *Starry Lake* another riveting story filled with mystery, intrigue, realistic characters, a dash of romance, a perfectly adorable little 'rapscallion' and clean humour, it is a story with an underlying faith message, complete with struggles and challenges. Oddly enough as I read *Starry Lake*, I was away camping. Linda's story was so believable, every so often I would look towards the dense bush and wonder, what if ... *Starry Lake* is a fine work of fiction and I would recommend it to anyone who enjoys a clean read, yet one filled with adventure and page-turning action.

— Glynis M. Belec
Co-creator of the *Chicken Soup for the Soul Series*
Author of *Jesus Washes Peter's Feet* and *Jailhouse Rock*
Angel Hope Publishing
www.glynisbelec.com

A Campground Mystery #3

STARRY LAKE

Dear Jillian,
God is Indescribable!
LD Stauth

L.D. STAUTH

STARRY LAKE
Copyright © 2018 by L.D. Stauth

All rights reserved. Neither this publication nor any part of this publication may be reproduced or transmitted in any form or by any means, electronic or mechanical, including photocopying, recording or any information storage and retrieval system, without permission in writing from the author.

This book is a work of fiction. Names, characters, incidents and setting (with the exception of a few named cities or towns) are fictitious and are a product of the author's imagination. Any similarity between persons (living or dead), places or events is purely coincidental.

Printed in Canada

ISBN: 978-1-4866-1584-1

Word Alive Press
119 De Baets Street, Winnipeg, MB R2J 3R9
www.wordalivepress.ca

WORD ALIVE PRESS

MIX
Paper from responsible sources
FSC FSC® C016245

Cataloguing in Publication may be obtained through Library and Archives Canada

*"He determines the number of the stars and calls them each by name.
Great is our Lord and mighty in power; his understanding has no limit."*
—Psalm 147: 4,5 (NIV-Zondervan 2011)

ACKNOWLEDGEMENTS

I can't believe *Starry Lake* is the third and final book in my Campground Mystery Series. I hope you have enjoyed the journey as you followed my characters: Maya and Kerrick, Blake and Karly, Harrison, Lily, and Jasmine.

During the creation of my novels it was a delight to share with you the joy of family, awe of nature, healing power of laughter, thrill of romance, and the all-encompassing joy and peace of God's love. Not to mention the apprehension of demented stalkers and murderers. :)

In case you were curious, the setting for each novel is an actual provincial park in Ontario, although I changed the names. Perhaps you recognized the area by the descriptions and maybe even camped there yourself.

The novel titles tell a story, in and of themselves.

Stormy Lake suggests that it is often through the storms of life that we realize our need of a Saviour. When we go through difficult times, He will be with us.

Lake of the Cross highlights the cross and demonstrates that God's invisible qualities, eternal power, and divine nature can be clearly seen by His creation.

Starry Lake reveals the peace, joy, and love that are available when we finally embrace the truth of Jesus Christ.

In June of 2018, *Stormy Lake* won a Word Award, sponsored by The Word Guild, for Best Suspense Novel of 2017. This was truly a humbling honour.

Thank you to those who have made my author journey a reality. Feedback from my readers is always welcome. And just to save you an email, yes, I realize that you paddle a canoe and row a boat (kind of messed that up a little in my first novel :) Please contact me at glstauth@sympatico.ca or you can follow me on Facebook at L.D. Stauth.

To think each star in the heavens has a name blows my mind. How about you?

L.D. Stauth

PROLOGUE

Blending into the dark row of evergreens, Harrison observed the bride and groom skipping out on their reception. He watched until the Cessna flew off into the starry night. A jealous pang knifed him in the chest. Although he was happy for his friends, the pain was almost unbearable. The wounds were still too fresh. He had loved Karly, but had to step aside, as her heart belonged to another. Why was he always too late? Would there ever be anyone for him?

And what was all this religious stuff? Was it for real? He didn't know Blake well, but Karly's newfound faith seemed genuine. Being the level-headed person that she was, he couldn't imagine her making a major decision like this without valid reason.

Harrison sighed. Coming to this wedding was a big mistake. With his body weak from the recent trauma and his spirits low, he could barely find the energy to stand upright. Harrison tensed when a slender hand found its way into his palm.

Raven!

He withdrew his hand like he would from a hot stove. "What are you doing?"

"I thought maybe we could start over and put the past behind us, my puppy dog."

"We've been through this before. It will never work. And, I'm not your puppy dog."

"Don't you find me attractive?" A delicate finger traced a path up his arm.

He brushed her hand away. "You're attractive, Raven, but there's more to a relationship than appearances."

"But we were happy once, weren't we? Until that two-timing relationship wrecker came along and stole you from me."

"That's not how it happened, and you shouldn't speak ill of the dead. You and I were having our own problems. Jessica just brought them to the surface."

"We were having problems? What were they?" Raven stepped in front of him, partially obscuring his view of the moonlit lake.

"Raven, I don't have the energy to re-hash things with you. Just believe me, we're through. Along with everything else, your spiteful and vindictive actions the last few years have cemented my decision to end our engagement."

"*My* actions? Really? You should be lucky I would want you back after *your* despicable behaviour," Raven snarled, poking a finger at his chest for emphasis.

"My behaviour?" He was aware his voice was raising several decibels, but he didn't care. There was no one around anyway.

"You practically drooled all over Jessica, and then Karly, and the whole community knew it. Now you look like a sad puppy who's lost and can't find his way home."

Harrison's anger suddenly deflated. The truth slammed into him like a ton of bricks, her words hitting home with an intensity he wasn't prepared for. For a moment he remained silent, reeling from the impact. Then he took a deep breath.

"You're right, Raven, I'm sad and lost. For the last few years, I've been travelling in circles, getting nowhere, trapped in a life that has done nothing but disappoint me. I don't know the answer, but one thing is clear; it isn't you."

"That was harsh," Raven huffed. "Fine, have it your way." She whirled her tiny body around with amazing speed, flew through the line of trees like a nighthawk in flight, and disappeared into the blackness that was as dark and abysmal as his soul.

As he dropped to his knees, every ounce of him spent, a sob left his mouth and echoed across the water. The despondency in his soul was crippling. He welcomed the stabbing discomfort in his side that his impulsive action caused. Pain was a welcome distraction from his hellish downward tailspin.

He'd never felt this low his whole life. Deeper and deeper he spiralled into the menacing chasm of gloom and desolation. Would the emptiness ever go away?

A searing hand touched his shoulder and a bolt of heat sprinted through his body. The sensation was so ethereal that his senses reeled. What had just happened? He looked around. No one was near.

A flicker of hope stirred deep within his chest. Faint at first, it grew in intensity until it propelled him to his feet. Something wonderful was happening and he couldn't help but embrace it. It was tangible and swallowing him whole.

Something was out there. Something more real than anything he'd ever experienced in his entire life. Harrison twirled in a circle, his hands high in the air. Crazy—but he almost felt like dancing.

He gazed across the moonlit lake and blinked. *Is that...?* No, it couldn't be. It had to be a reflection from trees or a structure nearby. But there was nothing around except dense bush. Nothing manmade that could account for its presence. And it hadn't been there a minute ago.

A shiver ran through him as he stared at the silhouette of a cross on the surface of the lake. With it came an inexplicable and bizarre desire to remove his sandals—even though the thought made no sense to him.

Barefoot and gazing at the cross, he couldn't help but feel, even in his infantile knowledge of God, that the place he was standing was holy ground.

CHAPTER ONE

As Harrison Somerville rounded the heavily treed and secluded section of campground road, an ear-piercing, heart-halting screech assaulted his ears with such intensity that a bolt of fear charged through his body, leaving a sour taste in his mouth. Slamming his foot on the brake, breath coming fast, his eyes scanned all directions before he turned off the engine.

Where had that noise come from? His insides churned like the turbulent waters of a thunderstorm on Lake Huron. With it, a horrifying thought ran through his brain, almost freezing him to his seat. Piney Campground was without a doubt the busiest park he had ever been employed at. People and children were everywhere. Had he crushed a child beneath his wheels as he absentmindedly patrolled the campground?

With trepidation, he stepped from his vehicle just as another yell assailed him from directly above his head. Gaze shooting upward, he caught a glimpse of a pair of scrawny bare legs attached to polka-dotted purple and white shorts, dangling in mid-air.

"Don't just stand there and stare. Help me down, mister."

As the young girl's bossy command left her mouth, a pink flip-flop fell from her foot and bounced off his face. Harrison made a quick assessment of the precarious situation. *I need to think of something fast.* Thin as a rail and hanging by one arm from a low-hanging branch of the oak tree about ten feet above him, the girl probably didn't have the strength to last much longer.

Before he had a chance to come up with a plan, her petite body plummeted. He opened his arms in time to accept her lightweight frame. Although she wasn't heavy, he stumbled forward a step at the impact, but managed to regain his balance.

"Thanks," she smiled, keeping her left fist closed tightly over an object in her hand. "Your timing was impeccable. Now put me down."

Impeccable? Harrison held back a smile as he set her on her feet. "Do you make a habit of climbing trees? And where are your parents?"

"It's just me and my mom. I left her relaxing at the campsite, reading her book and enjoying her afternoon tea. She needs her alone time. I'm quite a handful."

Harrison Somerville crossed his arms and attempted to glare at the high-spirited girl, likely about ten years of age, squelching the grin that was desperately attempting to break through to his face. "Is that so? What's in your hand?"

"Nothing."

The park naturalist squatted to her level and frowned. "It's an egg, isn't it? Do you hear that frantic squawking? Mother bird is already crying because her baby is missing."

The eyes of the small child darted back and forth through the trees as distressed shrieks pierced the air. A guilty look crossed her dirt-smudged face, but it quickly disappeared. "Preposterous," she snapped, nose tilted upward. "I have no idea what you're talking about."

"Oh, I think you do," he challenged, just as a cacophony of strange sounds—a skidding noise, spraying gravel, and a loud thud—reached his ears. He spun around. A young woman had driven her bicycle into the back of his parked truck. She lay on her side, the bicycle on top of her.

Harrison jumped up and raced to the woman's aid, lifting the bike, with one wheel still rotating, from atop her. The little girl screamed again—a screech that could literally stop a grown man's heart. As Harrison dropped to one knee to check the woman's injuries, the little girl was suddenly at his side.

When she draped her small torso across the woman's prone frame, his eyebrows drew together. Before Harrison could figure out the connection between the two, the child let loose.

"Mom. Don't die! It would be unbearable if you left me. I know you'd be going to heaven, but I don't want you to leave yet." Torrents of tears ran down the child's face as she yanked on her mother's arm. "Come on now. Get up. You can do it. It's just a scrape. Pull yourself together."

The woman opened her eyes and blinked. Then she blinked again. "Do something, Mister. Please help my mom."

Harrison extended a hand toward the prone cyclist. "Are you okay, miss?"

Ignoring his offer, she sat up. Awkwardly, she stumbled to her feet. Her tan-coloured shorts were smeared with dust and oil from the road and her short, wavy, russet-coloured hair stuck up at weird angles. With her yellow tank top, her entire appearance reminded Harrison of a Cedar Waxwing. The crazy thought of likening the woman to a bird lodged in his brain. Before he knew it, the grin he'd been trying to hold back broke through to his face.

"Why are you smiling? Do you think it's funny that my mom could have died?" The young child's enormous jet-black eyes drilled him.

Harrison sobered. He hadn't realized his thoughts were so easily read. Although he *had* been told before that he carried his emotions on his sleeve. Apparently on his face too.

"Good grief, Jasmine. Aren't you the drama queen. I'm not going to die. I just had a little accident." The woman brushed twigs from her shorts and patted the top of her head to flatten her unruly hair. When her hazel eyes met his, her cheeks flushed a rosy pink.

"Are you in need of first aid?" Harrison pointed at a trail of blood making its way from her scraped right knee to her one shoeless foot.

"No, thank you. I'm fine. Nothing a little bandage won't cure." She hobbled toward the wayward sandal, picked it up, shook it free of gravel, and slid her foot into it.

Harrison glanced at the child, who was still without her flip-flop, and couldn't help but compare mother and daughter at that moment. Both seemed to have trouble keeping their shoes on their feet.

"And don't forget the antibiotic ointment." The young child put a finger in the air. "By the way, Mom, why did you ride your bicycle into the back of that man's truck? Weren't you watching where you were going?"

The woman's cheeks grew deeper crimson. "I was looking for you." Her voice cracked. "How many times have I told you to stay on the campsite? No wandering off without me. You could get yourself injured or lost or..."

The young girl sighed and tossed her head from side to side. "I know. A bad man could take me. Honestly, Mom, you worry too much."

Ignoring that, the woman turned to Harrison. "I'm Lily Martin." A shaking hand suddenly thrust itself toward him. "I'm really sorry about your truck. Did I damage it?"

He clasped her trembling hand. "Harrison Somerville. The truck is fine. I'm more concerned about you. Are you sure you're okay?"

When she nodded, Harrison let go of her. "I think you should be aware of what happened here a few minutes ago. I was patrolling the campground when your daughter's screams alerted me. I found her dangling from that branch by one hand." He pointed upwards.

Lily's eyes widened as she covered her mouth with a hand. "Jasmine. How many times have I told you not to climb trees? It's dangerous and not very lady-like."

"I don't want to be a lady." The belligerent child stomped her one sandaled foot on the road, scattering small stones. "Besides, I saw the nest earlier and I wanted to check it out."

"Jasmine Martin." Lily's voice raised a notch. "What's that in your hand? Did you steal an egg?"

Whipping her clenched hand behind her back, the insolent child clamped her lips tightly together and glared at her mother.

Not having children of his own, Harrison keenly observed the mother-daughter scene. What happened next surprised him, since he had already been leaning toward the assumption that this young mother had entirely no control over her pugnacious child.

"Hand it over." Lily extended a palm.

The child opened her fingers to reveal a crushed blue shell, then broke into wails that could have been heard from the space station. "Now look what you made me do."

"Stop carrying on right now. I've had quite enough of your outbursts. Get your flip-flop and march right back to the tent, where you will take a time-out and think about what you did." Lily gestured down the road.

Her daughter took one step in that direction, but her mother stopped her with a firm hand on her shoulder.

"One more thing before you go." The mother spoke loudly enough to be heard over her daughter's sobs. "You owe this man an apology for having to take time from his busy duties to rescue a naughty child."

"That's okay, Mrs. Martin. It wasn't an inconvenience. I was patrolling..."

But when she held up a hand toward him, he closed his mouth.

"We're waiting, Jasmine."

Mercifully, the wails reduced in intensity, dropping to whimpers and then to an occasional hiccup. "I'm sorry." As the child's lower lip quivered, an object appeared in his peripheral vision, barrelling toward him at a high rate of speed. He ducked just in time to avoid being divebombed by a frantic female robin.

Harrison shook his head and looked down at the little girl. "That mother bird is really angry."

When the bird flew between the branches of a tree and dove at their heads again, Jasmine's eyes grew large. She dropped the crushed egg, covered her head with her hands, and ran down the road, screaming all the way.

Harrison laughed. Perhaps Jasmine would think twice before raiding a bird's nest again. But when he looked at Lily Martin, she did not appear amused. Not at all. In fact, her lower lip quivered as though she might burst into tears at any moment.

The urge to laugh fled as Harrison bent over, picked up her bicycle, and held it towards her. She took it without a word, grimacing as she swung her leg over the bar. As he watched her pedal away, her back-tire wobbling, the frenzied robin made a last-ditch attempt to torment him. Harrison dove into the safety of his truck, closed the door, and breathed a sigh of relief. It was only a bird, but nature could be terrifying at times.

As Harrison reached for his key, images of the last few minutes replayed in his head. He hoped the panicked attack of the mother robin had been enough to scare Jasmine into leaving nature alone.

More importantly, he hoped the child had learned the importance of listening to her mother. If he hadn't come along when he did, her fall from the tree might have resulted in serious injuries.

And speaking of injuries, I hope Lily Martin is okay.

He started the truck and drove slowly along the campground road, his nerves still reeling from the last few minutes. He couldn't help but shake his head.

What a strange day.

CHAPTER TWO

Harrison stared at the full moon that glimmered across the calm waters of Lake Huron and fought the feelings of depression and sadness attempting to overtake him. This was a bad idea, gawking at the large luminescent lunar ball. Why did he continue to put himself through this?

It had been ten months since his quest had begun—ten months since he had run away from his job, friends, family, and everything familiar, in search of... he wasn't even sure what. So far, each full moon had accomplished nothing but remind him of his past failures. Yet, an inexplicable compulsion drove him to this odd, self-inflicted, lunar ritual each month.

Harrison plunked himself down on a large piece of driftwood, stretched out his legs and crossed them at the ankles. Despite his best efforts, memories flooded back and sank him deeper into the pit of despair. They began almost four years ago with his broken engagement to Raven George, a waitress in the small town of Aspen Ridge, Ontario.

At first, her alluring indigo eyes and shiny midnight-black hair drew him. But her outward beauty quickly faded when he discovered her insides were as ugly as a turkey vulture.

So, when Jessica Wakely, a stunning blonde, was hired at No Trace Campground, he was very drawn to her. That revelation helped Harrison to see that he wasn't ready for marriage, and his engagement to Raven was wrong. So, he ended it.

But Jessica had a long-time boyfriend and made it clear that she wasn't interested in Harrison, beyond friendship.

Then, in a cruel twist of fate, Jessica vanished. And Harrison was accused of her murder. For two long years, he lived under the burden of suspicion, until her body was found, and the killer finally revealed—a middle-aged park employee named Heather who had, ironically, murdered Jessica out of a secret, demented love for him.

As if his heart had not already suffered enough damage, Karly Foster came into the picture. Another employee, she was hired as a park naturalist at No Trace Campground about two years ago. Feisty, head-strong, and gorgeous, he couldn't help but fall head-over-heels for the tall, slim blonde.

He knew her feelings for him were not quite where his were, but at least her friendship was real. Patiently, he waited for her feelings to catch up, but then another unforeseen event had sent him reeling backwards again into loneliness and despair.

An ex-boyfriend of Karly's had unexpectedly appeared in her life after three years, and they were married before the month was out under a full moon. It was not like they had even planned to meet again. It just happened. Was there a power out there that controlled such things?

Harrison slapped his palms on the sun-bleached branch. Then his shoulders slumped.

For some reason, he couldn't be angry at Karly or her husband Blake. Despite the situation, the three had become good friends. Maybe it was the horrendous danger they had all faced, being tracked by Heather during the annual No Trace Canoe Race. Maybe it was the life-threatening injury he'd sustained when Heather had stabbed him in the side and left him to die.

Due to Blake's faith in God, Karly had made a life-changing decision and chosen to put her faith in that same God. From what he knew of Karly, she was a strong, intelligent woman. Even for the love of a man, she wouldn't pretend to adopt new beliefs just to please her husband. Maybe God *was* something to consider.

Harrison uncrossed his legs, pressed his hands on the driftwood and got to his feet. Hands stuffed in his pockets, he ambled along the beach in the darkness, oblivious to the night hawk squawking loudly above. His mind wandered back to his ethereal encounter when he'd seen the cross on the water and felt that touch on his shoulder. That experience had left him with such an impression that soon after he left his job at No Trace and made a drastic move to Piney Campground on the shores of Southern Lake Huron. But was it all for naught?

A teenage girl's laughter reached his ears as a group of young people jumped in the lake, several feet ahead of him. He had a sudden urge to do the same. Forget the worries and cares of this life and just throw himself into the water, laughing. This truth trek was just too hard.

When was the last time he had laughed without inhibition? Harrison smirked, remembering his encounter with Jasmine Martin and her mother. Did that even count as a laugh, given that his outburst seemed inappropriate at the time?

He had learned one thing over the last few months. Although his move had come at the expense of leaving behind his aging mother and the security and familiarity of his job in Northwestern Ontario, it wasn't all bad.

Piney Campground was one of the busiest around with over a thousand campsites spread out over more than six thousand acres, with three main campgrounds and ten trails.

It was home to the globally rare Oak Savanna forest, sixty butterfly species, and, most importantly, hundreds of bird species. Having his Masters in Ornithology, that was his love and area of expertise.

As a park naturalist, nothing compared to leading a group of enthusiastic birders into the bush. In the spring, the search for warblers could consume him if he wasn't careful.

Harrison sighed as he shuffled through thick sand toward the wooden staircase. He really liked it here. So why was he so sad? Why so unfulfilled? Was it his longing for a family? He wasn't getting any younger; his fortieth birthday was fast approaching.

His foot on the bottom step, he turned and took one last look over his shoulder at the teasing lake and the mocking moon, half-hoping for another miraculous divine intervention, but feeling more like a fool. So far, he had no answers on his pilgrimage to discover the true meaning of life.

No cross glimmered across the water. No searing hand touched his shoulder. No supernatural feeling of holiness consumed him and gave him hope.

Perhaps he had imagined it all. There was no God. No truth. No love. A heaviness settled in his chest. The longer he went without answers, the more likely that possibility existed.

He tore his gaze from the pitted orange ball. The despair was so great, he could almost feel it wrapping itself around him like a boa constrictor attempting to squeeze his life away.

As he trudged up the wooden staircase in his hiking boots, one thing was clear. This lunar trek for truth couldn't go on indefinitely. There was a limit to his endurance.

If he didn't have an answer soon, he'd give up this crazy pilgrimage and believe what he'd always believed. Life was only what you made it.

CHAPTER THREE

Lily Martin tossed and turned all night long. Judging by the chirping sounds that were beginning to seep through the canvas tent, it had to be very early dawn.

No matter how hard she tried, she couldn't get comfortable. At thirty-four years of age, hitting the back of a parked vehicle, while riding a bicycle, didn't come without physical consequences. How could she have been so careless?

Her right knee and elbow throbbed in unison, and her left side was bruised and tender from the bicycle's handlebar that had stabbed into her on impact.

But the physical pain paled in comparison to the mental. Ramming into the back of the park truck was humiliating enough, but her daughter's rebellious behaviour was even worse. Hence the reason for her accident—a desperate search for a missing child. Being a single mom was hard.

Lily stifled a groan as her daughter's knee jabbed her in the back. At this rate, morning couldn't come fast enough. She'd love to get up and make herself a coffee but moving now would awaken Jasmine. Although she loved her daughter dearly, she wasn't quite ready to face another day—especially not one like yesterday. She felt so inadequate to be Jasmine's mother.

To add to her restless night, memories of her failed marriage flooded in unannounced. Both hands flew up and held the sides of her head. What did she hope to accomplish with a journey down nightmare lane?

Ross Martin had been a popular young man in the College and Career group, and extremely handsome to boot. Although he hadn't attended her church while growing up, he became a regular attendee from the age of eighteen when invited by a friend. His faith seemed genuine as he often played his guitar on the worship team and participated in youth events and weekly Bible studies.

Lily was attracted to him, but he rarely took notice of her. He did seem interested in almost every other girl in the group, however. And no one seemed to mind his flirtatious ways; in fact, he was the secret desire of every girl's heart.

So, when he finally asked Lily out, she was skeptical. Deep inside she figured she was just another notch in his growing list of conquests, but despite her inhibitions, she fell for his charming ways, smooth talk, and declarations of undying affection.

Everyone was shocked when they became engaged. The rumor was that quiet, unassuming Lily had tamed the handsome prince.

How could she have been so wrong about him? That was one of the questions that haunted her night and day. The other was equally upsetting. How could he call himself a Christian and behave that way?

The hardest part to understand was why God would allow her to go through such a painful thing. Why didn't he warn her?

Her husband's first indiscretion came a few months into their marriage when she was newly pregnant with their daughter. She thought her world had been ripped right out from underneath her. His betrayal shattered her happy life into jagged pieces.

After his heartfelt confession, counseling, and a promise to never ever stray again, she reluctantly took him back. What a fool. She should have called it quits the first time.

The second tryst happened after Jasmine started kindergarten and carried on until last year. For five years she suspected something, but this time he was smarter and covered his tracks with cunning and deceit.

All those late nights at the office and weekend business trips out of town set off alarms. But over and over he denied anything was going on, constantly accusing her of harbouring unforgiveness.

To cast doubt on his infidelity, he flung Scripture at her. She remembered one of his favourite lines, when she would give in to her suspicions and confront him, "How many times does God ask you to forgive? Isn't it seventy times seven? And you can't even do it once?"

When his adultery was finally exposed for the second time, she was done.

Less than a year ago, she became a single mom on paper. Realistically, she'd been a single mom all along. Not only had Ross failed to be a husband to her, he had never really been a father to Jasmine.

It was despicable enough of him to break their wedding vows and promises. But to ignore their beautiful, unique, and gifted child tore at her insides and made her angry. He didn't even want parental visiting rights. It was as if he wished to erase any connection to his former wife or life.

Would she ever get over the pain and rejection or understand why?

But when she opened her eyes and stared at the pretty little darkhaired beauty beside her, she knew one of the reasons. God had given her Jasmine.

CHAPTER FOUR

"Mom, your back tire is going to fall off," Jasmine yelled from behind her.

Lily cast a quick glance over her shoulder at the offending tire. "I think it'll be okay. Besides, I promised we would hike the Turkey Trail today." Lily wasn't exactly sure how long the wheel would stay attached. When it came to mechanical things, she was not so inclined. She just hoped and prayed that somehow it would function properly for the remainder of the trip, at least until she could get it home and have her father look at it.

A warm feeling flowed through her at the thought of her parents. They had been a lifeline to her through all the ups and downs of her troubled ten-year marriage. Without them, her church family, and ultimately God, she had no idea how she would have made it through.

Because of the generosity of her parents and wise financial planning, she was able to afford the mortgage on her small home. Sadly, Ross was one of those dead-beat dads, negligent in his responsibilities. In fact, she hadn't seen or heard from him since the divorce. It was as if he had disappeared off the face of the planet.

Lily pedalled hard toward the sharp incline ahead of her. It took every ounce of strength she had to get up the hill. Yesterday's crash was not only physically and emotionally distressing, but the damaged bicycle required extra exertion.

Sweat dribbled down her forehead and stung her eyes. Even at ten o'clock in the morning, the sun was blazing hot. Of course, it *was* the middle of July.

Relief flooded through her when she spotted the sign for the trail. She pedalled across the parking lot and guided her damaged vehicle into the metal bike rack. Jasmine did the same. Lily arched her shoulders back and did a few shoulder shrugs to stretch out her taut muscles. Why had she chosen one of the most difficult trails in the park, today of all days, considering her aching body?

Then she remembered. Last year, while camping with her parents, they had spotted two large turkey vultures sitting on a dead branch near the highest point of the trail. Jasmine had been so excited at the discovery that even a year later she hoped they would still be there.

Lily marvelled at her daughter's naivety, but at the same time loved her enthusiasm. Jasmine had a remarkable memory and knowledge of God's creation. The child was like a sponge, absorbing anything nature-related. In fact, Lily couldn't keep up with her thirst for knowledge.

"Hurry up, Mom. You're slower than Uncle Bobby with the gimpy leg."

"Jasmine, don't be disrespectful." Lily chugged another swig of water, re-capped her bottle, and started up the trail. Every step brought discomfort, but she'd never complain. Her daughter didn't need to add concern for her mother's injuries to her list of insecurities. Jasmine suffered enough with an absentee father; her biggest fear was losing her mother, as evidenced by the frantic outburst yesterday.

Could Lily blame her? If anything happened to her, her parents were young and healthy enough to gladly take Jasmine under their wings. That thought brought comfort, but it wouldn't help relieve Jasmine's fears. Ten minutes of steep climbing later, her daughter stopped.

"This is the spot." Jasmine scrunched up her nose. "And they're not here."

"Are you sure? I thought it was a little farther up the trail."

"No, I know because I scratched my initials here." Jasmine grabbed her hand and led her to a wooden bench nearby. "See, it says J.M."

"Oh, Jasmine, I don't think you should have marked park property like that."

Jasmine's shoulders lifted. "Will you look at all the other initials carved here? It's a thing people do. Honestly, Mom, you have so many rules."

"Just because others do it, doesn't make it right." Lily placed her hands on her hips.

Jasmine stuck out her lower lip. "It doesn't matter anyway. The vultures are gone."

"Let's continue on to the lookout at the top of the trail. Maybe we'll see some there."

Jasmine trailed behind her, kicking at stones in their path and clearly sulking. Within a few minutes, they climbed the steps to a platform. Joy raced through Lily at the view. From the highest point in the park, she could see the patchwork of fertile farmer's fields, towering grain silos, a verdant blanket of trees, and the glistening sapphire waters of Lake Huron. Although she'd witnessed the magnificent panoramic delight several times, she never tired of it.

"Isn't God amazing?" Lily whispered, her hazel eyes wide.

"True, but he'd be even more spectacular if he threw in a few turkey vultures."

"Maybe they're out for breakfast," Lily offered with a grin. "I wonder what they'd be eating?"

"Fresh carrion, I would think. Did you know that turkey vultures have such a keen sense of smell that they can detect gasses produced from decaying carcasses?" Jasmine held a finger in the air as she often did while spouting interesting facts.

"No, I can't say that I knew that." Lily shook her head. Her daughter's intelligence never ceased to amaze her. "I guess we're out of luck today. Do you want to head back?"

"No way, I'm staying until I see one. Those scavengers love to soar on thermal air currents and the top of this trail is a very good place to do that."

Lily flopped down on the wooden bench and stretched out in the hot sun. "Suit yourself. I'll just take a little rest."

As Lily closed her eyes, her daughter's small hand brushed her bangs off her forehead. "You relax, poor little lamb. You must be exhausted. I'll peruse the area while you take a tiny cat nap."

Peruse the area? Poor little lamb? Lily smiled at Jasmine's choice of words—a combination of her intelligence and an endearing phrase she'd picked up from spry old Mrs. Groves. Last Easter, Jasmine had accompanied Lily as she sang with the church choir for the seniors at The Garden's Nursing Home. Jasmine and Mrs. Groves instantly bonded, especially after Jasmine stuck her finger in a birdcage and the feisty cockatoo snipped at it and drew blood. Mrs. Groves tended to her daughter's injury, calling her a poor little lamb.

Jasmine was a unique child. And Lily loved her with all her heart.

Lily yawned deeply. A catnap sounded so inviting. Despite her aching muscles, the wooden bench felt as comfortable as a pillow-top mattress. With the warm sunlight and caressing breeze, she felt her body relaxing.

When a dark shadow blocked the sun's rays, Lily opened her eyes. A man in sunglasses and a black ball cap stared down at her. She bolted upright so quickly, her head spun. "Can I help you?"

"I'm good, thanks. Just checking on you. You seemed dead to the world."

"Jasmine!" Lily's feet hit the platform. "Where's my daughter?"

"There's a little dark-haired girl perched in the bush with binoculars aimed at a turkey vulture. Is that her?" The man pointed to the trail below.

"Yes, that would be her, thank you. I'm going to kill her. She's always running off." Lily got to her feet.

The man chortled, deep and hoarse. "That's cruel and unusual punishment, I'd say."

"Of course," Lily back-pedalled. "It was only a figure of speech."

She reached for her water bottle, scrambled down the stairs, hit the dirt trail, and took off running. An uneasiness came over her and she looked up. The man stared down at her over the platform's railing.

"Take care, Lily." He waved.

Lily swallowed the lump in her throat and picked up her pace. The uneasiness intensified. How did he know her name? A few steps around the first bend in the trail, she spotted her daughter. "Jasmine. How many times...?"

"Shush, mom, you'll scare Fred."

"Don't be shushing me. Fred?"

"He looks just like our old neighbour with the sunburned bald head and hook nose. So, that's what I named him."

A rapid flapping of wings and the vulture was airborne.

"Now look what you've gone and done." The child stomped her foot. "You frightened him off."

"That's the least of your worries. How many times do I have to tell you not to go off on your own?"

"But you were sleeping, and I saw Fred land in that tree right there." Jasmine's eyes filled with tears. "It wasn't far, and I figured I'd be back before you even knew I was missing."

"You figured wrong. Am I going to have to give you another time-out in the tent?"

Tears spilled down her child's bright pink cheeks, already flushed from the heat. "You just don't understand. No one understands," Jasmine wailed and took off running.

In a few steps, Lily caught up with her daughter. She hugged her tightly. "Mommy's not mad, honey. I was just worried." As she rubbed the back of her daughter's head, she remembered the strange man and held her daughter out at arms' length.

"Listen, sweetie, I'm sure we'll see more vultures. I'm sorry I scared Fred, but I have something very important to ask you."

Jasmine lifted her small face and made a swipe at her dripping nose with the back of her hand. "What?"

"Did you see a man on the trail with a black ball cap and sunglasses?"

Her daughter's head moved up and down.

"Did he talk to you?"

"Yes."

"What did he say?"

"He was very nice. Did you know he likes turkey vultures too?"

"What else did he say?"

"He asked me why I was all alone in the bush, and I told him that I wasn't alone—that my mom was right up there having a nap."

"Did he bother you?"

"No."

Lily's grip on her daughter's shoulders tightened slightly. "Now listen very carefully. Did you tell that man my name?"

Jasmine's forehead wrinkled. "No... yes... I can't remember. Why? You look worried, Mom."

"I'm fine, honey. Let's get back to the campsite and make some lunch. I'm starved." Lily tickled her daughter until tiny giggles burst forth. She assumed a runner's stance. "I'll race you back to our bikes. On your mark. Get set. Go!"

As they hurried back down the trail, jumped on their bikes, and pedalled away, Lily couldn't help but glance repeatedly behind her. They didn't see the man again, but something didn't feel right. How did he know her name? Perhaps she'd met him before and didn't remember. That's probably all it was. Like her daughter constantly reminded her, she worried too much.

Or did she?

CHAPTER FIVE

Harrison sauntered across the rolling boardwalk, admiring the work and dedication that 'Friends of Piney Campground' had accomplished over the last few years. With financial donations and hours of sweat, volunteers had taken on the project with a goal to protect and preserve the sand dunes. Together, they had constructed several boardwalks which could be rolled out and back, depending on the season.

Hands on hips, Harrison looked around and smiled as he observed healthy Pitcher's Thistle, Yellow Puccoon, and Bearberry. Without the boardwalk, their growth may not be possible, since sand dune vegetation was extremely vulnerable. The project appeared to be working.

As he made his way toward the beach, trickles of sweat slid between his shoulder blades. It was another hot and humid day, meaning the beach would be teeming with throngs of people hoping to refresh themselves in the cooler waters of Lake Huron.

As he broke through the tree line and stepped from the boardwalk, an on-shore breeze refreshed him. A hand flew up to shield his eyes as the glare of the sun on the water was blinding. He fished his sunglasses out of his shirt pocket and donned them.

That was better. And he was right. Two o'clock in the afternoon and there was barely a free spot of beach as far as the eye could see in either direction. The beach ran for ten kilometres and was one of the most beautiful he had ever seen. Lots of sand and shallow water made for great swimming and relaxing.

Multi-coloured umbrellas dotted the landscape while beach balls and Frisbees sailed through the air. Children filled pails with water and lugged them back and forth to construct sandcastles.

All alone, a toddler with water-wings ambled awkwardly through the sand toward the lake. Harrison relaxed as the child's mother jumped up from the towel she'd spread across the sand to scoop him up into her arms.

Off to Harrison's left, a family played a game of bocce ball. Just beyond that, a pair of pre-teen boys filled cups with lake water and doused two sun-bathing girls about their age. After the girls yelled hysterically, they took off in hot pursuit of the boys.

Harrison sighed, the weight of last night's moon-gazing returning with a vengeance. He turned and clomped back across the boardwalk. No sense dwelling on what he couldn't change. It was time to get back to work.

Harrison climbed into his truck and headed toward the canoe rental dock at the Placid River. As he drove over the bridge, he wasn't surprised to see the river dotted with canoes, kayaks, and hydro bikes. Campers were taking advantage of the hot weather and enjoying time on the water.

He parked his truck in the Piney Store parking lot and strolled past several patrons, faces and shoulders red from the sun, lined up for ice-cream cones at the newly-constructed snack shop. He tipped his hat at a few familiar faces as he passed. After waiting for several cars and a family of four on bicycles to pass by, he crossed the road, leaned on the railing, and watched as many fished from the wooden dock below.

A child caught his eye. She reached into a package of hotdogs and broke off a chunk. Harrison nodded. He'd often seen people use wieners as bait. The young girl attached the chunk to the end of a hook that dangled from a piece of fishing line, tied to a long thin branch. He blinked. Someone had made their own fishing pole? Now that was rarely done anymore.

As soon as the section of meat hit the water, a school of eager fish surrounded the bait, fighting for the treat. The young girl's excitement grew when the wiener was instantly snagged by a small but colourful sunfish.

A large snapping turtle came out of nowhere and swam toward the sunfish, swallowing it whole before the girl could yank her line from the water. Harrison grimaced. That poor old snapper would soon discover that he had gotten more than he bargained for. Now the young child had a turtle attached to the end of her hook, the weight of it bending and stressing the homemade rod. She teetered on the edge of the dock.

The horrific screech the panicking child emitted slammed his heart against his ribcage. Even his palms began to sweat. That peace-shattering sound couldn't belong to anyone other than the tiny rascal he had rescued from the tree yesterday.

When she turned and yelled for her mom, Harrison' suspicions were confirmed. The deafening squeal did indeed come from Jasmine Martin.

Lily rushed down the dock. Harrison held his breath. A turtle of that size could easily pull a child of that meager weight into the river before anyone could stop it. He let out his breath in a rush when Lily reached her daughter and grabbed the pole for support.

Harrison hurried down the steps and made his way through the curious crowd of on-lookers. "Can I be of assistance?"

Enormous jet-black eyes, almost too large for Jasmine's face, met his. They were wide with excitement. "Hey, you're the man from yesterday."

"Yes." He nodded. "I am."

"Look what I caught? Isn't it just so... catastrophic?"

It nearly was. Harrison smirked. "I believe that would be classified as the catch of the day."

"I think I'll take you up on your offer of assistance since my mom has a sore arm from her accident yesterday. She'll be useless in bringing this sucker in. His pull is strong."

A few chuckles rippled across the small crowd. Harrison cast a quick glance at Lily, whose cheeks and neck had flushed a deeper red than they had the day before, after her header into the back of his truck. Now an explosion of freckles dotted her nose and forehead. Funny, he hadn't noticed the freckles yesterday.

He reached for the rod, but despite her daughter's request for help, Lily Martin averted her gaze and held on to it tightly. "Jasmine, we can't keep a turtle."

The girl planted her free hand on her hip and stamped one foot. "Why not? Do you always have to say 'no' to everything? I caught him and he's mine."

Harrison cleared his throat. "I'm afraid your mother is right. It's one thing to land a small fish, but another entirely to haul in an old snapper that weighs at least thirty pounds. That old guy isn't called a snapper for nothing; he'll bite off your hand in a second if you get too close."

The young child kept her eyes riveted on the turtle. "The Common Snapping Turtle or, scientifically, the Chelydra serpentine, is rarely combative. He'd rather flee than fight because he is too large to hide in his own shell. He'll feast on anything he can swallow. And that's how he ended up on the end of my fishing pole. But as for dangerous, I highly think not."

Harrison's jaw dropped. Her information was not only accurate but astounding. "Since you know so much about snapping turtles, then how about his belligerent disposition and the fact that, if cornered, he will bite with his powerful beak-like jaws?" He contemplated the turtle. The reptile struggled to get away, leading Jasmine and her mother back and forth across the dock.

"True, but if we lift him carefully, we can avoid being bit. If he makes a hissing noise, then we'll know he's cranky."

"Surely, an aspiring park naturalist such as yourself would know you wouldn't want to take this old fellow from his Chelydridae family. Imagine if someone came into your home and took you from everything familiar. Would you be happy?"

"I guess not. But if we free him now, he'll be in pain with that hook in his mouth. Maybe we should take him to a veterinarian that specializes in aquatics." Jasmine craned her neck to look back at him, her dark eyes pleading.

Harrison squatted beside her. "I know it seems cruel but letting him go is the best thing to do in this situation. In most cases, the hook will rust and fall out. You will cause poor old Mr. Snapper more upset and possible injury by trying to yank him from the water and plunk him on an operating table. And the nearest aquatics veterinarian is several hours away."

Jasmine stuck out her lower lip. "I don't want to see him suffer."

"I know it's a wretched dilemma, but it's the right thing to do." Harrison reached into the holder on his belt and retrieved a pair of scissors. "Do I have permission to cut your fishing line?"

"No," she said curtly, reaching for the scissors. "If I'm going to be a park naturalist one day, I figure I'd better get tough. Hand them over."

Harrison's forehead wrinkled. *What a kid.* He handed her the cutting apparatus, and, without a moment's hesitation, she snipped the line and the captive disappeared underwater. Other than a slight tremble in her lower lip, Jasmine showed no signs of distress as she handed him back the scissors.

Lily let go of the rod and took a step back as the crowd of onlookers dispersed.

Harrison reached into his pocket and pulled out a barbless hook. "In the future, why not consider using one of these?"

Jasmine's hand closed over the hook as she stared out over the river and whispered, "I'm sorry I injured you, Grandpa Snapper. I didn't mean it. Please forgive me. I hope you don't swallow that hook. I wouldn't want it to tear your anus when it exits your digestive tract."

Harrison straightened quickly, shifting his weight from one foot to the other and clamping his lips tightly together. It took everything in him to squelch the laughter.

His outburst yesterday, when Jasmine had covered her head and run down the road while pursued by the frantic robin, had only seemed to upset her mother. He glanced at the woman from the corner of his eye. *Don't want to make that mistake again.*

A hint of a smile played at the corner of her lips. And that's all it took. He couldn't help himself and laughed aloud.

And this time Lily joined him.

CHAPTER SIX

Lily stared at the dying embers of the fire and thought about the day's events. Why did that same park employee, Harrison, have to be the one to come to their aid again? Twice in two days. She could have slithered under the dock and hid from embarrassment.

He probably thought she was the worst mother ever. His assumptions were partly true. Every day she crawled out of bed on a mission, to do her best. Most days she felt like a failure when she crawled back under the sheets at night.

Lily glanced at the tent. Earlier, her daughter had fed about a third of a bag of peanuts to a family of raccoons before falling asleep in her arms. She hadn't stirred when Lily had stood up and carried her into the tent, not even when she'd zipped the sleeping bag up around her shoulders. Lily sighed as she stepped back outside. No doubt the night bandits would soon be back for more.

Lily rubbed her arms and reached for her sweatshirt that she had dropped in the lawn chair beside her. She should have been firmer and not let Jasmine feed the wildlife. Sometimes, single parenting was exhausting. The way Lily looked at it, she'd save her no's, for the more important things in life. If tonight they had contributed to the obesity rate of raccoons, or their delinquency in the park, she'd feel bad, but in the grand scheme of life, that took second place to her daughter's happiness. At least this one time.

Lily added more wood to the fire and stirred life into the dying embers with a long, thick branch. In moments, flames roared to life. Mesmerized, she watched as tongues of fire lashed hungrily at the underside of a low-hanging maple branch. As the fire crackled and danced, a feeling of contentment came over her. The great outdoors was a balm for her hectic life and injured heart.

From the time she was a little girl, she had enjoyed camping with her parents. Tenting, hiking trails, swimming at the beach, and watching the birds and animals brought her fulfillment. Somehow, she felt closer to God in nature.

Lily relaxed in her lawn chair and her mind wandered to that tall, dark-haired employee and his conversation with her daughter at the dock about being a future park naturalist. Had he unknowingly given Lily a clue for direction in her daughter's life?

It made sense when she thought about it. Jasmine consumed scientific facts about nature and her environment like ravenous grackles at her sunflower seeds in springtime.

A glimmer of hope stirred inside Lily. Perhaps she should encourage her daughter more in this area. Harrison seemed good with children and Jasmine responded well to him. Perhaps he had a few of his own. It was probably the lack of a father figure in Jasmine's life that brought about a subconscious desire to listen to a male. Lily wasn't even sure if that made sense, but perhaps she'd gleaned some knowledge from the psychology course she was required to take for her job.

Lily drew shapes in the dirt with her poker stick. Although she loved her job, this vacation was much needed. Her position as a support worker in one of her city's nursing homes was challenging and exhausting. But rewarding all the same. Taking care of the needs of the elderly and infirmed gave her a sense of accomplishment and joy. Sometimes it came with heart-wrenching situations, but she wouldn't trade it for anything.

Leaves rustled behind her. *Probably raccoons returning for more treats.*

"Such a lovely lady sitting there all alone."

Lily's fingers froze around the stick in her hand. The man's cavernous voice sent tingles of fear zipping up and down her spine. She jumped up from her chair and whirled, poker stick at the ready.

But she couldn't see a thing. "Who's there?"

"Relax, Lily, I didn't realize you were such an uptight chick." The man's voice came from somewhere in the bush. But he wasn't far away.

Lily squinted. After staring at brilliant flames, the darkness seemed blacker than ever to her. "Who are you? How do you know my name?" Was this the guy in the ball cap and sunglasses from earlier today?

"I'm insulted. I can't believe you don't know who I am." He chortled.

"Why don't you show your face? What do you want?"

The man stayed in the bush, out of sight.

"Fine. I'm calling park security." Lily reached into her pocket and pulled out her cell.

"Good night, Lily. See you tomorrow."

Leaves and twigs crunched beneath his feet as the stranger fled deeper into the woods behind her tent. Her hand trembled as she stared down at her cell. Should she call for help? What would she say? The man hadn't exactly threatened her, although somehow it had felt that way.

As she contemplated what to do, a vehicle approached her loop of remote campground road. Lily hid behind a tree on her site, in case the stranger had returned with his vehicle. When she recognized the campground logo on the white park truck, relief surged through her. She stepped out in front of the slow-moving truck and raised her hand to halt its progress.

Hurrying to the driver's window, she was pleased to discover the same park employee who had come to their rescue twice already. Despite her earlier embarrassment, his face brought comfort.

"Lily?" Harrison looked concerned.

"I might need your help," she blurted.

"What's wrong? Is your daughter missing again?"

Warmth rushed into her cheeks. "No, she's sleeping soundly inside the..."

Her mouth went completely dry. *What if...*

Lily whirled around and made a bee-line toward her tent. Harrison's footsteps echoed behind her. She grabbed her flashlight from the picnic table, released the zipper, and shone the light inside. Relief flooded through her. Jasmine slept soundly, her arms wrapped tightly around Cinnamon, her stuffed monkey.

"Everything okay?" Harrison's voice came from close behind.

Lily turned, nodded, and put a finger to her lips. He took a step back as she re-zipped the tent closed. She led him away.

Lily's stomach churned. "I owe you an explanation." After she had shared both unsettling appearances of the odd man, Harrison rubbed his chin.

"I'll pass the word to security to watch for a thirty-something man of average height and thin build, in black ball cap and sunglasses, acting suspiciously. I should warn you that it will be like searching for a needle in a haystack. Do you know how many men that could describe in a large, busy park such as this?"

"I know. That's why I hesitated about phoning security. I don't have much more of a description. And he hasn't really threatened me."

"I know the campground is at full capacity, but I could check and see if there are any yurts available. Your site is in an isolated section. I could move you tonight."

"I think I'll be okay. He ran off that way." Lily pointed.

"Give me a minute. I'll be right back." Harrison grabbed a flashlight from his belt and disappeared behind her tent. The beam of light made its way up the hill and, a few minutes later, down again.

He re-emerged from the woods, tucking the flashlight back into the holder on his belt. "I didn't see anything unusual, but it's very black out there. Are you sure you don't want to re-locate?"

Lily shook her head before lowering the flashlight until it dangled at her side.

"I'll give you my cell number. Call me anytime, day or night, if he bothers you again."

"You'd do that for me?" Lily pulled out her cell and added him to her contacts.

"You've had a rough couple of days. We need to make sure nothing else happens to you and that little girl of yours."

Some of the tightness in her chest eased. "Thank you."

"I'll also have security make a few patrols through your area tonight. Does that make you feel a little better?"

"Yes; I'm sorry to be a bother."

"You're not a bother." The park employee headed back to his truck, which was still idling with the lights on. "I'm done my shift soon, but I'll check in with you first thing in the morning, if that's okay."

"I'd like that. Good night."

When he opened the door, interior lights revealed kindness in his eyes.

Harrison tipped his hat to her before closing his door. Lily watched him drive away and in a few quick strides was beside her tent. By now, her fire had burned down to a red glow and the air held a chill. Hugging herself tightly, she hurried inside. Harrison's offer of protection brought her a measure of peace.

Now, if her bladder could only make it until morning. She had no desire to traipse to the nearest outhouse in the dark with that weirdo lurking around. And there was no way she was leaving her daughter alone.

Tucked into her sleeping bag, she closed her eyes and prayed. Almost instantly she could sense a protective wall with surrounding angels and the presence of God's peace in her heart.

CHAPTER SEVEN

Harrison patrolled the remainder of the Sandy Dunes Campground, keeping his eyes open for a man fitting Lily's description. First, he checked out who was camping nearby.

The site to the left of Lily contained a young couple, roasting hotdogs over their campfire and seemingly oblivious to any goings-on around them. On the right, a group of about eight seniors encircled a campfire and appeared to be enjoying each other's company, judging by the amount of laughter bouncing into the night air.

It appeared the man who had been harassing Lily was not staying nearby.

As Harrison turned onto the main road that led from the Sandy Dunes camping area, he slammed on the brakes. His headlights illuminated a bicycle crossing in front of his truck at a high rate of speed. And the man fit Lily's description of the stranger.

Bingo. He followed the cyclist until he veered off the main road, onto a dirt path that led up a steep incline to the outdoor amphitheatre and Nature Visitor Centre. *Drat!* There was no way Harrison could catch him now.

He followed the road around until he reached the Nature Centre parking lot, then he pulled into a spot concealed by trees, shut off his truck, and waited. Harrison could see the path that led down from the hill. Perhaps, he'd catch him. But after ten minutes there was no sign of the cyclist.

Just as he put a hand on his key to leave, a horrendous crash shattered the stillness of the night. His windshield smashed into a million pieces in front of his eyes. The shock made his mouth go dry and his heart rate increase. Harrison shoved open the door and flew from his vehicle.

"Who's there?" he yelled. "And what do you think you're doing?"

Not a sound. Only the whip-or-will, whip-or-will, whip-or-will of a nearby bird.

Harrison flipped the switch on his flashlight and surveyed the area for the offending weapon. When he spied a sharp-edged rock the size of a softball lying in the parking lot beside his truck, he knew he'd discovered the artillery. The more important question was, who had carried out the assault?

An uneasy feeling came over him. Unless the attack had been instigated by delinquent teenagers goofing around—and there was no evidence of any teenagers in the area—or a piece of meteorite, and the rock didn't look as though it had come from space to him, it had most likely been thrown by the stranger who had been harassing Lily. There was a high possibility that the biker he had passed was indeed Lily's threatening offender. And he was warning Harrison to stay away. Now Harrison was worried. And angry.

He grabbed his radio and made a quick call to park security. An inexplicable desire to protect this mother-daughter pair welled up inside him. Of course, he would come to the aid of any camper. But in this case... perhaps it was the vulnerability of the beautiful, unique child? Or the tears Lily had so desperately tried to hide yesterday? No matter the reason, he'd make every effort to see to it that they remained unharmed while staying in his campground.

Then again, he always was a sucker for a woman's tears.

❖

The digital numbers on the clock in his replacement truck read 7:13 in the morning as Harrison crawled around the farthest loop of the Sandy Dunes Campground. As promised, he was checking in on Lily Martin and her daughter.

He slowed as he passed the Martins' campsite. An object hit his windshield and he slammed on his brakes. What were the odds of another attack against him, and so soon? But when no cracks appeared in the glass, and an upside-down, pink flip-flop sat on his windshield, he blew out a breath.

The flip-flop could only mean one thing. Harrison leaned forward to peer out the front window, tilting back his head to gaze upward. The mischievous, dark-haired rapscallion smiled down at him.

Harrison threw his truck into park and climbed out. He stared up at her and swallowed the lump in his throat as he remembered the last time he found her up a tree. "You seem to be having some difficulty keeping those sandals on your feet. Perhaps it would be safer if you climbed the tree in running shoes next time." *What was he saying?* "On second thought, perhaps it'd be safer if you didn't climb at all. I don't think your mother will be happy." Harrison glanced around, but hurriedly fixed his gaze on the daring rascal. "By the way, where is your mother?"

"At the facilities. But guess what I saw?"

"A nest?"

"No." She giggled. "That's too obvious." Jasmine held onto smaller branches and made her way across a larger one until she was directly overhead.

"A chipmunk?" A few slivers of bark broke free and sailed past his face. Harrison's breath hitched in his throat. If Jasmine slipped...

She tossed her head sideways, sending her long hair flying.

"A bird?" Harrison's eyes were glued to her. How did parents do it? This wasn't even his child, but his knees weakened with her every move.

"You need to be more specific than that. There are over 325 species in the park."

Had the young child memorized the campground pamphlet? "Well, young lady, birds just happen to be my specialty. Let me think." He tapped a finger against his chin.

The little girl squealed. "Are you an ornithologist?"

Although he should expect it by now, Harrison still blinked, caught off guard by her vocabulary. "That I am. Did you see a woodpecker?"

Her giggles, pure ripples of delight, ascended and descended the musical scale, like a pianist tickling the ivories. He was fascinated and intrigued at the same time.

"How did you know it was a woodpecker?"

Harrison shrugged. "Lucky guess."

"But the park has several species of woodpeckers. Which one did I see?" Jasmine dropped to a sitting position on the branch and swung her legs wildly.

Harrison's palms grew clammy as a large gust of wind caused the branch to sway and groan. "Why don't you get down first and then I'll make my final guess as to which species of woodpecker. I don't expect your mother would be pleased if she knew you were up that tree. Besides, we don't want a repeat of your accident the other day."

"She'll never know." Jasmine searched the road through the tree branches. "I'll be down before she ever has a clue. Unless," the girl's tone turned slightly accusatory, "someone tells her."

Not having children of his own, Harrison wasn't quite sure how to respond to her sassy boldness, but he'd give it a whirl. He paced beneath her branch, in case his next words came true. "What if you fell? How would you explain your accident?"

"I... um..."

"Precisely. You see Jasmine, parents make rules to keep you safe. And even when your mother is not watching, you need to obey her."

An indignant pout marred her pretty, china-doll features. "I suppose it's kind of like being God's child. My Sunday school teacher told us that nothing is hidden from God. So, do you suppose God is displeased with me when I don't obey my mom?"

Harrison stopped pacing and stared up at her. He had no clue about God and his ways, but if there was an all-knowing deity, it made sense that he would want Jasmine to obey her mom. Fortunately, he was saved from having to respond when a sleepy-looking, tousled-haired woman in bluish-green flannel pyjamas and a white hoodie approached. Now the rebellious child would have some explaining to do.

When Lily's eyes met his, her hand flew up to the top of her head where she patted down unruly curls.

Harrison suppressed a grin. "Good morning, Lily."

She dropped her hand and folded her arms across her chest. "Good morning. I wasn't expecting you so early."

"How are you this morning?" Harrison tilted his head, keeping Jasmine in his peripheral. "An uneventful night, I hope?"

"Why are you asking if our night was uneventful?" Jasmine yelled down.

Lily's neck craned upward at the sound of her daughter's voice. "Jasmine. Not again." She slapped her hands on her hips.

"I'm sorry, Mom. There was a..."

Lily sighed. "Whatever am I going to do with you? Do you want to spend the rest of your vacation confined to the tent?"

"No, but..."

Lily raised a palm toward her. "I don't want to hear it. There is always an excuse for your disobedience. Get down from there right now."

The child whimpered as she stepped across the swaying branch and descended the tree trunk with the agility of a monkey. When her feet hit the ground, Harrison wiped his damp palms against his jeans.

"But I didn't get to tell that man what kind of woodpecker I saw," Jasmine protested.

"You can tell him later. For now, go read your devotions and think about your behaviour. Then we will talk." Lily pointed toward the tent.

Her stern authority was intimidating. As much as he worried about her hurting herself, Harrison was glad he wasn't Jasmine at that moment. His heart went out to the tiny, rambunctious child. Harrison could understand her curiosity about all things nature. He had been exactly that way as a boy. In fact, he still was.

The little girl limped toward the tent, reminding Harrison about the flip-flop that was still sitting on his windshield. He reached for it and handed it to Lily, who had grabbed her daughter's arm and was steering her across the campsite.

"I believe this is your daughter's." When she stopped and reached for it, he asked again, in a lowered voice this time, "Are you okay, Lily? Seriously, no more issues?"

"You head inside, Jasmine. I'll be right there."

She waited until her daughter had disappeared inside the tent before turning back to him.

"No, he didn't bother us anymore. To be honest, I'm more worried about Jasmine. She continues to defy me at every turn. I'm at my wit's end."

Harrison removed his cap and raked a hand through his hair. "I can't help you there. I've never had kids of my own."

Her hazel eyes widened slightly. "Really? I would have pegged you for a father."

"Nope, no kids and never married."

Silence followed.

"What about her father?" As soon as the question left his mouth, Harrison wished he could take it back, as a twinge of pain crossed her face. "I'm sorry. It's none of my business." He snapped and unsnapped the plastic adjustment strap on the back of his cap.

"That's okay," she replied softly. "You couldn't have known. Jasmine's father and I were married for ten years. It didn't work out. The divorce was final a year ago. And he's not involved in her life in any way."

"I'm sorry."

"Ross wasn't a father to Jasmine when we were married, and he's not a father now."

"I'm sorry to hear that. Maybe Jasmine acts out because of her missing father."

"You're probably correct. I've thought of that, but I don't know how to fix it."

Words of wisdom popped into his brain and tumbled out of his mouth before he could stop them. "Keep being the great mother that you are. You have a precious daughter, full of enthusiasm for life. With the correct guidance, I have no doubt she will turn out to be absolutely wonderful."

He plunked his cap back on his head and lifted a shoulder. "Don't ask me where that came from, I haven't a clue."

A laugh, with identical musical tones to her child's, only richer, trickled across her full pink lips. And accompanying the delightful sound was one large dimple that graced her left cheek. None on the right. Unusual, but kind of cute. Before he knew it, he was laughing with her.

Stop staring. Harrison sobered and cleared his throat. "Well. If that man should bother you again, or you have any concerns, just give me a call."

"I'll do that. You're very kind to watch out for us."

"It comes with the job. Good day." He touched the brim of his cap, climbed into his truck, and drove away.

CHAPTER EIGHT

Laughing together with that man left Lily feeling deliciously warm. For one tiny, unbelievable moment, she hoped the man's attentiveness might go beyond the call of duty. What would it feel like to have someone care deeply about her again?

Disappointment surged through her at the thought of his parting words. Of course, his concern came with the job. He got paid to ensure that all the campers in the park were safe, not just her and Jasmine. She shook her head as if that action would dislodge the thought and send it flying out her ears. Besides, even if he cared, could she let her heart love again? Baffled and shaken that she'd even allowed her mind to go in that direction, she hurried inside the tent to deal with Jasmine.

"Children obey your parents in the Lord." Lily read the verse directly from the Bible. "So, you see, honey, this is God's command. It's not just something I ask."

"I'm sorry, Mom. I'm trying." Her daughter's earnest confession was a balm for her self-doubt.

"Come here, sweetie." Lily held out her arms. "I know this has been a really hard year for you. I want you to know that I love you with all my heart and my rules are for your benefit, not mine."

"That's what that nice park man said to me."

"He did?" Lily's eyebrows lifted. "What else did he say?"

"He said that even when you weren't watching I should obey, because I could fall and have an accident."

Lily's eyes widened. "He actually said that?"

"Yep, and did you know he's an ornithologist?"

"Is that someone who specializes in dental surgery?" Lily's lips twisted sideways.

Hysterical giggling shook her daughter's tiny frame. "That's an orthodontist."

"Are you laughing at me?" Lily tickled her daughter's ribs.

"Really, Mom, I can't believe you don't know." Jasmine giggled some more.

Lily stopped tickling her daughter and threw her palms in the air. "What is an ornithologist, oh wise daughter of mine?"

"It's someone who studies birds." Jasmine shook her head, as though she couldn't believe her mom had lived that long and never learned that.

Lily crawled toward her backpack. "You're never too old to learn something new. Now get dressed. I have a surprise for you."

"You do? What is it?"

"It's not a surprise if I tell you, is it?" Lily searched her backpack and pulled out her white shorts and lilac tank top. "We're going on a little trip."

A high-pitched screech caused Lily's heart to skip a beat. "We're going to Grand Beach, aren't we?"

"Not if you give your mother a heart attack. Please control those outbursts. You'll scare away all the wildlife in the campground or, worse yet, a nearby camper will report me to park security. What would you say to breakfast at Aunt Bessie's?"

Jasmine leapt into Lily's arms, practically knocking her off balance, since she was standing on one leg, trying to pull on her shorts.

"You read my mind. How did you do that? Come along now, Mother, let's quit lollygagging."

Lily pressed her lips together. Laughing would only encourage her daughter. "Can I finish dressing first?"

"I think that's a great plan. And Mother?"

"Yes?"

"Wear your emerald t-shirt and jean shorts."

"Why?"

"Because you look very pretty in that outfit and you've got to look your best for that ornithologist."

"Jasmine Martin." Lily did up the top button on her white shorts. The young child snickered. "It's obvious he's into you, Mom."

"What? He's not *into me*. He's just doing his job."

"Whatever." Jasmine ducked out of the tent.

Lily grabbed her purse and zipped the tent closed. "There will be no more of that silly nonsense, Jasmine." With difficulty, she ran a brush through her daughter's tangled silky hair then tried to tame her own unruly curls.

"You are so beautiful, Mom; I wish I looked just like you."

"No, you don't. My hair has a mind of its own."

"It's funky."

Lily laughed. "Is that what you call it?"

"And the colour is so unique, like a rusty nail."

"A rusty nail? That doesn't sound very attractive to me."

"Believe me, it is. And I'm sure that nice ornithologist thinks so too. I saw him watching you when you weren't looking."

"All right, enough. Let's go for breakfast before the place fills up. You know how popular it is."

"Waffles and strawberries. I can taste them now." Jasmine rubbed her tummy in circles, making Lily smile. Oh, how she loved her daughter.

✣

Lily felt nauseated. Her scrambled eggs, bacon, toast, and jam swam around in her stomach, reminding her of the plight of the agitated snapping turtle that Jasmine had accidentally snagged. It couldn't be him. Could it?

"Mom, what's wrong? You look like you've seen a ghost or something."

If only she knew. "It's nothing. My breakfast isn't sitting too well. That's all."

"I hope you're not getting sick. We've got lots of camping left to do."

"No, I'll be fine. Just finish up your waffles so we can do some serious shopping." Lily glanced around, desperate to vacate the restaurant. She'd recognize the back of her ex-husband's head anywhere. He had a double crown, so his jet-black hair swirled in protest near the top of his head. Gobs of hair gel were necessary to curtail its rebellion. That and the width of his shoulders, the way he turned his head. It had to be him. It had been over a year since the divorce and, although she hadn't seen him since, she'd know him anywhere. When he laughed aloud, the unique guffaw sealed any remaining doubts.

As unobtrusively as possible, Lily studied the unfamiliar woman across from him; she wore enough bling to blind a pilot from thirty thousand feet. Should she warn the poor woman of what the future held for her? Of the adulterer she was sharing breakfast with?

No, it wasn't her place. Her biggest problem now was how to exit the restaurant without being noticed. Even if it didn't seem fair to Jasmine, in the long run it would spare her much pain. She couldn't imagine what it would feel like being rejected by your own father. Hers was so loving and kind.

But her daughter could read her like a book. "Who are you staring at, Mom?" Jasmine turned. "Dad? Is that you?"

Leaping from her chair, the child made a beeline toward his table. The surrounding patrons couldn't help but observe the scene unfold as Jasmine exuberantly threw her arms around her father's neck.

Lily held her breath. *Please, God, let him be glad to see her.*

"Jasmine!" Ross's voice carried genuine surprise as he hugged her tightly and planted a kiss on her cheek. "It's so good to see you, honey. What are you doing here? Is Mommy with you?"

"Yep." Jasmine pointed at her. "She's right there behind you."

When Ross turned, and their eyes met, Lily was surprised to feel... nothing. No, that assessment wasn't entirely accurate. As he set Jasmine down, got up, and approached Lily, her heart plodded along heavily, waging a silent revolt.

"Lily. What a surprise. I hadn't expected to see you both today."

"No, I didn't expect to see you either." *Especially with another woman.* She bit back the spiteful retort for two reasons—to spare her daughter and because it wasn't true. Other women were the reason her marriage had fallen apart. Her eyes flew to the festering glares of his latest fling, whose eyelashes were so long and upturned, they looked like hairy caterpillars before a cold winter's approach.

"Mom and I are camping at Piney Campground. Why don't you come by and see us?" Jasmine clasped her father's hand tightly and swung his arm back and forth.

No. Panic rose in Lily's chest and she fought it back. *Please say you're busy.* Although she couldn't blame Jasmine for wanting to be with her dad, she couldn't bear the thought of dealing with him. Over the last year, she'd done a decent job, or so she thought, of burying the pain of his betrayal.

"Really? I would love to. If it's okay with your mom." Ross turned dark, pleading eyes on her.

You won't be bringing her, will you? Again, she bit back the words that were fighting to slip out. She couldn't break her daughter's heart. "Sure."

"What campsite are you on? How long are you there?"

As she answered his questions, the other woman suddenly shoved back her chair with such force it crashed against the window sill behind her. Clomping toward them on her several-inch pumps, short skirt, and enough intoxicating perfume to be considered biological warfare, she'd obviously had enough.

"Ross? What's the meaning of this little charade? Who are these people?" The fingers on one hand wiggled toward them, each adorned with sparkling rings.

Ross's face blanched. "Morgan, this is my ex-wife Lily, and our daughter Jasmine."

Gum popping sounds echoed throughout the small dining room as his latest girlfriend chomped angrily. "Really?" She whipped her long, bleach-blonde hair off her shoulders. "I wasn't aware you'd been married."

"Now you know," Ross replied, keeping his tone matter-of-fact.

"Then I'm out of here, babe. I'm too young to be saddled with that kind of baggage."

Ross shrugged "Your loss." Morgan stalked across the wooden floor, whipped open the glass door, and disappeared into the morning sunshine.

"Daddy?" Jasmine's forehead wrinkled. "What did she mean when she said she didn't want to be saddled with baggage? Aren't horses saddled? And I don't see any bags lying around."

"You know what, little princess, it doesn't matter." Ross touched a finger to Jasmine's nose. "The main thing is that we get a chance to visit. I've really missed you."

Lily bit her lip. Did he mean it? Could she trust him? For Jasmine's sake, she desperately hoped he meant what he said. Because her daughter's heart depended on it.

CHAPTER NINE

Lily averted her eyes as much as possible from the display of flesh parading itself up and down the streets of Grand Beach. Next to the scores of bikini-clad girls and shirtless men that meandered along the main strip of the popular tourist town, Lily felt as though she had donned a parka and snow pants instead of her white shorts and lilac tank top. And she knew, even as Ross held Jasmine's hand and seemed to enjoy his daughter's company, his eyes were lusting. It wasn't *entirely* his fault. The flagrant, flaunting, fleshy procession would be hard for most people to avoid.

A large-chested girl in a slinky black string bikini and jean shorts about two sizes too small strutted past them. "Now why couldn't you have dressed like that for me? Maybe our marriage would have had a chance," Ross whispered in her ear.

Lily's breath caught in her throat. She skittered her gaze toward him. Ross hadn't changed at all. His words were so hurtful, she could hardly breathe. The only credit she could give him was that he said it quietly enough that Jasmine didn't hear.

Take the high road, Lily. "Look at this bathing suit, Jasmine." Lily pointed at a cute purple and pink one in the window display.

The three entered the store. Lily found the rack of bathing suits and located the one from the window. She held it up. "What do you think?"

Jasmine rolled her eyes. "That's ugly. Besides it's a one-piece. Those are for old ladies. I want a two-piece just like the one she's wearing." Jasmine pointed to a young teenage girl who was wearing a blue plaid bikini top and a short silky wrap around her bikini bottom.

Lily pulled her daughter aside and spoke softly. "Jasmine, I believe we are to treat our bodies with modesty. As long as I still have a say in your style of clothing, you are not going to dress like that. Besides, one-piece bathing suits are more practical and comfortable. So, if you like, we will continue to search for a bathing suit. If we can't agree on one, then you will have to make last year's do since it still fits."

"Ah, lighten up, Lily. Don't make her old-fashioned like you. Get with the times." Ross shoved back his shoulders and glared at her.

Lily's pulse spiked. She pressed her lips together. Twice in the last few minutes, he'd inflicted painful jabs. Everything in her wanted to snap back at him. She rubbed her temples. "I've developed a headache and I'd like to get back to the campground. Let's go, Jasmine." She tugged on her daughter's hand.

"But, Mom, I haven't seen Dad in a really long time. This isn't fair." Jasmine yanked her hand away and stomped one sandaled foot.

"She's right, Lily. What if I kept her for a few hours and brought her back, say around four p.m? You can relax and have a nap to get rid of... that sudden headache." Ross smirked.

Alarm charged through her at the thought of leaving Jasmine with her ex. She had no reason to suspect that he would harm her, but he'd never shown any interest before. Why now? Had he finally come to realize the value of his daughter?

"Come on, Mom. Please say yes."

"Can I talk to your father alone for just one minute?" Lily gave her daughter a tight smile.

"Okay." Jasmine slipped a few aisles over, but kept hopeful eyes glued on her. How could she disappoint her little girl?

Lily took a steadying breath. "What's all this about, Ross? And I want you to be honest. You've been AWOL for the last year of our lives. Why would you suddenly take an interest in being with your daughter?"

Ross shrugged. "You're right. I've been negligent in support payments and visitation. But all of that is about to change. I've been seeing a counselor and I'm making some positive changes in my life. I was about to contact you when I ran into you at Aunt Bessie's."

Lily tilted her head as she contemplated his words. As much as she wanted to believe him, there was the matter of the woman in the restaurant and the outrageous claim that Lily's style of bathing suit had hurt their marriage. The idea that he had changed was absurd.

But Jasmine would never forgive her if she said no.

"All right, Ross, but there are a few stipulations. She needs to be back to my campsite by four p.m. sharp or I'm calling the police. And there is to be no skimpy clothing purchased. After all, she is only ten."

"No problem. I'll abide by your wishes." Ross shoved his hands in his pockets.

Lily waved a hand toward Jasmine, who darted across the shop towards them.

"You can go with your father." She gave Jasmine a big hug. "I'll see you later. Have fun."

She watched the two of them as they disappeared outside, the bells above the door jangling. Clasping her hands together, Lily breathed a prayer that her daughter would be safe, and that she would have fun. Although, until Jasmine was safely back with her, Lily certainly wouldn't.

CHAPTER TEN

Even though Lily figured Ross didn't believe her, she did have a headache. Oddly enough, it had developed after she saw him at the restaurant. Clad in sunglasses, Lily relaxed in her zero-gravity lawn chair, her book sprawled across her lap. Even her novel, as interesting as it was, couldn't keep her mind from flitting back to the events of the morning.

Would Jasmine be safe? If anything happened to the love of her life, she didn't know if she'd be able to go on. Jasmine was the only reason she got up in the morning. Well, that wasn't entirely truthful. There were also a few other reasons.

Mom and Dad had been pillars of strength through her difficult marriage and recent divorce. If she gave up, she'd only worry her parents. In their aging years, they didn't need her to fall apart.

Despite the heart-wrenching betrayal of an unfaithful spouse, the worries of inadequacy as a mother, the stress of her job, and the financial strain that single parenthood brought, there was an underlying, inner peace.

Without a doubt, she knew who was responsible for that peace.

Her mind wandered to the words of one of her favourite poems, "Footprints in the Sand", which seemed to parallel her life. God had promised to never leave her, and he was keeping true to his word. The poem was so very personal to her. As she looked back through the storms and trials of life, when only one set of footprints was visible in the sand, as the poem stated, God was not absent but carrying her.

Lily closed her eyes and whispered a prayer of thanks. Then she asked God to forgive her for the worries she'd allowed to creep in. She would continue to trust that he would carry her through whatever she faced in the future.

Lily opened her eyes and glanced at the time on her cell. She had an hour before Ross was to return with Jasmine. Perhaps a quick trip to the beach would refresh her and alleviate the throbbing in her temples.

She slipped into the stifling-hot tent, changed into her navy and white striped, one-piece bathing suit, and pulled her white terry cover-up over her head. Then she tossed her beach towel, sunscreen, and cell phone into her floral beach bag. Hopping on her bike, she wobbled her way out of the campground and followed the main road to the beach.

In about ten minutes, she arrived. Lily swiped at her brow with the back of her hand. *My, it's hot.* After leaning her bike against a tree, she hurried across the boardwalk and descended several steps to the beach area.

She struggled through the deep sand in her neon-green flip-flops, searching for a vacant spot of shoreline. Finally, she found a tiny area, away from the water, near the tall dune grasses, where she could drop her beach bag.

Lily yanked her terry cover-up over her head, kicked off her flip-flops, and hurried toward the lake, dodging sunbathers, beach umbrellas, picnic hampers, and sandcastles. She hobbled across the gravel at the water's edge, wincing occasionally as stones poked the soft undersides of her feet, before her toes began sinking into the soft, sandy bottom. It was shallow for a long way out, but the coolness on her lower legs felt wonderful. When deep enough, Lily dove under the water and a wave of refreshing flooded over her. She did a front crawl, then the breast stroke toward deeper water. Lily loved the sounds that water made as it splashed and trickled over her body.

Floating peacefully on her back, she gazed at puffy white clouds drifting lazily through an intense sapphire sky. One cloud instantly stood out to her. The countenance of a bearded man mesmerized her with his kind smile, tender eyes, and wholesome visage. Could she be seeing the face of God? Was that possible?

Just what would God look like?

Lily smiled. Her thoughts drifted back to her childhood. Being the oldest of three, she had liked to entertain her siblings every night at bedtime. And she had a great audience since all three shared one room.

Lily chuckled at her remembrance of the 'toilet paper people'. Some nights, Lily would slip to the bathroom, steal a wad of toilet paper, wet it under the tap and bring it back to the bedroom. Then she'd form the soggy tissue into shapes of people and stick them on the wall—hence the name.

Another memory popped in. To this day, her brother Nathan still teased her about the night she tried to convince her siblings that a race of people lived inside the nightlight bulb, in another dimension invisible to the human eye.

What a crazy imagination. She giggled aloud before remembering she was out in public. Embarrassed, she jerked her head up and searched the lake. Thankfully, no one had heard. In fact, she had to squint to see the shoreline. Oops. She'd drifted a little far in her trek down memory lane.

Thankfully, she was a strong swimmer. Years of lessons at their local YMCA had paid off. Soon, she found herself approaching a group of young men tossing a football in the lake. When an errant throw landed with a splash directly in front of her, she picked it up and hurled it back.

"Good throw." One of the young men grinned. "Want to join us in a game of keep-away?"

"No thanks." Lily had never responded well to flirting. Not before Ross and certainly not now. Besides, she was older than she looked.

Sloshing out of the lake, she laid out her towel, flopped onto her back, and closed her eyes. The sun was deliciously warm.

Lily delighted in the sounds all around her. Happy screeches of children, squawking seagulls, and crashing waves brought her contentment. She sighed. Her headache was almost a distant memory.

"Alone again, I see. That doesn't seem proper for such a beautiful woman."

Lily's eyes shot open as her heart ricocheted off her ribcage. He was back again. This time he was bare-chested and wore black, knee-length swimming shorts. Dark sunglasses covered his eyes and he still wore a black ball cap on his head.

"What do you want? And who are you?" Lily sat up, reached for the beach bag, and clutched it against her chest.

A crusty belly laugh rang out as he dropped to the sand beside her. "Quit playing games with me, Lily."

"Honestly, unless you tell me who you are this instant, I'm going to report you to the campground authorities for harassment." Lily's hand shook as she searched the bag for her phone.

His fingers dug into her arm, halting her search. "Chill out. You don't need to contact security. I'm insulted you think of me as a threat, and I'm deeply hurt that you don't remember me." He pressed his other hand over his heart in dramatic fashion.

"Maybe this will help." He let go of her arm, removed his sunglasses, and smiled widely, as if posing for a photo. She stared at a pair of small, beady brown eyes, a flattened bridge of nose, and a mouth overcrowded with teeth. Try as she might to recall that face, she was almost positive she'd never seen this man before. Certainly, she would remember. Lily was terrible with names, but never forgot a face.

"Think, Lily, think. You see me twice every week."

Lily pulled her bottom lip between her teeth. How could she see a man twice a week and not remember him? Chills zipped up and down her spine. Did this guy have all his mental faculties about him?

"Harvester Breads? Any bells ringing yet?"

Lily shook her head, her heart rate sprinting wildly.

"The Gardens Nursing Home? The elderly need to eat as well as the rest of us." He smirked.

Lily's mouth went completely dry. He knew where she worked?

"I deliver bread at eight in the morning every Monday and Thursday. Don't tell me you haven't noticed me. I've certainly noticed you." One side of his mouth hitched up.

A sick feeling began in the pit of her stomach and a shudder raced through her at his creepy leering.

"Once last winter I rang the backdoor buzzer, and you came along to let me in. We met then, don't you remember?"

No, she didn't remember. Lily swallowed the enormous lump in her throat. She had to get away from this man. She did a frantic scan of the beach-goers nearby. Just who could she reach out to for help? She was at the highest point on the shoreline. Almost everyone was below her and facing away, toward the lake. No one would even notice if he hauled her away. Unless she screamed. Which she wasn't opposed to doing.

"When I deliver bread, I can see you in the dining room spoon-feeding that silver-haired old biddy... the one with birds and flowers on her sweatshirts. You smile when you see me waving at you through the kitchen serving window."

Lily's stomach tossed some more. Her hands grew clammy as she listened to the stranger. She had no recollection of waving at the bread man.

"My work in the nursing home keeps me extremely busy and focused. Perhaps you're confusing me with someone else." Lily's voice trembled.

"Nope. It's you. It doesn't matter anyway." He replaced his sunglasses. "The main thing is that we're finally together."

Together? Warning bells clanged in her skull. Her heart was pounding so rapidly, she felt dizzy.

"I've waited a long time for this moment—for the chance to finally talk to you. I'd like to get to know you better." He reached for her hand.

"Let go of me." Lily jerked her hand away and scrambled to her feet.

"Since you don't remember me, let me introduce myself. My name is Brad Pit, like the actor, but minus one 't'." He stared up at her blankly.

Lily's eyes widened as she jammed her soggy, sandy towel in her beach bag. Was he joking? "I'm really not interested in dating anyone right now."

For a split second, the idea to scoop up a pile of sand and throw it at his face crossed her mind, but it probably wouldn't accomplish much of anything, since he was wearing sunglasses.

Lily took off running through the blistering sand. Was he following her? Would he get the message that she wasn't interested and finally leave her alone?

Lily tripped up the boardwalk stairs on jelly-like legs. Reaching her bike, she hopped on the seat and pushed her bare feet against the pedals. In her panic, she'd left her flip-flops in the sand.

What was wrong? She wasn't getting very far, very fast. Had the tire finally become so loose it was malfunctioning? Lily hopped off her bike and her stomach sank. Both tires were flatter than pancakes. Had Brad Pit sabotaged her bike?

She threw a worried glance behind her. The creepy man stood as rigid as a soldier, arms crossed, staring at her from the top of the boardwalk stairs. What was she to do now? She probably couldn't outrun him, especially since she was barefoot, not to mention she could run about as far and fast as a snail.

Harrison. She let her bag slip from her shoulders. She just had to locate her cell. She reached in and began a desperate search. When her fingers closed over the palm-sized device, she breathed a sigh of relief. Her fingers shook as she punched in the number.

"Hello?"

His calm voice eased her fear. Slightly. "It's Lily. I'm sorry to bother you, but I'm at the Sandy Dunes Campground Beach and that man is here again. I'm afraid, Harrison." She kept her eyes glued on the worrisome stranger who approached a blue bicycle leaning against a tree.

Harrison urged her to get back to the beach, told her that there was safety in numbers, and assured her he'd be there as quickly as possible. Lily ended the call just as the stranger cycled toward her.

Heeding Harrison's advice, Lily sprinted across the sandy cliff and scampered downward among tall dune grasses. One bare foot caught a sharp root and she yelped. The pain caused her to drop to her knees momentarily. She scrambled to her feet again and gained speed as she raced down the hill.

She angled a worried glance over her shoulder. When she saw the freaky stranger staring down at her from the top of the dune, a wave of fear charged through her again. Still running, she turned and ran smack into the chest of... the flirtatious football dude.

"Hey, what's the rush? Is there a rabid raccoon after you?" He rested steadying hands on her shoulders.

Lily bent over, hands on knees, gasping for breath. "No. It's worse and it's human. Can I stay near you until park security arrives?"

The man scoured the sand dune behind her. "Is that him?" Football Guy pointed upward.

Lily forced herself to look. Brad Pit, or whoever he was, held something in his hand and had aimed it in her direction. *Oh no.*

She dropped to the sand and covered her head. "Get down. He has a gun."

"It's only a green water pistol," Football Guy replied calmly. "I noticed him earlier, carrying it as he walked across the beach. What happened? Did that man hurt you?" He crouched down beside her.

"It's a water gun? I'm sorry. I guess I panicked." Lily sat up but couldn't bear to look.

"No worries. I can see why you're concerned. That guy seems a little off." He waved a hand to his two friends who were raiding a nearby cooler for drinks. "See that guy up there with the water gun in his hand? He's been bugging... what's your name?"

"Lily."

"We're going to stay with Lily until park security arrives."

"No problem," answered a short, plump guy with long, blond frizzy hair.

All three men surrounded her, staring up at the strange man. That must have been enough to scare him off, because when Lily did summon up the courage to glance up the hill, he had disappeared. Football Guy squeezed her shoulder. "It's okay, he's gone now."

Lily didn't have the energy to get up. Instead, she sat in the sand and hugged her knees to her chest. "Thank you. I don't even know your name."

"Shane. And I see a white park truck arriving. That must be security." He held out a hand to her.

Harrison climbed out of the truck. The tight muscles across her shoulders relaxed a little. She was safe now. Lily grasped the proffered hand and allowed Shane to pull her to her feet. Her gaze shifted to the spot where she'd last seen Brad Pit.

Why was he bothering her? Deep down, even with Harrison's approach, she didn't feel safe.

Camping was supposed to be relaxing and a break from the stresses of life. But so far, between the strange man harassing her and Ross re-appearing in her life after a year, it wasn't turning out that way at all. Nope. Not one little bit.

CHAPTER ELEVEN

From the top of the dune, Harrison scanned the large crowd of beach-goers as he searched for Lily. A woman with hair the length and colour of Lily's, in a navy striped bathing suit, sat in the sand, knees drawn up to her chest. She turned her head and looked in his direction. Yep, that was her.

The young man standing beside her took her hand and pulled her to her feet, and a crazy protective pang barrelled through his chest. Was that the creep that had been harassing her?

Sprinting full-speed toward the wooden staircase, he charged down the steps, two at a time, clambered through the thick sand, and stopped in front of the man. "Who are you and what do you want with this woman?"

Lily stepped between them. "Harrison, it's okay. This is Shane. He and his friends have been helping me."

Harrison's chest heaved rapidly as he tried to catch his breath. "I'm sorry. I misunderstood."

Shane shook his head. "No apology necessary. But you may want to find the strange dude running around up there. I think he's one brick short of a load. He aimed a water gun in our direction." He pointed to the top of the sandy bluff.

"Really?" Harrison probed the pale face of Jasmine's mother. "Are you okay, Lily? Did he hurt you?"

"No."

"Why don't you come back to the park office with me? We'll talk with our head of security." He slid an arm around her shoulders.

They trembled under his arm, striking a chord in his heart.

"Thank you for watching out for her." Keeping his arm around her, Harrison shook hands with her three protectors.

Shane nodded. "It was our pleasure."

Harrison lowered his arm to press a hand to the middle of her back and guide her as they turned to leave. Lily took a step forward and stopped. "I left my flip-flops and cover-up here somewhere..." Her eyes searched the area. "There they are." She pointed.

Harrison let go of her, reluctantly, and fetched the items. Despite the unsettling circumstances, his eyes couldn't help but admire her slim, shapely figure as she wrestled to slip the terry material over her head.

"Why are you limping?" His eyes narrowed as they approached the stairs and he glanced down at her feet

"I'm fine. I just stepped on something sharp when I was running down the sand dune. I'll be fine."

At the cliff top, Harrison examined Lily's flattened tires before he threw the damaged bike into the back of his pickup. Both tires had been slashed. His forehead wrinkled. *Not good.*

As he drove, Lily filled him in on the latest with the weird man. He was surprised to learn that the stranger claimed to deliver bread to the nursing home where she worked.

"It seems you've been unaware of this man's attentions towards you, Lily. In his demented mind, he thinks his feelings are being reciprocated."

"Did I tell you that he says his name is Brad Pit? He told me that it's spelled differently than the actor. It's missing a 't'."

Harrison shrugged. *It's not the only thing he's missing.* "I suppose it's possible his parents gave him that name." Although he doubted that was true. "His actions have me more concerned."

Half an hour later, the head of security, Jason, assured Lily they would keep watch for her stalker. Harrison wasn't surprised when a scan of all registered campers came up blank for the name Brad Pit. Clearly, the man had used an alias, which would make finding him nearly impossible.

Lily glanced at her cell then raced for the office door. "Oh no. My daughter. I needed to be at my campsite thirty minutes ago."

Harrison nodded at Jason before following Lily out the door. "I'll drive you back. Where has Jasmine been?"

"With her dad."

Harrison pressed his remote to unlock the truck and opened the passenger door for her. He frowned. "I thought they didn't have contact." He fastened his seatbelt and turned the key.

"They didn't until today. I took Jasmine for breakfast at Aunt Bessie's and there he was. I was flabbergasted that he wanted to visit with her for a few hours. I warned him to have her back by four or I'd call the cops. Ironic, isn't it, that I'm the one who's late?"

"It's not your fault. The circumstances were beyond your control."

Lily fidgeted with the drawstrings on her beach bag. As they pulled up to her campsite, Harrison noticed a tall slim man with a full head of jet-black hair tossing a Frisbee back and forth with Jasmine. So, this was Lily's ex. It was apparent that his daughter had inherited his genes, at least in the hair department, but Jasmine seemed to have gotten her mother's petite build and features.

"Thanks for everything today. I appreciate you coming to my aid at the beach." Lily unfastened her seatbelt.

"No problem. Do you really think you'll be safe camping here? Maybe you should pack up and head home." *I don't want her to go.* That fleeting idea skidded through his brain and then it was gone. Harrison sat up straighter, confused by his own thoughts.

"I don't think that will deter the man. If he followed me here, he probably knows where I live." Her hazel eyes met his.

"I guess that makes sense." Harrison rubbed his chin. "My offer for help stands. Any time of day or night. Just call me."

Lily slipped from the vehicle but paused with her hand on the door. "Thank you. I don't know what I would have done without you today."

Did her lower lip quiver slightly? Harrison's chest tightened. As he watched Lily close the door and hurry towards her daughter, something stirred inside him and left his emotions in an upheaval. He had to admit he was very worried about Lily and Jasmine Martin. How dangerous was the strange man to these campers?

Bang, bang, bang!

Harrison jumped at the loud knocking on his driver's window. Lily's ex fixed him with a cold stare. *This ought to be interesting.* Harrison pressed the button to lower his window.

"I'm Ross Martin. If you're thinking of making any moves on my wife, you'll have to go through me first," the man snarled.

Making moves on her? His cocky tone irritated Harrison. "Your *ex*-wife needed protection today. Where were you?"

Ross shifted from one foot to the other, his hands splayed on his thighs. "I was with my daughter. Wait. Why did Lily need protection today? From what?"

Harrison rested his arm on the open window ledge. "Why don't you ask her?"

"Okay, I will. In the meantime, Lily and I are working on reconciling, so back off, unless you want my fist to connect with those perfect white teeth of yours."

Harrison's eyebrows rose, and a corner of his mouth hitched up. "Good luck with both ventures." He couldn't resist. He pulled down the sun visor and grinned a large toothy smile into the mirror. "They are quite white, aren't they?"

Before Ross could react, Harrison stepped on the pedal and drove away.

What a jerk! He wished he'd had the nerve to say those words to the man's face. Maybe he was a coward for not confronting Ross Martin about his 'deadbeat-dad' status and lack of involvement in his daughter's life, but it wasn't his place. Besides, no sense riling the man further for no reason. He wasn't planning on making any moves on Lily. His goal was to keep her safe and allow her to have an enjoyable camping experience.

Absolutely nothing more than that.

CHAPTER TWELVE

Lily approached the drying line, bathing suit and cover-up in hand.

"You're late." Ross glared at her from his lawn chair.

"I know. I'm sorry, but it was unavoidable." Lily draped her damp articles of clothing over the line.

"Are you seeing that guy in the truck?" Jealousy tinged his voice. Although he had never physically abused her, his tongue was often the deliverer of verbal barbs.

"What? No. It's not what you think." Lily sank onto her camp chair, slipped one foot from her flip-flop, and examined the bottom of her heel.

"Really? Then explain why you were in his truck."

"Because my bike got two flat tires and he kindly drove me back from the beach." Lily decided to leave out the information about the frightening confrontation with the unnerving stranger, since Jasmine was listening, and she didn't want to worry her. Besides, Ross wouldn't care. He'd never taken any interest in her life before. Why now?

"If that's the case, then where's your bike?"

"I forgot to get it back from him. It's still in his truck." Lily studied the small cut on her foot. "Jasmine will you bring me the first aid kit, please?"

"Sure, Mom." Jasmine headed for the tent.

"Likely story," Ross snapped, when Jasmine was out of earshot.

"Believe it or not, it's the truth." Lily felt a tad guilty. It wasn't the *whole* truth. But it was the truth. "Besides, if I *was* seeing Harrison, it wouldn't be any of your business. We're divorced, remember? And weren't you with a woman today? Did I throw a thousand questions at you about her?" She normally didn't let Ross goad her like this, but for some reason she felt like donning her verbal boxing gloves today.

"Oh, so it's Harrison now. Not just a nameless park employee." Ross narrowed his eyes at her as Jasmine approached with the kit.

Heat crawled up Lily's neck. She was mortified at her body's involuntary response. There really was no reason for it. It wasn't as though anything was going on between her and Harrison.

"Will the two of you stop arguing?" Jasmine dropped the kit in Lily's lap and clamped both hands over her ears.

Oops. How much had she heard?

Lily mentally kicked herself. She knew better than to let Ross get under her skin. "I'm sorry, honey, you're absolutely right."

"Yes, listen to the wisdom of our daughter. And by the way, I'm famished. How about something to eat? An invite to supper would be nice."

That wasn't fair. He had her trapped. For Jasmine's sake, she couldn't refuse. Lily slapped a Band-Aid on her foot and closed the first aid kit before getting up from the chair. "We're roasting hotdogs over the fire. You're welcome to stay."

"Thank you, *dear*. That sounds delicious." Ross stepped to her side and wrapped an arm around her shoulder.

"Yippee!" Jasmine screeched. "I'm hungry. Let's eat."

When Jasmine ran to the picnic table to retrieve the metal hotdog skewers, Lily shook off Ross's arm. "Don't touch me. You had your chance. Ten years of chances. But you didn't want me. I was never good enough. Now, it's too late."

"Come on, honey, you know what God says about forgiveness."

"I do forgive you, Ross. But that doesn't mean I have forgotten what you did. Do you know how much you hurt me? And your daughter?"

Ross blanched. Her words appeared to strike a blow, almost as if she'd slapped him. Could he truly be remorseful for his behaviour? Was he really receiving counselling? Would he start to spend time with his daughter and pay child support?

"Come on, Dad, let's get the fire going."

Lily massaged her temples as Ross prepared the fire and Jasmine gathered the condiments, hotdogs, and buns. Thankfully, her daughter was very capable of preparing the simple meal as Lily's heart wasn't into it and neither was her head.

As she dropped onto her lawn chair and allowed Ross and Jasmine to prepare supper, her mind wandered. Although she wasn't thrilled he was there, she could see two benefits to Ross's visit. Jasmine was happy, and perhaps Brad Pit would keep his distance. Should she tell Ross about the stranger? Would he even care? How long would he stay? What did Harrison think about her ex-husband's sudden re-appearance in their lives?

That last thought surprised her. Why was she concerned about what the park employee might think? Ross had been talking with Harrison at his truck window. What could they have been discussing?

When Ross presented her a paper plate with a hotdog fixed the way she liked it, thoughts of Harrison drifted away.

"Thank you." She reached for the plate, avoiding eye contact with her ex.

Considering the circumstances, the remainder of the evening went well. Jasmine regaled her father with stories of her mother's bicycle crash into the back of the park truck. Then she relayed every single detail about the snagging of the giant snapping turtle and the fact that the nice park employee helped her make a difficult decision in releasing him to the wild.

Ross stayed and stayed. He tucked Jasmine into her sleeping bag and promised that he would see her soon. Lily hoped and prayed that he would keep his word.

And then she was alone. Alone with her ex. Taciturn, she stared at the flames. She didn't know what to say. It had all been said before.

"I want us to start over."

Lily tensed. "Pardon? Didn't you hear me earlier?"

"I understand that I betrayed you. I shattered the trust thing. But can you give me time?"

"Time for what?"

"Time to prove I'll be faithful."

"You had ten years to prove that. Besides, if that's the case, explain the woman in the restaurant today. Explain why you've been AWOL from Jasmine's life for the last year."

"There's an easy explanation for the woman. I'm lonely. I miss you. Since we're technically divorced, I'm not cheating. Besides, I just met her this morning as I walked along Grand Beach. Nothing happened between us, and believe me, nothing will."

"What about your absence from Jasmine's life?"

Ross crossed and uncrossed his long legs. "Through counselling, I'm just beginning to understand what it means to be a father. If you remember correctly, my father was absent for most of my life. I don't know how to be a dad."

Guilt charged through Lily. Had she been unfair to Ross? He had had a difficult childhood. Had she been too hard on him?

"Please, Lily, I beg you, for Jasmine's sake. Can we try again? I know I messed up big time. We can go to counselling together. I'd even agree to that."

Lily rubbed her temples some more. She'd already told him she was done. Why all the pressure? Her mind recalled his cutting remarks in Grand Beach today and her stomach roiled in protest. "I'll think about it. That's all I can promise for now."

"Fine, I'll accept that. I suppose staying the night would be out of the question?"

"You got it." Lily stood, hoping he'd take the hint that it was time to go. Although she certainly felt safer with him nearby, especially with that weirdo lurking around, she would still prefer that he go. Lily's gaze skittered toward the dark woods.

Harrison had promised to come if she needed him. Oddly, she felt safer and more secure with the park employee than she did with the father of her child.

Ross skulked away into the dark, toward his vehicle, like a dog with his tail between his legs. If that dramatic exit was supposed to inflict guilt, it didn't work. Perhaps she'd hardened her heart toward him a long time ago. And a hard heart wasn't a good thing. Was it?

Lily stared at the dying embers, a fitting metaphor for her dead marriage. Suddenly, the fire pit blurred in front of her. She swiped at a tear that slipped down her cheek. No. She refused to cry anymore. God knew she'd cried more tears over the last ten years than the volume of water pouring over Niagara Falls. Unfortunately, her ex's plea for reconciliation had resurrected memories of her horrible marriage.

She'd promised Ross she'd think about reconciliation. More importantly, she'd pray. A few minutes later, after retrieving her Bible, she turned to a passage in Nehemiah.

"... Do not grieve, for the joy of the Lord is your strength."

Lily's breath hitched in her throat at the first verse she read. God's tender love never ceased to amaze her. God knew she was crying. He was up there watching her right now. Lily tipped back in her zero-gravity chair and was treated to the sight of millions of glittering, shimmering stars—a stunning display of uncluttered brilliance.

As she stared at them in awe, a warmth began in her chest and spread throughout her entire body. "Thank you, God, for loving me," she whispered.

The peace that followed was like nothing earthly she'd ever experienced.

CHAPTER THIRTEEN

Harrison spent most of the day preparing for his talk. Tonight, at the outdoor amphitheater, he would present an educational session on the brown-headed cowbird. To make his lecture interesting, he gathered photos and loaded them onto his computer. He loved taking scientific facts and relaying them to people in an interesting and informative way. Maybe he should have been a teacher.

But no, that would involve spending most of his day in a building. He was born to be in nature. He shuddered at the thought of how stifling and constrictive an indoor career would be. As a park naturalist, he could teach and enjoy nature simultaneously. In his mind, he had the best of both worlds.

Even though his personal life had been filled with disappointments, at least he could be thankful for his job. He wouldn't trade it for all the money in the world. If only he could figure out why he felt so empty inside. His life seemed to lack purpose. Yes, the job brought great fulfillment, but something was missing. Did he need a wife? No. That didn't necessarily bring happiness. He knew a lot of marriages that had ended in divorce or were heading in that direction. He sighed. So many questions but very few answers. And so, his truth trek continued.

After a quick supper of lasagna left over from the night before, Harrison finished up some paperwork, then climbed into his truck, set his computer on the passenger seat, and made his way to the amphitheater.

In a few minutes, he was set up and ready to present his topic. Slowly, interested campers began filling the bench seats. Clearly some had read about the educational program in their campground pamphlet and were arriving with their families.

Others likely happened to be cycling or hiking past and, out of curiosity, decided to stay. Either way there was not a seat to be found when nine o'clock rolled around. Harrison estimated that there were approximately a hundred people filling the benches and standing along the back and sides.

"Good evening, fellow campers and nature lovers. My name is Harrison Somerville. I'm a park naturalist employed with Piney Campground and tonight I would like to tell you about a very nasty bird. He's from the Genus, Molothrus and the Species, Icteridae. By chance, does anyone know what bird this might be?"

Someone near the back thrust an arm into the air and waved wildly. "Oh, I know, Harrison. Pick me. Pick me."

A few laughs rippled across the audience, especially when the dark-haired girl jumped to her feet, still waving her arm frantically. He should have known. It was the pretty little rapscallion he'd encountered several times over the last few days. How could he say no? "Okay, Jasmine, would you kindly share the answer with us?" He had no doubt in his mind that she knew the answer.

"Gladly," she replied, bouncing up and down on the balls of her feet.

Harrison smiled as she climbed on the wooden bench so that she would be visible to the entire crowd.

"The nasty bird that Mr. Somerville refers to is the brown-headed cowbird. He is actually a brood parasite." One finger pointed heavenward. "I suppose you are all wondering what a brood parasite is? Let me tell you, it's practically criminal. If I was the bird police, I'd arrest this delinquent fellow for his terrible behaviour."

The corners of Harrison's mouth hitched upward. He knew Jasmine was not an ordinary child, but her intelligence still captivated him. And apparently, the entire audience too.

Harrison shifted his gaze toward Lily, who was biting a fingernail. She was obviously worried about her daughter's outburst. But there was no need. Every eye and ear were glued to the excited young girl and almost everyone in the crowd was smiling. Harrison had no intention of interrupting this budding naturalist.

"Jasmine, I think everyone will hear you better from up here. Would you like to join me on stage?"

"Would I." She squealed as she jumped to the ground and slapped all the way to the front in her fuchsia flip-flops, her long ponytail bouncing wildly from side to side.

"Thank you for coming up here, Jasmine. We would all love it if you would enlighten us with your profound and accurate scientific knowledge."

Jasmine's science lesson continued as though she hadn't missed a beat. "The brown-headed cowbird is so busy following around cattle to eat the insects stirred up by the herd, that when they do lay their eggs, they don't have time to take care of them. Imagine that."

Harrison's lips twitched. The mannerisms and animated expressions of the unusual child were endearing. There was something very special about Jasmine Martin.

"But that's not the worst of it. Mrs. Cowbird dumps her eggs in other passerine nests, especially those that are cup-shaped. Then she goes back to following the cattle and expects the host bird to feed her young."

As Jasmine took a deep breath, Harrison saw his cue to politely interrupt. "Jasmine, I suspect that most of these campers don't know what a passerine is. Would you like to educate us?"

"Of course. A passerine is another name for a perching bird."

A middle-aged gentleman raised his hand. "Miss, can you give me an example of a passerine?"

A puzzled expression crossed her face.

Harrison rubbed his chin. *Finally, she's stumped.* Someone had asked her a question she couldn't answer.

Jasmine tapped a finger against her cheek. "You can correct me if I'm wrong, Mr. Somerville, since you have your master's degree in ornithology. I'm sure you know the answer. I believe passerines such as yellow warblers and blue-grey gnatcatchers cover over half of all bird species. Is that correct?"

Harrison's eyebrows lifted. She wasn't stumped at all. "You are absolutely right."

A hush of admiration settled across the amphitheater. He wasn't the only one blown away by the intellect of the young girl.

"Cowbird eggs have been documented to have been found in the nests of as many as two hundred species of passerines. I hope that has answered your question sufficiently, sir."

"Yes, and I think you deserve a round of applause." He stood to his feet and began to clap. Just as others were about to join in, Jasmine held up her palm.

"Thank you, Mister, but I'm not nearly finished yet."

"Oh, pardon me." The man threw his hands in the air, smiled, and plunked to his seat.

Jasmine paced back and forth across the stage, but stopped suddenly, a serious expression on her face. "Some cowbird eggs are recognized by the host and rejected. But that's not necessarily the wisest thing to do, because the revolting cowbird retaliates by sending in the mafia."

Laughter erupted across the entire crowd. Harrison couldn't help himself and chuckled along with them.

"What's so funny?" Jasmine turned and glared at him, wide-eyed and indignant.

Harrison pressed his lips together to try and gain control. "I've never quite heard it put that way before." He had difficulty eliminating the picture from his mind. All he could see was a flock of felonious cowbirds, dressed in pin-striped suits, carrying Tommy guns and storming a nest.

"You obviously have heard of 'mafia behaviour'?" She drilled him with her gaze, hands on her hips.

"Yes, I have, and you are absolutely correct." Harrison nodded and took a deep, steadying breath. "Can you explain to the crowd what mafia behaviour is?"

"When Mother Cowbird learns that her baby has been rejected, she returns to ransack the nest. This forces the host to build a new one which, of course, Mrs. Cowbird finds and drops her eggs in again."

A young boy of about eight years old sitting in the front row yelled at Jasmine, "How'd you get so smart?"

Jasmine shrugged. "I read a lot."

"Why?"

"Because it interests me."

Harrison decided it was time to publicly thank Jasmine for all her helpful information. Just as he opened his mouth to speak, she opened hers and on she went with more amazing facts.

"Another big problem with brood parasitism is that cowbird chicks grow big very fast. That means they hog all the food and, sadly, many of the host young die. If they don't die of starvation, the big mean cowbird baby pushes the smaller frail birds from the nest. So, the next time you see a brown-headed cowbird..."

"I'll shoot it with my pellet gun," a man's deep scratchy voice called out from somewhere near the back of the crowd.

When Harrison traced the guttural remark to a young man in a black ball cap and sunglasses seated directly behind Lily, alarm bells rang in his head. Was this the stranger who had been harassing her?

Before he had a chance to voice his opposition to the camper's suggestion, Jasmine's angry response said it all. "No. It doesn't matter how repulsive this bird's behaviour is, God made the brown-headed cowbird and there is never any excuse to shoot or kill something in nature unless you plan to eat it, or it is threatening someone's safety."

Her stern rebuttal silenced the man. In fact, across the entire crowd, the only sound was the whimpering of a large golden retriever who was objecting to his master's command to sit and obey, while a chipmunk scampered back and forth between his paws.

A plan hatched in Harrison's mind. "At this time, I would like to turn the slide presentation over to Jasmine." He quickly showed her how to run through PowerPoint.

He had no doubt she'd know exactly what each photo represented, but just in case, he kept one eye on the screen and, as unobtrusively as possible, made his way off the stage.

The first photo showed a passerine's nest with six similar eggs and one large spotted one that clearly did not belong. As Jasmine expertly conducted the presentation, he slipped toward the back and stopped beside Lily's row.

Lily glanced his way with a tight smile, worry in her eyes. She must know that her stalker was behind her. Harrison nodded ever-so-slightly, hoping she caught the subtle movement.

As he reached for his radio to contact security, the strange man jumped up, charged clumsily past some very annoyed campers, and disappeared down the trail into the encroaching darkness.

Harrison placed a call to security anyway, hoping that somehow, they would catch this weirdo. He waved at Lily. She slipped from her seat and moved to stand by his side as Jasmine continued her presentation flawlessly.

"Are you okay?" he whispered.

Lily nodded, but her complexion was pale.

Harrison took her elbow. "The presentation's nearly over. Come with me."

She followed him to the front. As he climbed the few steps to the stage, she slipped behind a large planter off to one side.

"You're just in time, Mr. Somerville. I was about to have to repeat the whole collection." Jasmine turned to him, still clutching the remote in her one hand.

"Well, nature lovers, this has been an unusual night for me." Harrison walked over to Jasmine and rested a hand on her head. "Never, in all my years as a park naturalist, have I encountered such a vast wealth of knowledge in someone so young. Can we all give Jasmine Martin a round of applause?"

The entire crowd stood to their feet and clapped. The young girl curtsied, her ponytail flouncing forward. As the thundering applause continued, Harrison angled a glance at Lily. Her hands covered her face and her body shook. Was she crying?

A sinking feeling gripped him. So much for staying detached. He always was a sucker for a woman's tears.

CHAPTER FOURTEEN

As the crowd dispersed, and Harrison made his way toward her, Lily sucked in a shuddering breath. What was wrong with her, anyway? The tidal wave of emotion that swept over her was ill-timed.

As she sat in the corner of the stage, behind a wooden planter containing tall grasses, Harrison squatted down to her level. The concern in his eyes was touching.

"Are you okay, Lily?"

She swiped at her wet cheeks with a trembling hand. No sense trying to speak. At this point, any words would come out completely garbled.

Harrison placed a hand on her shoulder and squeezed. "We'll catch that guy yet. I'm sorry that he's doing this to you."

His hand shot warmth through her. It was so unexpected, yet desirable, that she dared not look him in the eye. Instead, she shook her head and fingered an ornamental blade of grass from the planter beside her. Could she tell him the real reason for her tears? That, although she was worried about the strange man, and even a little afraid, there was an entirely different reason for her emotional meltdown? Would it be appropriate? She barely knew him.

Lily glanced toward her daughter, who was fielding questions from a small group of campers that had come forward to talk to her. Jasmine looked so happy.

Harrison followed her gaze. "You have an amazing daughter. She is very, very special."

Bingo! That was all it took to make the world around her blur again.

"How did you get here tonight?" Harrison's eyes were sympathetic.

"We walked," she croaked.

"Don't go anywhere without me. I'll take you and Jasmine home after I tidy up and your daughter is finished with her steady stream of admirers. I don't want you to run into that man again."

Pull yourself together. Lily gave herself a pep talk as Harrison walked away. What must he think of her? That she was an overly emotional female? *No more tears.* Lily sniffled and clambered to her feet.

Jasmine's last admirer left as Harrison approached with equipment in hand. "I'm ready and it appears your daughter is too."

"Mom." Jasmine half-ran, half-skipped toward her and pointed at the back of a retreating gentleman. "You won't believe it. That man with the silvery hair is a Friends of the Piney volunteer. He invited me to join the group."

Lily hugged her excited child to her chest. "That's great, honey."

Jasmine looked up at her with wide eyes. "That's not all. He wants me to accompany them on their yearly bird count."

"That's incredible. And I'm so proud of you. You did a wonderful job up here today."

"Thanks, Mom. Can I go? Please? Please? Please?" Jasmine jumped up and down.

"I don't see why not. Of course, I'll come too." Lily adjusted the hair elastic on her daughter's ponytail, which had loosened during her animated hopping.

"No problem. I don't mind. Then you'll truly understand the difference between an ornithologist and an orthodontist."

A rush of heat suffused Lily's neck and cheeks as Harrison arched one eyebrow in her direction.

"I know the difference. An ornithologist studies the teeth of birds, right?" Lily lifted both shoulders. Why had she just said that?

Jasmine giggled and pressed a hand to her stomach. "Mom, you are so silly. Birds don't have teeth."

"I know. I wanted to see if you were paying attention." Lily ignored Harrison's curious stare. He was probably trying to figure her out. One minute she was crying, the next making crazy jokes.

Finally, Harrison turned toward her daughter. "You'll learn so much. Most of the Friends of the Piney are avid nature lovers with years of experience. But I suspect you will also teach them a thing or two."

Jasmine screeched. "This is the best day ever. Well... almost. Seeing my dad yesterday tops it by just a little." She pinched her thumb and pointer finger together for emphasis.

"Follow me, ladies. I'm parked in the Nature Centre's parking lot." Harrison strode the path that led down the steep hill.

"Ladies. He called us both ladies." Jasmine's tinkling laugh warmed Lily's heart.

When they arrived at the twilight-shrouded campsite, the headlights of Harrison's truck illuminated a mess. Lily inhaled sharply.

One of her coolers lay on its side and a raccoon was gorging itself on the corn-bacon casserole she'd intended to heat up for tomorrow night's supper.

"Will you look at that, Jasmine? That's what happens when we feed the wildlife." Lily stepped from the truck.

"I'm sorry, Mom, but they were so cute." Jasmine looked up at her, worry in her eyes.

Lily gave a playful little tap on her daughter's backside. "It was my fault too. Not only did I help you feed the coons, I forgot to put the cooler in the back of the car. If you grab a garbage bag, I'll help you clean up the mess."

Jasmine hurried toward the mischievous raccoon, which scampered away and disappeared into the dark woods.

"Would you like a cool drink?" Lily walked over to the blue cooler under the tent's awning.

"A cool drink sounds wonderful." He ducked under the awning to stand beside her.

"Okay, I have iced tea, water, lemonade, and Kool-Aid jammers." Lily unlocked the secure metal snap and rooted through the melting ice and other drinks. Thankfully, their bandit raccoon didn't appear to have been thirsty, or had been unable to get inside this cooler.

"I haven't had Kool-Aid since I was about twelve years old. If Jasmine wouldn't mind sharing, I'll take one of those." He removed his cap and played with the adjustable strap, snapping and unsnapping it again.

He had to stop doing that. The awkward, shy action not only endeared him to her, it increased his good looks by leaps and bounds. Lily tore her eyes from the rich brown hair that so perfectly complemented the shade of his eyes and the dark shadow on his lower face. Harrison was a very handsome man.

"Jasmine won't mind. In fact, I drink them myself." Lily pulled out three cherry-flavoured drinks. "Will you close the cooler for me?"

Harrison slapped his cap back on his head, shut the lid, and secured it in place. Lily set the three drinks on the picnic table. She un-wrapped a straw, poked it through a bulging foil bag, and held it toward him.

"Oops." A hand flew to her mouth. "I'm so used to doing this for Jasmine. I didn't mean to treat you like a child."

Harrison chuckled and reached for the drink. "I don't mind. It's kind of nice to be waited on. I've lived alone for nearly twenty years. I can't remember the last time someone catered to me."

"Thank you for bringing us home tonight. In fact, thank you for everything over the last few days." Lily removed the plastic wrapper from her straw and walked a few steps to drop the wrappers in the large green garbage bag that Jasmine was now filling with food remnants. While walking back, she jammed the straw into the container a little forcefully, and red liquid oozed out the top and down her fingers. Lily shook her hand free of the cool, sticky drink.

"You're welcome." He took a long gulp and sighed. "I'd forgotten how refreshing this beverage is."

Lily took a sip of hers. "It does kind of hit the spot, doesn't it?"

"Maybe we're both kids at heart." A corner of Harrison's mouth hitched up. Then his eyes narrowed. "You can tell me it's none of my business, but I'm concerned about your situation. You have a lot going on. Is there anything I can do to help?"

Lily motioned toward a lawn chair. "Do you have a moment?" What was she doing?

"I do, but those flimsy camp chairs don't cater to my bulky frame. Picnic tables work better. Unless you have the extra-sturdy type of chair." Harrison plunked himself down on the top of the table and rested his feet on the bench.

"Actually, they are the sturdier type, since Ross needed that too. But this is fine." Lily climbed up and sat beside him. "You're very kind to ask about me. After my breakdown at the amphitheatre, I feel like I need to explain. Believe it or not, those were happy tears."

"Happy tears?" Harrison tilted his head.

"Don't men ever have those?"

Harrison took another large draw on his straw. "Not that I'm aware of."

"Well, anyway, Jasmine is different," Lily whispered, as she angled a glance toward her daughter, who seemed to be distracted with the cleanup.

Harrison tipped an ear a little closer. "Pardon?"

"I'm sorry. I don't want her to hear me." Lily's heart did an odd leap at his nearness.

"I've never met anyone like Jasmine. She's truly amazing." His husky voice, gushing with admiration for her daughter, made her stomach do a little flip and flutter.

Lily drew in a breath before continuing. "Jasmine doesn't do well in school. Her teachers don't understand her. Her classmates can't relate. And frankly, some days I can't figure her out either. She gets more than the average child's share of detentions, and I can't count the number of times I've been called into the principal's office to deal with Jasmine's outbursts."

"Outbursts?"

"She often corrects her teachers in the accuracy of their information—or lack thereof. Jasmine has a very high IQ and can't help but feel she needs to set her teachers straight. Although she means well, it comes off as disrespectful. Socially, she has very few friends. While her peers want to play dolls, she would rather research the Milky Way Galaxy or study the migrating path of Tundra Swans."

Harrison's eyes twinkled. "Tundra Swans do fly right over Piney Campground and land in a field nearby."

"She'll love that. Of course, there's also the matter of her father. He hasn't been a part of her life for so long. Even when we were together, he barely gave her the time of day." She nudged his arm with hers. "What you did for Jasmine today was like lathering honey on my heart."

Harrison's brow furrowed. "I'm not sure I'm following you."

"Today meant the world to me, because it meant the world to her." Her eyes misted over. "It was incredible to see the crowd respond in a positive way to my daughter. Jasmine was so happy. And that's what I live for."

Harrison had been resting his elbows on his knees, empty drink pouch in hand. He squeezed it until it made a crackling sound. "More happy tears?"

Lily nodded. "Thank you for allowing her the opportunity that you did."

"I have no idea what it's like to try and raise a child alone, especially one that is as gifted and intelligent as Jasmine. But from what I see, you're doing a fantastic job with her. She is truly a beautiful and special young lady."

"Thank you. Your reassurance means a lot to me." A deliciously warm feeling flowed down her arm to her fingertips. When had his shoulder come to rest against hers? She couldn't tear her eyes from his gaze, which pulled her toward him in a powerful way.

"You're welcome."

"Are you going to kiss my mom?"

A jolt passed through Lily. Jasmine was inches from them, gawking. "Because now's not the best time. Mom is supposed to be helping me clean up." She held up the green bag with corn remnants adhered to the outside and on her hands. "I'm a sticky mess."

Harrison jumped down from the picnic table, his hiking boots stomping the dirt loudly. "I have to get back to work. If you need me at all, don't hesitate to call." He yelled the words over his shoulder as he tossed his empty drink pouch into the green garbage bag at Jasmine's side and strode toward his truck.

"I ... will," Lily stammered, as she slipped from the picnic table and hurried to the drying line to retrieve the washcloth, attempting to avoid the curious eyes of her ten-year-old daughter as she did so.

"Good-night, Miss Jasmine, sleep tight. Maybe I'll see you tomorrow." Harrison waved before climbing into his truck.

"Oh, you will." She winked.

Lily skittered her gaze toward Harrison, who was peering at her over the top of his open driver's door. Her breath caught in her throat when a smile played at the corner of his lips.

Oh my!

Despite her best attempts to curtail it, a corner of her mouth turned up in response to his dashing grin.

God, help me!

CHAPTER FIFTEEN

"Backstroke, Mom, that's the only way we're going to get out of this mess."

"I know, Jasmine, I'm trying. My paddle is tangled in underwater weeds." Lily wrestled with the wooden instrument until it finally came free with a jerk. Carefully, she steered the canoe from the shallow, reedy area.

"Look at the pretty lily pads. Hey, I just thought of something. Those plants have your name. Isn't that funny?"

"Interesting, Jasmine, but I'll tell you something that's not very funny—the remark you made last night about Mr. Somerville kissing me."

"I didn't mean for it to be funny. I was just asking a question based on my observations. And I needed your help with the cleanup."

"What observations?"

Jasmine shrugged. "It's not rocket science, Mom."

"It isn't what you thought it was. We were just talking."

"And staring into each other's eyes."

Lily sighed. "In the future, there will be no more comments like that. I'm not interested in dating and I'm sure Harrison isn't either."

"Does that mean you and Dad will be getting back together?"

Lily's chest tightened. "That's highly doubtful."

"I'm okay with that. Since Dad's been gone, you're much happier. Although I want to see him more often, I understand that your marriage didn't work, and you are better off without him."

Lily sat up straighter. Was God speaking through her child to give confirmation about the question Ross had thrown at her about reconciliation?"

"Mom, duck!"

"Huh?" She should have listened first and asked questions later. The brush of the bird's wing across her hair was unsettling.

"That was amazing. We startled a great blue heron into flight." Jasmine's voice oozed with excitement.

Lily patted the top of her head, a little uneasy about the entire episode. "It certainly was a unique experience."

Leisurely, they paddled in the mid-morning sun. The pair had gotten an early start from the canoe launch area and now, an hour later, approached the road bridge that crossed the narrow tributary.

"This is the end. Let's turn around and head back," Lily suggested.

"No, Mom, it's not the end. We can climb out, portage across the road, and put our canoe in the river on the other side."

"Portage? Are you crazy? The two of us can't carry this big red beast."

"Can we try?"

"No, Jasmine. It weighs too much. Time to head back."

A family of cyclists—a mom, dad, and four boys—crossing the bridge above them stopped to wave. Two of the boys were very young and sat safely secured in child seats attached to each parent's bike.

Lily waved. The oldest boy, who looked about ten, shouted to Jasmine, "Hey, aren't you the girl that told us all about the brown-headed cowbird?"

"Yes, that would be me."

"Guess what we saw?" His features danced with animation.

"What?" Jasmine asked.

"Six enormous wild turkeys."

"You're wrong, Ian, those were turkey vultures." His younger brother pulled off his bike helmet, exposing a mop of auburn curls.

"No way, Connor," the eldest responded. "I'm sure they were wild turkeys."

"Guess what?" Not to be outdone by his brothers, a child of about three years of age, straight blond hair sticking out from under his colourful cartoon helmet, piped up from the seat on the back of his father's bicycle. "I feeded chipmunks, lots and lots and lots of peanuts." He stretched his arms wide apart.

Lily laughed. "I'm sure those chipmunks have really full tummies."

The toddler grinned from ear to ear as his head bobbed up and down.

"Where did you see the turkeys?" Jasmine asked the oldest boy.

"Back there on a trail." He pointed behind him.

"Thanks for letting me know. I have a spectacular occurrence that you will appreciate since I can tell you love nature. While my mom and I were canoeing, we startled a great blue heron. When he flew away, his wing tip touched my mother's head."

"Cool!" All three boys spoke in unison as if directed by an unseen familial bond.

The baby on his mother's bike squealed as though he understood the whole conversation and wanted to say his part.

As they waved goodbye and rode off, their happiness hovered in the air after them.

Lily dipped her paddle in the water to turn the canoe around, but a movement along the riverbank below the bridge caught her eye. Her breath caught in her throat when a man popped up from his hiding spot behind some bushes. *No. Not again.*

"Good morning, Lily." The stranger's unexpected presence sent chills up and down her spine.

"Let's go, Jasmine. Now. Paddle hard." Lily dug her paddle into the water, fast and furious.

"What's wrong, Mom? Who is that man?" Jasmine dropped her paddle into the water with a splash.

"I don't know. We'll be fine. Let's just get back to the canoe dock as fast as possible." Lily's attempt to reassure her daughter would hopefully help calm her own nerves too. *Please, God. Keep us safe. We're an hour away from help.*

"How does he know your name?"

Lily paddled with everything she had, intensely studying the riverbank as it sailed past. So far, no more sightings of the weird man. "Push, Jasmine, push."

"I'm paddling as hard as I can, Mom. You sound worried."

"Remember when we did the Turkey Trail and you met a man asking about the turkey vultures?"

"Yes."

"That's him, and I don't want to alarm you, Jasmine, but I don't feel comfortable around him. I don't want either of us anywhere near him. If you see him hanging around, please let me know."

"Okay." Jasmine's voice quivered.

"I'm sorry, honey, I don't want to worry you. I didn't want to tell you, but I think now I've been wrong. You need to know so you can also be aware. Whatever you do, do not, under any circumstance go with him anywhere. If you see him, let me know immediately. If by chance I am not with you, run to the nearest person or campsite and have them contact park security or ask for Mr. Somerville."

"Okay, Mom, don't worry. We'll be okay. God is watching over us, remember?"

"You're absolutely right." Despite her faith in God's protection, an eerie feeling came over her at the thought of being alone on the Placid River with the odd stranger on the bank somewhere, probably leering at them from a concealed position. What would stop him from jumping in and swimming towards them? The river wasn't that wide.

From her unsettling incident on the beach, she recalled Harrison's suggestion that there was safety in numbers. She couldn't agree more, but right now there were no other canoeists in sight. Most didn't venture as far as they had.

Maybe the scary man's appearance was a coincidence and he was taking a break from biking along the trail. A few minutes later that hope was dashed when, off to her left and at the top of the riverbank, she observed her stalker sitting on a picnic table, staring in their direction. Hopefully Jasmine didn't see him. Lily didn't want to alarm her even further.

Harrison had offered to help if she needed it. Should she call him on her cell? Would he start to get annoyed with her constant cries for assistance? Maybe he thought she had imagined her stalker. But no, Brad Pit had sat behind her at the amphitheatre and Harrison was aware of his presence then. And her male protectors at the beach verified the stranger's presence to Harrison.

Would Brad Pit be waiting for them as they disembarked? Maybe a quick call to Harrison would be wise. If he wasn't busy, his presence at the dock would be comforting for her and frustrate the stranger.

Before she had a chance to pull out her phone, her daughter screeched and pointed. "Hey, there's Mr. Somerville on the dock. I'm not surprised. I told you we'd see him again." Jasmine turned and grinned at her. She'd obviously forgotten all about the worrisome stranger. How did kids do that?

Lily scanned the small crowd that had gathered near Harrison. Thankfully, her stalker wasn't a part of it. Everyone was staring down at something on the dock. Lily gently turned the canoe until one side bumped up against the wooden platform. A teenage girl, probably a student hired for the summer, squatted, grabbed the rope, and tied it securely around the large metal loop. She held the side while Lily and Jasmine climbed out.

Lily stepped toward the circle of curious campers to see what all the interest was about. Her stomach heaved as she stared in horror at... a bloody, severed appendage.

CHAPTER SIXTEEN

"What is that?" A young boy bent over, hands on knees, and gawked at the body part. "My family found it lying on the shore partway down the river and we brought it here."

"And your name is?" Harrison asked.

"Gabriel."

"Well, Gabriel, it appears to be the appendage of a snapping turtle. Notice the scales and large claws." Harrison pointed at the leg.

"Very good, Mr. Somerville. Does anyone know why the claws are so large?" Jasmine drilled the group of on-lookers.

Lily rolled her eyes. Not again. Why did her daughter feel the need to take charge? That was the park naturalist's job. But the ear-to-ear smile on Harrison's face proved he was not the least bit offended.

When no one volunteered an answer, she continued. "The large claws enable turtles to climb up steep riverbanks and onto floating logs to bask in the sun."

"As far as you can tell, what happened to this turtle?" Harrison tilted his head toward Jasmine.

"He got old, died, and was ripped apart by a vulture or coyote."

"Maybe, but I suspect otherwise. If you look closely, you'll see the limb was severed by something sharp. It appears to be a recent accident of some sort, possibly by a boat's blade." Harrison squatted down again and lifted the appendage with gloved hands.

A teenage girl standing nearby gasped and covered her mouth. She took a step backward and bumped into a tall, dark-haired man, likely her father. Her younger sister pressed a hand to her stomach but didn't move.

"Good observation." Jasmine crossed her arms and tapped her flip-flopped foot.

As interesting as this was, Lily craned her neck up toward the road, searching for the odd man again. Hopefully, he was gone for good. But she highly doubted it.

"Let's hope he didn't suffer." Harrison remarked. "We will, however, take this for further examination and study. Thank you to the Stewart family for bringing this to our attention. I'm sorry this is so upsetting for your daughters." Harrison nodded toward the father of the teenaged girls.

"Don't give it another thought. They're afraid of their own shadows." He flapped a hand through the air. "We brought them camping to toughen them up."

His wife, who looked as young and pretty as the teenage daughters, chimed in. "Last year when we were canoeing, we glided a little too close to a beaver lodge. One of the beavers swam under our canoe and bumped the bottom. That sent our daughters into hysterics."

Harrison shook his head. "I'm sure today won't be a highlight on their list of best camping experiences either, but to give them credit, at least they didn't scream."

The crowd began dispersing as an attractive young park employee with long silky blonde hair stepped to Harrison's side, carrying a pail. "You can deposit that in here." She held out the container.

"Thanks, Megan." Harrison set the leg down carefully in the bucket.

Megan began to walk away then turned toward Harrison. "Are you coming?"

Lily studied Harrison's beautiful co-worker and a clawing twinge gnawed at her insides.

"I'll meet you at the truck. Just give me a minute." Harrison looked her way. "How are things today with you two fine ladies?" His smile obliterated the worrisome canoe ride from her mind and reminded her of the unexpected closeness they'd experienced last night.

"Good." Lily beamed.

"Be honest, Mom." Jasmine slapped her hands on her hips. "They are anything but good. We saw Mom's stalker. First, he was at the bridge, then a couple more times along the riverbank as we paddled back. My mom is scared, although she puts up a brave front. And interestingly, God always seems to plant you nearby when we have trouble."

Harrison's brow furrowed. "I don't know about God planting me here, but I'll be happy to be of assistance. What can I do?"

Lily wrapped her arms around herself as her thoughts returned to the worrisome man. "I'm not sure."

"Are you coming?" Harrison's co-worker yelled from the railing above them. "Don't forget we have a meeting in ten minutes."

Harrison shifted from one foot to the other. "Be right there, Megan. Sorry, I need to get back to work. Are you sure you're okay? I can call security."

Lily shook her head. "No, we'll be fine to walk. I don't want to be a bother."

"If you need me, don't hesitate to call." Harrison took a step to leave, but Jasmine barrelled into his stomach and wrapped her arms around his waist.

"Thank you, Mr. Somerville."

The eyes that met Lily's over her daughter's head widened. "You're welcome, Jasmine."

Did his voice just crack? And was that moisture in his eyes?

Harrison jogged toward the steps. An odd and unfamiliar feeling settled in the pit of Lily's stomach as she watched him climb into his truck, seated beside his perky young female employee. Jealousy? Of course not. That would be ridiculous. There was nothing between her and Harrison; he was free to sit beside whomever he wanted.

When Jasmine begged for an ice-cream cone at the newly-constructed snack shack, the unsettled feeling fled. "That sounds like a great idea, honey."

A few minutes later, mother and daughter sat at a picnic table underneath an outdoor umbrella, licking their treats furiously before the sun's heat melted them away.

"Can we stop at the Visitor Centre before we head back? There are always interesting birds there," Jasmine pleaded.

Lily reached for her daughter's hand. "Sure, honey, we'll stop there first. It's on the way."

As they sat under the elevated gazebo near the Visitor Centre, Jasmine scanned the feeders with her binoculars.

"Mom, there's a red-headed woodpecker at the side of the building. Have a look."

Lily took the binoculars and scanned the area until she found the bird. "Good spotting, Jasmine."

She handed them back, and for the next several minutes, Jasmine delighted in finding downy woodpeckers, tufted titmice, and white-breasted nuthatches. Lily sighed contentedly. Jasmine was the most alive when in nature. The more she thought about it, the more confident she was in her decision to steer Jasmine in the park naturalist direction. Harrison's advice was taking root in her heart.

A pair of binoculars was suddenly thrust in front of her face. "Quick, before it gets away. There's a spectacular rose-breasted grosbeak on the branch of that tree right there," Jasmine squealed.

Lily searched the deep woods through the eyepieces. "I can't find him. He must have flown away."

"Look harder."

"I'm trying. There are so many leaves in the way. Bird-watching is definitely easier in the spring."

"Just look for black, white, and red. Those colours are obvious among the green leaves."

Lily snorted. "Maybe for you. Wait a minute. I see some black. And some red. But it doesn't look like…"

The binoculars slipped through her fingers and crashed to the wooden deck with a loud clunking noise. Lily grabbed Jasmine's arm and yanked her away from the gazebo railing.

"Mom! What are you doing?"

"We're running."

"Why?"

"Just trust me."

Lily dragged her daughter at full speed down the wooden walkway, past a startled-looking older couple, and through the doors of the Visitor Centre. Once inside, she bent over to take a breath and put a hand on her chest to slow her racing heart.

"My binoculars," Jasmine wailed.

"We'll send someone to get them." Lily straightened up and placed a hand on Jasmine's shoulder.

A baby-faced teenager with a camp shirt on approached. "Can I help you? Is something wrong?"

"Yes, I need park security here now." She didn't mean to sound bossy, but this was an emergency. "Then can you send someone to retrieve my daughter's binoculars? I dropped them at the gazebo."

"Definitely." He hurried away and picked up a phone at the main desk. When he'd hung up, the young man made a swift exit from the main doors and returned with Jasmine's binoculars a few minutes later.

"What happened, Mom? Did you see that man again?"

"Yes." Lily could hear the quiver in her own voice.

Lily paced the small building until a buff, broad-shouldered man, with the words SECURITY written across his navy vest, pushed his way through the glass doors and headed over to the main desk. When he removed his sunglasses, Lily recognized him as Jason, the employee she'd met after the incident at the beach.

Lily's legs wobbled like jelly. "I'm Lily, the lady who requested help. Can we speak privately, please? Wait right here by the desk, Jasmine. Don't go anywhere." She leaned toward the young man who helped them previously. "Will you please keep an eye on my daughter?"

He nodded. "I will."

"Jasmine, under no circumstance do you leave this building."

The words fell on deaf ears; Jasmine was already engrossed in the pages of a nature magazine.

Once inside the small room, Lily plunked onto a chair and spilled the upsetting event in a fast ramble.

"Let me get this straight. Through a pair of binoculars, you spotted this horrifying sight deep in the bush?"

"Yes, it was completely by accident. My daughter wanted me to find a rose-breasted grosbeak, and suddenly, there he was in my view."

"Your stalker had a severed, bloody turtle head in his hand and he held it up in your direction, as though taunting you?"

She nodded, wishing she could dislodge the alarming image from her mind.

"Can you show me where he was standing?"

"If I have to." Lily's stomach pitched and rolled as she led him to the general location. When Jason suggested that she go back inside and stay with her daughter, he didn't get any argument from her.

About twenty minutes later, Jason returned. "I'm sorry, Lily, he's long gone. But I did find the severed turtle head."

Lily winced at the memory. "You may want to bring this matter to Mr. Somerville's attention, because the leg of a turtle was found along the riverbank this morning. My daughter and I were canoeing and arrived at the dock when he was examining the body part a family had found and brought to him. He suspected the turtle's appendage had been severed by a boat. He will want to know about... the head." Lily swallowed back a wave of nausea as she imagined the suffering of the poor, unsuspecting turtle.

"Sure, I'll let him know. This guy is clearly disturbed, if you ask me. Be careful out there. Let me make a quick call then I'll accompany you back to your campsite." Jason pulled his cell from his shirt pocket and walked a few feet away.

Lily was shaken. She'd certainly allow the security man to accompany her and Jasmine back to their site. After that she had a decision to make. Perhaps she should go home. But if this guy was as sick as he appeared, would home be much safer? Harrison Somerville's face flashed into her mind. Oddly, she felt more secure at the idea of having the enormous, tender-eyed giant nearby than being alone in her own home. Ultimately, God was in control. She sent up a quick prayer for wisdom and protection.

Her teeth clenched as defiance swept through her. There was no way that strange man was going to steal her precious vacation away from her. Nope. None whatsoever. Lily might be small, but she could be feisty when need be.

When the security guy jammed the phone into his pocket and looked her direction, she stood a little straighter and pushed her shoulders back.

Look out, Brad Pit... or whoever you are. You don't want to mess with Lily Martin.

CHAPTER SEVENTEEN

The report from security troubled Harrison to the core of his being. It sounded to him as though they had a very demented man on their hands. Now, he was even more worried about Lily and Jasmine Martin.

At what point should he contact the Ontario Provincial Police? Did the stalking of one of his campers and the dismemberment of a snapping turtle constitute police involvement?

Perhaps he should meet with the park superintendent and obtain his advice. Settling on his latest idea as the most feasible, he contacted Randy Wilson and set up an appointment to share his concerns at four o'clock that afternoon.

Until then, he'd keep himself busy with Megan, organizing and planning tomorrow morning's birding trek on Tapping Trail in search of woodpeckers. That trail seemed to house more of those species than any other in the park. A smile came over his face as he imagined Jasmine on the trail with him, asking questions, but mostly offering intelligent information.

Come to think of it, he never did discover the type of woodpecker she had spotted the other morning when he found her up the tree adjacent to her campsite. He'd have to remember to ask her that question. Should he let her know about the birding expedition in the morning?

A warm feeling flowed through him at the remembrance of her spontaneous hug at the Placid River canoe dock. An incredibly large lump had formed in his throat at the gesture. The emotion that coursed through him at that moment was baffling and very foreign. What did it mean? Why had that tender act from a child almost reduced him to a whimpering, sentimental fool? He shook his head. Time to think of something else. "Megan, do you think we're ready for tomorrow?"

"I think so." She organized a pile of pamphlets on the desk.

"Then I'm heading out if you don't mind. I have a meeting with Randy Wilson in a few minutes."

"Okay, see you tomorrow morning." She stopped organizing and covered his hand with hers. "Is something troubling you? You haven't seemed yourself the last few days." Her eyes probed his.

Harrison slowly removed his hand. Her question surprised him yet didn't at the same time. Had he been that obvious? He grimaced. No matter how hard he tried, he could never disguise his emotions. "I'm fine. Thanks for your concern." Harrison smiled, then turned toward the screen door, shoved it open, and made an impulsive decision to stop by the Martin campsite before his meeting with Randy.

As he rounded the secluded bend on the Sandy Dunes road, his heart hammered loudly. Mother and daughter lay curled together on a hammock in the shade of the branches of a large maple tree. The tender scene both moved and puzzled him.

The sight tugged at his heartstrings in ways he didn't understand and couldn't explain, but he was totally taken aback by Lily's behaviour. How could she be so unguarded at a time when a psychotic weirdo could be stalking her? Wasn't her total disregard for her own safety and that of her daughter foolish?

He slowed his vehicle as he neared, contemplating whether to disturb them. The decision was made for him. The sound of his engine must have alerted Lily, as she bolted upright and stared in his direction. Even sleepy-eyed and with hair tousled, the mother-bear protectiveness was starkly evident on her face.

He knew the moment recognition dawned for her, as her shoulders relaxed, and a timid smile came to her face. Harrison threw his truck into park and clambered out.

Lily slipped from the hammock as Harrison reached it, and together they stared down at Jasmine.

"Sleeping beauty," he whispered.

"I know." Lily nodded. "I'm very blessed to have her." She put a finger to her lips and waved a hand toward him as she stepped to the far side of the campsite.

Harrison followed her. She was barefoot. She'd probably kicked off her sandals before flopping into the hammock. "I read the latest report from security, so I came by to make sure you were okay. I also wanted to invite both of you to join me on a birding expedition on Tapping Trail tomorrow morning. I thought Jasmine would really like it."

Lily's eyes sparkled. "That's so kind of you. I'm sure Jasmine would love to go searching for woodpeckers."

Harrison lifted a shoulder. "I'm curious to know what else she can teach me."

Lily giggled softly; the high-pitched tinkling, like glass wind chimes in a tender breeze, stirred something deep within. And that dimple... yikes.

"Have you thought of contacting the police over your situation?"

"It's crossed my mind. Do you think I should? He hasn't tried to harm Jasmine or me." Lily coaxed a lock of curly hair behind her ear and looked up at him, worry in her hazel eyes.

Harrison pursed his lips. "Any man who would kill and dismember helpless wildlife has serious problems. In fact, I'm meeting with the park superintendent in a few minutes to inform him of this latest incident. There's a penalty for killing wildlife. At the very least, he'd be fined and evicted from the park."

"If you catch him." Lily raised her palms.

"True. To be honest, my bigger concern is you and Jasmine. Maybe you should not only contact the police but consider going home."

"You're probably right. But the thought of cutting short my vacation because of him makes me angry. I've waited a long time for this break. And Jasmine is so alive in nature. She's in her element here." She pushed her shoulders back and stomped one bare foot, sending a pinecone skittering across the grass. "I'm not going to let him win."

The corners of Harrison's mouth twitched at her gutsy reaction, then fell into a frown. His emotions were changing direction faster than the weather vane on the roof of the Visitor Centre on a windy day. "It's just that, as much as I want to help you, I may not always be available. What then? And if security can't get here fast enough..."

They both turned at the sound of tires crunching the gravel road.

"Oh, that's just great." Lily grumbled and slapped her hands onto her hips.

"What's wrong?"

Lily bit her bottom lip. "It's Ross." A shaky hand raked through her auburn curls. "What does he want now?"

The black Ford Focus pulled onto the campsite directly in front of them. Ross Martin killed the engine and glared at Harrison through the windshield.

Wonderful. Lily's ex was back again. Why? To carry through on the threat to his pearly whites?

"He probably wants to know what brand of toothpaste I buy." Did he say that out loud?

Lily's brow wrinkled as she tilted her head in his direction. "Huh?"

Oops. What had he done? He had to stop speaking without thinking first. If he explained that statement, it would probably only exacerbate the situation. Lily didn't need to know that Ross had threatened him.

"Nothing. I should probably go." Not waiting for a response, Harrison strode toward his truck. He didn't want his swift exit to appear cowardly but avoiding a confrontation with Ross was likely best for Lily and Jasmine.

A horrific screech cut the air as he opened his truck door. Jasmine tumbled from her hammock and sprinted toward Ross. "Daddy! You're back."

Harrison jumped into his vehicle, stepped on the gas, and made a hasty exit from the Sandy Dunes Campground area. His fingers tightened around the steering wheel. How did he get himself in the middle of this complicated mess? Where would it all end? Maybe he should just step back and stay out of things, especially since Ross seemed bent on reconciliation. And really, what did it matter to him? It was none of his business. He had a job to do and that's what he would do. Ensure the safety of his campers.

But how did he ignore the tug on his heartstrings from the little dark-haired rapscallion? Or the even stronger pull of Lily's warm hazel eyes and perfectly-shaped dimple that appeared when he least expected it, weakening his knees.

Harrison shook his head, trying to shake free any mandates other than those that lined up with his mission. And that was to find the meaning of life.

Harrison pulled into the parking space outside the park office, resolved to keep his priorities straight. Job first. Mission in life second. Or should it be the other way around? Hmm.

No matter. There was no clause in his mission's mandate for his personal life. At least not right now.

CHAPTER EIGHTEEN

Lily stared at the swirling dust cloud left in the wake of the retreating vehicle. Oh, how she wished he hadn't gone. And that Ross hadn't reappeared. Her forehead wrinkled. What had Harrison meant by that remark about toothpaste? She sighed. He was a perplexing man.

Lily tore her eyes from the rapidly-disappearing truck. Ross was pulling a tent from the trunk of his car. She stared blankly, rooted to the spot, as Jasmine wrapped her arms around her father's waist.

"I'm joining you guys." Ross lugged the canvas bag to the far corner of the campsite. "After seeing you both the other day, I realized how much I missed you. So, here I am."

Her ex-husband unzipped the tent bag and pulled out the crumpled canvas.

"Jasmine, can you grab that end please?"

"Yippee! This is turning out to be the best camping trip ever." Jasmine skipped toward the corner of the canvas.

Lily's feet felt as though they weighed a hundred pounds each. The best camping trip ever? From her perspective, it was exactly the opposite. How dare Ross assume he'd be welcome here? How could she tell him that his presence wasn't wanted, especially in front of her excited daughter? The only positive slant to her ex's unexpected visit was added protection from the twisted Brad Pit. Lily pressed her lips together. Maybe this was an answer to Harrison's suggestion that she pack up and go home. Now she could stay.

Was she being foolish with her life and the life of her precious daughter? Should she report this latest incident to the police? Should she tell Ross about the frightening stalker?

So many questions, but absolutely no answers.

❖

As Harrison had suspected, Randy Wilson listened intently, but in the end decided that, even though the events were disturbing, a crime had not been committed. The decision to involve the police rested entirely with Lily Martin. His supervisor assured him that the OPP were not going to waste their time looking for a bread man going by the name of Brad Pit for dismembering a turtle, unless the camper filed a stalking or harassment complaint.

His supervisor did say that if park security caught him, the man would be evicted from the park and barred from entering again. And they were going to do their best to apprehend him.

Harrison had to admit that the whole scenario would appear ludicrous to a police officer. If someone had told him the story, he'd probably think it was all one big joke. But he knew otherwise, and somewhere deep inside felt compelled to take this man's behaviour seriously. Even though the smashed windshield couldn't be definitively linked to the stranger, he suspected it was the work of Brad Pit. Just how dangerous was this man?

A chill shuddered through him. That was the question.

Harrison drove through Piney campground after sunset, his spirit deeply conflicted. Although his shift was done, he was restless. He couldn't keep his thoughts from drifting, almost obsessively, back to Lily.

Even though he didn't want her to leave, a thought that surprised and baffled him, her safety and that of her daughter was most important. Did she really believe that God would protect her from that crazy man? He personally knew two women who had been murdered, Jessica Wakely and Madison Springfield. Where was God then? How had he allowed that to happen?

He took a deep breath. What about Ross Martin? Was he planning to visit Lily and Jasmine every day now? A horrible thought struck him. Maybe he'd come to stay with them. Would Lily allow that?

He forced his shoulders to relax. Despite the tension that had wafted from Lily as she observed her ex's approach, if Ross was going to stick around, Harrison could place a positive spin on it. Maybe the man's presence would deter Lily's stalker. And the safety of the campers was of the utmost importance.

He straightened in his seat. If Ross was there, Lily wouldn't have to leave. *Oh boy.* Why did the thought of her going shake him so much?

Harrison had parked at the Sandy Dunes Campground beach as darkness descended. Now, he ambled through the thick sand, stepping over a stinky pile of rotting debris that had washed ashore. Tilting his head, he stared up at the amber, waning, gibbous moon. Bone-weary, he dropped onto the same piece of driftwood he had found the other night and listened to the gentle sound of waves lapping the shoreline.

Harrison took a deep breath. Why did he care so much anyway? It wasn't as though he had feelings for Lily. And even if he did, Lily wasn't the least bit interested in him.

He picked up a stone that had been lying at his feet and hurled it into the lake.

He was just about done with this lunar trek to discover the meaning of his disappointing life. As far as he was concerned, you were born, you died, and if by some miraculous chance you found love in that time or accomplished something great, you could count yourself lucky. Then life was over and that was the end. You returned to dust to be forgotten, along with the billions and billions of other people that had walked this meaningless earth.

The hope he felt that night at Shadow Lake was fading fast. In fact, it was nearly gone.

CHAPTER NINETEEN

Harrison lumbered behind the group of enthusiastic birders along Tapping Trail. Even though this was one of his favourite trails in the park, he couldn't summon the excitement or energy needed to guide everyone else along it today. Thankfully, Megan seemed up for the challenge, so he let her lead and do most of the talking.

Harrison had spent an anxiety-filled night, tossing and turning, his thoughts in turmoil over the Martin dilemma. He didn't realize how disappointed he had been that Lily and Jasmine hadn't joined him on the birding expedition until his spirit soared at the sound of Jasmine's voice behind him.

"There you are, Mr. Somerville. I'm sorry we're late, but my dad wanted to take a shower first and there was a long lineup." Jasmine skipped to his side.

Harrison's jubilance took a nosedive when he turned and observed the tall, handsome, dark-haired man walking by Lily's side, his hand on the small of her back. Talk about riding an emotional roller coaster. Of course. How had he forgotten that Ross had arrived?

His eyes met Lily's briefly. He didn't have time to try and analyze the look in them before her gaze slid away.

Harrison bit his bottom lip. He refused to make eye contact with her ex. To dispel the sudden awkwardness, he clapped a hand on the shoulder of the young girl. "It's great seeing you too, Jasmine. I'm so glad you've decided to join us. By the way, you forgot to tell me the species of woodpecker that you spotted the other day."

The child jumped up and down. Her child-sized binoculars, hanging by a strap around her neck, swung wildly. "Oh yes." She clapped her hands.

Harrison grinned, her excitement contagious. Where did kids get such boundless energy? "Well? Are you going to keep me in suspense forever?"

"A flicker." She beamed.

"That's wonderful. Piney Campground does have an abundance of them. The bird's markings are incredible. Don't you agree? I'm sure we'll see a few on the trail today."

"And if not, we'll most certainly hear their noisy calls," Jasmine added.

"Right you are." Harrison smiled down at her.

Megan appeared in front of him, drilling him with her gaze. Her arms dangled at her sides; one hand held a clipboard, which she tapped against her thigh. "Speaking of noise, can we keep it down back here? We'll never see birds this way."

Harrison leaned toward Jasmine and whispered, "Oops, I guess we've been told."

After Megan shook her head at him and slipped away to the front of the group, Jasmine pressed a finger to her lips. "We'll do our best, right, Mr. Somerville?"

"Right." Harrison winked, and a warm feeling flowed through him. How it had happened he had no clue, but in less than a week, Jasmine Martin had wormed her way into his heart. A fierce protectiveness came over him. If he had any say in the matter, Brad Pit, or even her very own father, had better not hurt a hair on this precious child's head, or they'd have him to deal with.

As the birding tour ambled slowly along, Harrison was pleased to find Jasmine at his side, instead of her father's. When the sound of hammering reached Harrison's ears, he stopped dead in his tracks. Jasmine stopped too. "Could it be a pileated?" Her eyes were wide with excitement.

"Me-thinks you are correct, young lady."

Jasmine snickered as she lifted her binoculars to her eyes and scanned the trees.

Harrison turned and faced Lily, his voice a low whisper. "Is it okay if I take Jasmine to the front for a minute?"

Lily nodded. Ross opened his mouth to object, but Lily silenced him with a raised hand.

Harrison ignored the dark looks hurled in his direction by Ross and whisked the little ebony-haired wonder to the front of the line beside his co-worker.

"I hope you don't mind, Megan, but I have an eager student who wants to be the first to spot Mr. Pileated."

She frowned. "Go ahead, but please be quiet and don't scare it away."

Harrison had never seen this irritable side of his co-worker. No matter. She took her job seriously, which was good. He gently tugged on Jasmine's hand as they stole softly down the trail, a few feet ahead of the group.

Harrison ducked as the air filled with the sounds of flapping and whooshing. It was all a crazy, exhilarating blur as a pair of pileated woodpeckers flew out of the trees and swooped through the air directly overhead.

"Wow. That was amazing," Jasmine squealed as she stared up at the sky. "Not one, but two."

"I told you guys to be quiet," Megan reprimanded them, arms folded across the clipboard pressed against her chest. "Now look what you did. You scared them away."

Harrison's shoulders drooped, and he stuck out his lower lip. "I'm sorry, teacher, but it wasn't our fault. They came out of nowhere and almost hit me in the head."

Jasmine began to giggle. She giggled so long and hard that she ended up holding her stomach and dropping to the ground in hysterical fits of laughter.

Suddenly Lily was beside him, staring down at her daughter. "What's going on up here? Jasmine get up from the dirt and settle down."

"I can't. It's impossible. He's so funny." Jasmine pointed up at him.

Harrison looked sheepishly at Lily and Megan. He threw his hands in the air. "What? I had no control over those birds appearing when they did. It wasn't my fault. That plucky pair of pileated were plotting pandemonium... just to get me in trouble." Harrison removed his cap and checked the top. "I wouldn't be surprised if they left me a parting gift as well. Nope. All is well."

Lily pressed her lips together, her eyes twinkling, while Jasmine continued to roll in the dirt, giggling.

"Funny or not, he's now going to the back of the line." Megan scowled. "Where he will stay."

Harrison cocked his head. No trace of humour there. None whatsoever. What was eating Megan today? He extended a hand to Jasmine and helped her to her feet.

Lily headed to the back of the line, with Harrison and Jasmine following, After Harrison checked to make sure Lily was far enough ahead to be out of earshot, he whispered to Jasmine, "Just ignore *Old Cranky Pants*. Megan always gets irritated if I spot a bird before she does." Harrison stuck a finger in the air. "But let's keep that our little secret."

Jasmine touched a dirt-smudged finger to her lips. "Sure, Mr. Somerville. It's our little secret." The cheery sound of her jingling laughter reached deep inside him, rivalling the musical masterpiece of the house wren. And that was beautiful indeed.

CHAPTER TWENTY

Lily stifled a laugh by covering it with a fake cough, knowing it would only irritate Ross. Harrison Somerville was a very funny man. And she'd never seen Jasmine so happy.

"I knew we couldn't trust you. What kind of shenanigans did you get my daughter into up front?" Ross barked.

Lily's gut clenched.

"If you call providing the opportunity for Jasmine to see not only one, but two pileated woodpeckers, shenanigans, then guilty as charged." Harrison held his palms toward him.

Ross glared at Harrison, shifting from one foot to the other as if contemplating his next move.

Harrison didn't say another word. He couldn't. Jasmine, who was still trying to restrain her giggles, glanced his way. But he drew a line across his lips, as if zippering them closed. Lily's heart warmed at his attempt to settle her daughter down. Jasmine cupped a hand over her mouth, but muffled laughter still escaped.

Lily marvelled at the relationship that had developed between the two of them. Go figure. In the few days since they'd met, the bond between Jasmine and Harrison had grown stronger than Jasmine's relationship with her biological father had ever been.

Lily winced as Ross grabbed her upper arm, his fingers digging in. "We're leaving. I've had enough of this." He dragged her backwards and she stumbled over a fallen branch.

"Ross, let go of me." Lily tried to wrench her arm away, but he held fast. He snatched Jasmine's wrist in his other hand and started pulling her along as well.

"But, Dad, there are still lots of birds to see," Jasmine wailed, somehow managing to wriggle free of his grasp.

"Another day, Jasmine. Come here now." Ross crooked a finger at his daughter.

"Let them go, Ross." Harrison's voice was quiet but firm. Jasmine slipped to Harrison's side, a terrified look on her face. He rested a hand on Jasmine's shoulder.

"Stay out of this, Somerville. It's none of your business. Go play with your birds." Ross spit the words out. "It's obvious to me what's going on here."

He turned to face Lily, who was still struggling to get free. "You, my naive Lily, are too blind to see it, but I'm calling a halt to it right now."

"Too blind to see? Call a halt to what?" Lily had finally yanked herself out of his grasp and was massaging her tender upper arm.

Ross pointed to Harrison who now stood, feet apart, arms crossed, and staring in their direction. "Not only is that man a bad influence on our daughter, but he's using her to get to you."

Lily stiffened. "What on earth are you talking about?" Thankfully, the birding group had traipsed around a bend in the trail and were unaware of the embarrassing scene. Except for Harrison.

"Don't deny it. I can see the way he looks at you."

"Ross, stop it right now. This is so humiliating," Lily cried.

Harrison had dropped his hands to his sides and clenched them into fists.

Jasmine whimpered. It tore at Lily's heartstrings to witness the transformation from giggles to tears, thanks to Ross.

Harrison stepped toward her ex-husband and stared him directly in the eyes, their faces inches apart. "Whether you like me or not doesn't matter to me. But your abusive behaviour toward your ex-wife and daughter is way out of line. And it won't be tolerated. Especially in my park. It stops right now, with an apology to Lily and Jasmine, or I'm calling security." He tugged the radio out of its holder on his belt. His finger hovered over the button.

Lily's stomach swirled with nausea. Her arm hurt. Her cheeks burned. Was it possible to die of embarrassment? Her gaze flew to her daughter, who was visibly trembling. Poor sweetie. Lily opened her arms and Jasmine barrelled into them.

Please God. Resolve this situation peacefully.

Ross ran a hand through his hair and sighed. "Okay, fine. I'm sorry, Lily. And Jasmine. I didn't mean to be so rough. It won't happen again. But I can't apologize for my remarks to him." He jerked his head in Harrison's direction.

"I don't need or want an apology from you, Ross Martin. I'll tell you this, though. If I hear that you have laid a hand on either of these two again, the police will be here so fast, you won't have time to blink. You're pathetic. You didn't know what you had, and you threw it all away."

"Whatever!" Ross hurled the word at him. "Stay out of our business. Who are you to interfere? Let's go, family."

"No, I'll go. Let Jasmine enjoy the rest of the tour. I mean it, Ross. Don't touch them again. Or so help me..." Harrison stepped past them. Without another word, he stomped down the trail and disappeared around a bend.

Ross looked at Lily and Jasmine, a sheepish look on his face. "I'm sorry. Really, I am. I didn't mean to hurt either of you. It won't happen again."

"I know, Daddy. I love you." Jasmine disentangled herself from Lily's embrace and threw her arms around Ross's waist. "Let's go find some birds."

The trio hurried to catch up with the rest of the group. Lily's cheeks were still warm and all she wanted to do was go back to their campsite and crawl into the tent. *I need to be strong, for Jasmine.* If only she could erase the whole horrible incident from her brain.

In spite of everything, somehow Lily believed Ross. He'd never been physically abusive before. He'd gotten carried away in the heat of the moment, allowing his unfounded jealousy to cloud his judgement.

His jealousy was unfounded, wasn't it? He'd never, ever in their marriage shown that emotion before. There was absolutely no reason for it now. Was there?

Jasmine's wink, and her insistence that Lily wear her jean shorts and emerald top because Harrison had been watching her, popped into her mind. Lily shook off the memories.

What about that intimate moment when her arm leaned against Harrison's at the picnic table? The heat between them had been enough to roast a marshmallow.

Hadn't it? No. It was an extremely hot July day. That's all it was.

But when Harrison had risen to the defense of her and Jasmine just now, her heart had beaten erratically at the look of indignation and outrage on his face.

You didn't know what you had, and you threw it all away.

Harrison's words echoed through her thoughts and settled in her heart.

And hope flickered. For the first time in ten years.

CHAPTER TWENTY-ONE

Inside his truck, Harrison clenched his jaw. Why did that man irritate him so much?

He glanced out the open window, waiting for the birding excursion to end and Megan to return. When no one appeared at the bottom of the trail, he allowed his head to flop back against the headrest and closed his eyes to the tinny call of a nearby nuthatch.

As his mind replayed the upsetting scene, he felt his blood pressure elevate. Maybe he should have decked Ross in the mouth and released some of his pent-up frustration. For Jasmine's sake he had restrained himself. Not to mention that he wasn't a violent man and was too professional to hit a guy on the job.

Of all the nerve. He couldn't believe Ross had accused him of using his daughter to get to Lily. Jasmine was one of the most unique and wonderful children he'd ever had the privilege of meeting. His fondness for the intelligent, spunky, child was genuine.

As for Lily... well, she intrigued him. That's all. But, if he were truly honest with himself, no matter how hard he tried to fight it, he couldn't deny the pull he felt when around her. Those warm greenish-brown eyes had a way of reaching deep inside him to clear away the cobwebs that had collected in lonely corners. And that dimple. When it appeared, he felt as if he was being sucked right into it.

Harrison slapped the steering wheel with both palms.

The last thing he needed was to get involved with a divorced woman who had a belligerent and jealous ex-husband in tow.

Besides, his track record with women was so painful, he had decided after his latest heart-wrenching disappointment with Karly Foster that it was safer to stay single.

First and foremost, in his mind, was his journey to discover meaning and purpose in life. Perhaps the answer would finally bring him peace.

If he could ever find the evasive, surreptitious answer.

Deep in thought, he jumped when Jasmine's face appeared in the window.

"It wasn't any fun after you left," she said softly. "It's all the fault of that 'Old Cranky Pants'. I restrained myself from correcting your co-worker because my mother told me it's rude to do so, but can you believe she identified a female American redstart as a yellow-rumped warbler?"

Harrison's lips twitched. "Imagine that."

"It's every birder's nightmare." She threw her hands in the air.

Despite his attempt to squelch it, a smile broke through to his face. "Don't be too hard on her. She's just a beginner. And for some reason today, she's got her knickers in a knot."

Jasmine snorted. "That's funny... knickers in a knot. I guess we can give her some slack then."

A wash of pure cuteness flooded over him. They didn't come more adorable than Jasmine. How could a father ignore such a precious gift?

"Come on, Jasmine, it's time to go." Ross waved a hand toward his daughter. "Let's leave the man alone. He's caused enough trouble for one day."

Harrison's smile disappeared. Ross Martin's quarrelsome remark left no doubt that the man was itching for a fight. Why couldn't he just let things go? In what way had Harrison caused trouble? By providing the opportunity for his daughter to see a woodpecker and inadvertently making her laugh? He didn't quite get it.

Lily stood behind her ex-husband, staring down at her feet. Was she embarrassed, or angry, or both? His heart went out to her. Harrison squeezed the steering wheel tightly, until an idea popped into his brain and his hands relaxed and fell to his lap. He knew exactly how to get to Ross without resorting to violence.

"Lily, I was wondering if you would like to go for a walk with me tonight, on the beach. I could pick you up around nine o'clock," Harrison blurted, before he could stop himself.

Ross blanched. Harrison gloated. Not very nice of him to take pleasure at someone else's discomfort, but after all, Ross deserved it. He'd been a thorn in Harrison's side since he arrived. He may as well give wings to Ross's jealousy.

"Sure, that would be fine. I'll see you then." Lily cracked a gutsy, gorgeous grin in his direction, and he thought he might slip into cardiac arrest. He hadn't expected her to say yes. Did he need to hang onto his jaw to keep it from falling open?

Ross's stony gaze drilled him then flew to his wife and back to him again.

Voices pierced the silence and all four of them turned toward the trail entrance.

Megan stepped from behind the large viewing board that contained a map of the trail, toting her clipboard and binoculars as she conversed with an older couple.

The arrival of the birding tour suspended the tension in mid-air. Ross stalked toward his car without another word. Lily and Jasmine followed him, but not before Jasmine hurled an exaggerated wink in Harrison's direction.

Megan opened the back door of the park truck and placed her clipboard, birding book, and binoculars on the seat. She slammed the door a little too forcefully and slumped into the passenger seat. "That was a complete bust. I needed your expertise. I think I confused a few species out there."

Suddenly feeling on top of the world, Harrison decided to tease his co-worker, hoping to lighten her mood. "I heard."

"You did? What camper enlightened you? Wait, let me guess. Was it 'Little-Miss-Know-It-All'?"

"Don't be so hard on her. She's very intelligent. It just comes naturally."

"I'm glad you see it that way. I find her rather annoying." Megan slapped her seatbelt across her chest.

"That's because you don't understand her." Harrison studied his rear-view mirror, waiting for the last camper to pass, then checked all directions before throwing the truck into reverse.

Megan rolled her eyes. "And apparently you do."

Harrison threw her a hooded gaze. Maybe Lily had been right when she said that most people didn't understand Jasmine. That thought made him sad. "I've gotten to know her over the last week and she's really an amazing and gifted child."

"If you say so. I do feel sorry for her. With a father like hers, maybe I should give her a break."

"What do you mean?"

"I noticed the condescending way he treated his wife and daughter. Plus, there's just something about that man I don't trust. I can't quite put my finger on it."

Harrison reflected on her words as he slowly bumped and jostled his way along the pitted campground road, meandering around cavernous potholes. He'd have to remember to put in a request for re-paving in this section of the park. "I'm hard pressed to find anything good about the man myself."

"I can't imagine what it would be like married to a jerk like him. I'd rather remain single."

"Lily and Ross are divorced. But apparently he's trying to get her to reconcile." A niggle of guilt settled in his chest. He shouldn't have shared that last bit of information. "Please don't repeat that."

Megan shrugged. "I won't. I know this is rather personal, but I've noticed that you and Lily seem pretty close. Is there something going on between you two?"

Harrison blinked. "Um... no." He slipped into a parking spot in front of the office, under the shade of a gnarly oak, and left the truck idling.

Megan's eyes narrowed. She released the clip on her seatbelt and whirled to face him. "Is there a reason for your hesitation?"

"Lily and her daughter have needed some help lately. And I just happened to be in the right place at the right time."

"I see." Megan folded her arms across her chest. "And why did you disappear? You were supposed to help me with the tour."

Harrison's palms grew clammy and he wiped them on his jeans. "This is quite the inquisition, Megan. I'd rather not get into it, if you don't mind. I was having a difficult day. I'm sorry that I left you to fly solo." Harrison would have grinned at the use of his unintentional pun, if his emotions weren't swirling like an approaching funnel cloud.

"Ha! You're so funny." Megan fired him a gaze that was anything but humourous before she slipped from the truck, grabbed her things from the backseat, slammed the door, and hurried up the path. Not even a goodbye wave.

What was up with his partner? She was acting odd lately. Harrison's stomach growled, reminding him it was time for lunch. As he drove toward his cabin, his thoughts were in turmoil. His pulse quickened when he remembered Lily's grin as she accepted his invitation for a walk on the beach. Did it mean what he thought it could mean? Jasmine's question about whether he was going to kiss her mom sliced through his swirling confusion. He definitely had wanted to kiss Lily right then. Who knows what might have happened if Jasmine hadn't shocked them with her untimely presence? Was he beginning to have feelings for Lily? He hadn't meant for that to happen. Not at all.

His chest tightened as he recalled the pain of losing Karly Foster less than a year ago. Could his heart handle another rejection?

What kind of cockamamie plan had he gone and cooked up now?

CHAPTER TWENTY-TWO

Harrison parked his truck on the edge of Lily's campsite and shut off the engine. Ross and Jasmine were roasting marshmallows over a small campfire. There was no sign of Lily. Had she changed her mind and decided not to come? Maybe she was having second thoughts like he was. After all, the only reason he'd set up this date was to get back at Ross. Wasn't it? Harrison had endured a tormented afternoon, wrestling with his vacillating thoughts on the matter.

Ross fixed a cold stare in his direction. And that was all it took. Harrison stepped from his vehicle, pushed back his shoulders, and approached the campfire. When Jasmine saw him, she dropped her roasting stick and ran toward him.

"Mr. Somerville, would you like to toast marshmallows with us?"

"I'd love to, Jasmine, but your mother and I are—"

A horrendous yell sliced the air. Ross leapt from his chair and did a funky kind of dance. What in the world?

"Jasmine Elizabeth Martin," Ross bellowed, as he reached down to remove a stick from the top of his sandaled foot. "You are such a clumsy child. You dropped that scorching marshmallow on me."

Jasmine's bottom lip trembled. "I'm sorry, Daddy." The child scooted toward Harrison's side. He couldn't help but place a protective arm around her shoulders. Worry charged through Harrison. Twice in one day, her father had reduced this sweet child to a bundle of nerves.

"What's all the commotion out here?" Lily stuck her head out of the tent.

"Your crazy daughter dropped a flaming marshmallow on the top of my foot when *he* arrived." Ross wagged a finger at him before turning back to Lily. "I told you he was trouble and I forbid you to go with him tonight."

Lily slipped from the tent and zippered it closed. Harrison's knees weakened. She was wearing jean shorts and an emerald tank top. The top not only accentuated her figure but popped her hazel eyes to a sea-green hue.

"Ross, we had this discussion earlier and there's nothing more to say. I trust you will take loving care of our daughter while I'm gone." Her words were placating yet firm. "Let me see."

Ross propped his foot on the bench of the picnic table.

"Remove your sandal for a moment." Lily inspected his skin. "I think you overreacted a little. All the sticky marshmallow is on the leather of your sandal, except for this one little spot on your middle toe. Very little landed on your bare skin."

Ross leaned down and examined his foot a little closer. "Oh. Well, I felt the heat just the same."

Lily looked in Harrison's direction. "Are you okay, sweetie?"

Harrison caught himself before he nodded. *Phew!* She wasn't talking to him.

"I didn't mean to hurt Daddy." Jasmine scurried toward her mom. "It was an accident."

"I know, honey. Daddy's foot is just fine. No worries." Lily pulled back a strand of hair from her daughter's face. "You two make up before I go."

Ross sighed. "I'm sorry for getting angry with you, Jasmine. Come give your daddy a hug." He held his arms open wide and Jasmine fell into them.

Harrison took in the scene before him. Although he had wanted to laugh aloud at Ross's dance inflicted by the searing sugary treat, he had to admit, a burn from a flaming sticky marshmallow might make him lose his cool. At least Ross had apologized. He was impressed with the way Lily dealt with everything.

"She needs to be in bed by nine thirty."

"Yes, yes, I know," Ross grumbled. "You don't need to remind me. Jasmine, will you get your dad a wet washcloth? I need to remove this sticky mess."

Lily accompanied Jasmine to the clothesline on the far edge of the campsite where a washcloth was pinned up, while Ross did a one-legged hop toward him.

Harrison crossed his arms, his lips twitching at Ross's theatrics. Why was the man hopping if the marshmallow didn't burn his foot?

"I think we need to get some things straight." Ross halted in front of him, breathing hard. "Lily and I may be divorced, but that's only on paper. We're in the process of reconciliation, so don't be making any moves on my wife." Ross snarled the words between gritted teeth.

Harrison could think of a million things to say in rebuttal, but any words would only aggravate the situation. He had the strongest desire to give a gentle push on the man's shoulder and topple him like an injured flamingo. That might ruffle his feathers a little. Instead, Harrison pulled his keys from his pants pocket and dangled them in front of Ross's face. "Are you ready, Lily?"

Sweatshirt in hand, Lily stepped to his side. "Now, I am. Let's go."

❖

"I'm sorry." Lily apologized as they strolled side by side along the Sandy Dunes beach.

"For what?" Harrison tilted his head.

"Ross. You don't deserve to be treated that way. I admire your restraint. A lesser man would have decked him, and I wouldn't have blamed him."

Harrison took a deep breath. "To be honest, I can't say that it didn't cross my mind a couple of times today."

"I think I know why you behaved as you did." Lily picked up a colourful pebble from the shoreline and studied it.

"You do?" Harrison quirked an eyebrow.

"Yes, for Jasmine, and I have to say it means a lot to me."

Harrison smiled. "I am very fond of your daughter."

"I can tell." Lily tossed the pebble into the water. It made a tiny plopping sound and a small circle of radiating ripples followed. "The lake is so calm tonight."

"I heard the weather's about to change." He studied the horizon. Far across the lake, a gigantic tangerine appeared to be falling off the edge of the planet. The sun was going down in a blaze of glory, streaking the twilight sky with shades of magenta, pink, and lavender, despite the thin layer of cloud rolling in.

"This view is incredible. I've heard that sunsets over Lake Huron are right up there with some of the best in the world." Lily eyes were wide as she looked out over the lake. "And have you ever noticed that the prettiest sunsets occur when clouds are present? It's almost as if God is saying that he's with us during the storms of life and he will make all things beautiful in his time."

Harrison blinked. Although he had made the connection before with high-level clouds and the colour of a sunset, he'd never thought about the link to God. Could there be some truth to what she was saying? It might be plausible if you truly believed there was a God.

Harrison shoved his hands into the pockets of his jeans as they began strolling again. He stopped at the bottom of a wooden staircase. "Would you like to climb up to that landing?"

Lily charged up the steps in front of him. She'd tied her white sweatshirt around her waist and the body of the shirt flapped as she ran. "I sure would. I bet the sunset will be even more incredible from up here. Did you know that in all the years I've been watching them, I don't think I've ever seen the same one twice?" Her voice trailed behind her, dropping excitement in her wake.

I guess she really likes sunsets. Harrison chuckled and jogged up the steps, taking two at a time to catch up with her. "It's funny you should say that. I've often thought that too."

Lily reached the platform before him, leaned against the railing, and pointed. "Look at that narrow line of cloud that has zipped in front of the sun. It appears to have split that sphere of hot gasses directly in half."

Harrison slapped his hands on the railing and laughed. "Sphere of hot gasses? Now I understand where Jasmine gets her scientific knowledge. Perhaps her mother also has an extremely high IQ?" Harrison studied the interesting phenomenon, which paled in comparison to the woman at his side. The more time he spent with Lily, the more bewildering she became.

"Nope." Lily's nose scrunched up. "I'm as average as they come."

A movement in Harrison's peripheral caused him to turn slightly. An Eastern Kingbird perched on a nearby branch. Harrison placed a hand on Lily's shoulder. When she looked up at him, he put a finger to his lips. Then he gently turned her until her back was to him. Keeping his hand on her shoulder, he leaned down and whispered in her right ear, "Eastern Kingbird at two o'clock."

A few seconds later, her gentle nod confirmed the sighting. "I'll have to gloat about our find to Jasmine." She turned to face him. "Thanks for pointing it out."

Harrison swallowed as she looked up at him. Nope. Not average at all. He really needed some water. How had he never noticed such striking attributes before? Lily was so incredibly pretty, with her light smattering of freckles and hair that fell in unpredictable waves around her face. And those eyes... luminous hazel-green with golden specks that almost glowed. Must be the reflection of the sun on the surface of the lake. But no, the sun had almost dipped below the edge of the horizon now. What would make them twinkle like that? It was almost as if someone had shone a flashlight on the back of Lily's irises.

Lily took a step back from him before making a beeline for the wooden bench.

Harrison blew out a breath. The attraction simmering between them was growing. She must feel it too. He leaned against the railing and folded his arms over his chest.

Lily crossed her legs and swung one wildly. "So, tell me a little about yourself. You seem to know a fair amount about my life. I know nothing about yours. Did I hear you say that you just moved here a year ago?"

Warmth filled Harrison's chest. He couldn't remember the last time anyone had cared enough to ask about him. He plunked himself down beside her and stretched his legs out in front of him.

Over the next few minutes, Harrison told her everything, from where he was born to the murders in No Trace Campground and last, but not least, his lunar-truth-trek after his bizarre happenstance at Shadow Lake. "I'm sorry. Am I rambling?"

Lily placed a hand on his knee. "You're not rambling."

Harrison met her gaze. "I've probably bored you to tears when all you asked was a simple question."

"You're not boring. In fact, just the opposite. That's quite the story, especially the murders. You've lived dangerously." While her smile reached deep inside him, her fingers were burning imprints on his skin.

"Not of my own accord, believe me. I'll take dull and uneventful any old day."

Lily jumped to her feet and clapped her hands. "I think I have the answer you've been looking for."

Harrison would have laughed at her antics, so much like her daughter's, but her last sentence made him sit up straighter. "Are you serious? I've been searching for almost a year. How could you possibly know?"

Lily rubbed her arms. "Your vision of the cross on the water and the searing hand on your shoulder gave me goose-bumps."

"I know what you mean. It had a similar effect on me."

"God is revealing himself to you." Her eyes were incredibly large.

Harrison removed his cap and raked a hand through his hair. "I don't know about that. Maybe it was just an unexplainable phenomenon, sort of like the split sun tonight. Besides, why would God care about little old me when there are close to eight billion people on the planet?"

"You're not the only one he cares about. God loves everyone, but not everyone chooses to love him."

"And you have made that choice?"

"Yes, and Jasmine too."

"What about Ross?"

Lily pursed her lips. "That's difficult to say. I met Ross at church and thought he felt the same as I did about God. But his actions over the years have made me wonder."

"What actions?" Harrison lifted his palms. "Wait. If that was too personal, you don't have to answer that question."

Lily wrung her hands together and paced in front of him. "Ross lost interest in church and ..." her voice softened until he could barely hear her, "... he was unfaithful to me twice in our marriage." A hand flew to her chest as if the memory was too much for her heart to bear.

Harrison's gut clenched. And he thought he had problems with relationships. How would it feel to marry someone and have them betray your love, not once, but twice? When she stopped in front of him, he rose to his feet and lightly grasped her arms. "I'm so sorry."

"I guess I wasn't good enough for Ross." Lily blinked several times, as if trying to clear away tears. "If I was, maybe our marriage would have worked. I guess I'm just too plain, boring, and average."

Lily was not plain. Or boring. Or average. Ross was a jerk. Harrison could barely take his eyes off her tonight. But he couldn't tell her that. Could he? Should he? Maybe she needed to hear it.

Lily spun away from him to face the twilight-shrouded lake. Her swift action startled the kingbird into flight. Or maybe it was the wind rustling the tall grasses below that had frightened it.

Harrison moved to stand behind her. "Would you like to know what I see when I look at you?"

"No. I don't think so."

"Lily, please look at me."

She hesitated before turning. His heart lurched at the sadness in her eyes. Before he could restrain himself, he grabbed the dangling arms of the sweatshirt she'd tied around her waist and gently pulled her forward. "I see a wonderful and caring mother who loves her daughter more than life itself. I see an honest, genuine human being."

She pressed her lips tightly together and wouldn't meet his gaze.

"I see a woman who has been wounded deeply."

She shuddered. A hand flew to her mouth.

Harrison opened his arms and she rushed into them, sinking against his chest. He tenderly stroked the back of her head. "I'm so sorry for what you've gone through. But you need to hear this, Lily. I'm not finished." He tipped her chin up to face him. "There's an unexplainable brightness about you that draws people to you." Harrison's voice grew raspy. "Not to mention those startling hazel eyes, adorable one-sided dimple, full rosy lips..."

Lily stiffened in his arms. She took a step back. "I'm sorry. I can't do this." She spun around and headed down the stairs.

Harrison felt like smacking his forehead with his hand. *Congratulations, you idiot!* Had he pushed things too far? Lily was a wounded bird and instead of offering healing, his words had only caused her wounds to fester.

Frozen to the spot, Harrison watched her reach the bottom and begin to walk back the way they'd come. He had to fix things. He started for the steps.

About halfway down, an excruciating bolt of pain radiated through the back of his right calf. The pain was so intense his knee buckled beneath him. Horrified, he felt himself falling. Over and over he somersaulted. His legs, arms, and torso slammed mercilessly and repeatedly against the unforgiving wooden stairs.

His body finally came to rest in a heap of soft sand at the bottom. Harrison struggled for a breath. As pain coursed through his frame in various locations, he fought the waves of nausea and dizziness that threatened to pull him into an even darker place.

He blinked to stay awake. Then he blinked again. Was he hallucinating? It wasn't the wind that had rustled the long grasses underneath the stairs. What he saw lurking between the slats of the open wooden staircase made his hair stand on end. He really wished it was a horrible nightmare.

Except that it wasn't.

CHAPTER TWENTY-THREE

"Harrison. Wake up. Are you okay?" A hand gripped his arm and shook it, but he couldn't seem to pry his heavy eyelids open.

"I think so. Who's asking?"

"Lily and thank God you're conscious."

"Of course, I'm conscious. Why wouldn't I be?"

"You took a terrible fall."

Harrison finally managed to lift his eyelids. He could barely make out Lily's face in the dim light. Pain coursed through his body. Why was he lying on the beach? In the dark? With Lily staring down at him? "What happened?"

"Like I said, you fell down those steps." Lily pointed behind her.

His mind began a recovery mission through some very confused grey matter. As the fog began to lift, memories came flooding back. "I was coming to make sure you were okay. I wanted to apologize for upsetting you."

A warm hand touched the side of his face. Her eyes were soft. "It's not your fault. You didn't do anything wrong."

Harrison tried to get up and groaned.

"Maybe you shouldn't move. Should I call an ambulance?" Lily's voice sounded worried.

"No ambulance. Will you help me get up?"

Lily grabbed his left bicep with both hands.

Harrison sat up. When the world stopped spinning, he took a deep breath.

"Are you steady enough to stand?" Lily squatted beside him in the sand.

"It's now or never."

She grasped his elbow. "Okay, let's try it."

Awkwardly, Harrison clambered to his feet.

"How do you feel?"

"A little bit of a head rush and kind of dizzy."

"Take some deep breaths." Lily rubbed his upper back.

Harrison did as he was told until the shoreline levelled out.

"Now try taking a few steps."

As he walked, the back of his right leg felt extra warm. Lily directed him to a large piece of driftwood, the same one he had used countless times to sit on and contemplate the meaning of life. She ordered him onto it.

"Oh, my goodness," Lily cupped a hand over her mouth. "You need medical help."

"I'm sure I'll be okay."

"No, there's a nasty gash on the back of your calf that is bleeding profusely. You'll probably need stitches. That's strange. You must have cut yourself on something when you fell."

A vile image flashed into his mind. Should he tell Lily what he saw while lying twisted like a pretzel in the sand? Harrison craned his neck toward the staircase.

"What are you looking for?" Lily removed her white hoodie, dropped to her knees, and tied it tightly around his calf.

"Nothing."

"Let's get you to the hospital."

Harrison limped to his vehicle. By the time he reached his truck, he was perspiring and felt woozy. He reached in his pocket and tossed the keys to Lily. "You should drive."

After climbing inside, Harrison slumped against the headrest. His leg was bent at a strange angle and throbbed painfully. He reached down and adjusted the seat so that it slid back as far as it would go. That helped a little.

"We'll head into Sarnia," Lily informed him. "The drive is about forty minutes. Will you be okay? Are you sure we shouldn't call an ambulance?"

"I'm sure. Let's go."

As Lily sped through the Sandy Dunes Beach parking lot, every pothole jarred him almost senseless with pain. His right side ached along with his leg. Honestly, he hurt almost everywhere. At thirty-nine years of age, that kind of fall wreaked havoc with his body. But there was a bigger concern than his physical pain. He couldn't tell Lily who had caused his dangerous fall down the steps. When the truck jostled violently, Harrison let out an involuntary moan and grabbed his side.

"I'm sorry. I didn't see that pothole in the dark."

Harrison gritted his teeth. "No need to apologize for potholes. It's not your fault they exist."

"You may have bruised your ribs when you fell." Lily's voice carried concern.

"I'll be fine. Do you mind if I close my eyes for a bit?"

"Don't go to sleep. Does your head hurt too? Did you hit it? Maybe you have a concussion." Lily gripped the steering wheel until her knuckles gleamed white in the moonlight.

Harrison chuckled. Big mistake. Perhaps he did have some bruised ribs. "You worry too much."

"I can't help it. Once a mother, always a mother." Lily wheeled onto the main road through the campground.

"But, I already have a mother and believe me, I don't see you that way at all. Nowhere near." Harrison's smile was weak and lopsided.

"Oh."

She didn't say any more, but her tone of voice told him he was treading on dangerous territory. Comments like those had made her leave the viewing platform in the first place.

Harrison yawned. In case Lily's warning had merit, he tried desperately to stay awake. The bright yellow Tim Horton's coffee shop sign blurred as they drove through the community of Sunset Grove.

"We're here."

Lily's voice made him jump. Oops. He'd fallen asleep after all.

Harrison blinked at the bright emergency sign. He felt foolish as he limped through the parking lot, down the ramp, and toward the automatic glass entry doors. Not only because he had a sweatshirt tied around his lower right calf, but because he was using up valuable emergency room time for those with more serious illnesses or injuries. Should have manned up and just slapped a bandage on his cut.

Besides, he didn't need to add this emergency visit to Lily's stressful life. She had enough on her plate with her ex's reappearance, the challenges of being a single parent, and a stalker harassing her.

A security guard nodded at them and stepped out of the way to allow them to pass. Harrison scanned the waiting area. Standing room only. Oh boy. Another reason to leave. He leaned down toward Lily who was holding his arm for support. "Let's go. I'll be fine. We'll be here all night."

"Don't be ridiculous. I think you need stitches." Lily pointed at the triage nurse. "Get in there and get registered."

Harrison's lips twitched at her bossiness. "Fine. I'm going." He slipped behind the glassed-off triage area and plunked his aching frame onto the chair.

A frazzled-looking nurse droned in a monotone voice. "What brings you into the emergency tonight?"

Harrison glanced briefly into the waiting area before answering. He wanted to make sure Lily was out of earshot. "I think I've been stabbed."

The nurse's eyes widened. "What do you mean you *think* you've been stabbed? And have the police been notified?" It was interesting how that one sentence of his had removed the monotony from her tone. Entirely.

Harrison sighed and unloaded all the gruesome details. The nurse took one look at his lower calf with Lily's sweatshirt tied to it and paled. He followed her gaze and his stomach lurched. The sweatshirt was no longer white. And he was bleeding all over the floor.

She cleared her throat. "What's your pain level out of ten?"

"A strong eight point two five."

The nurse shook her head. "In all my years of asking that question, I've never had anyone decimalize it before."

Harrison shrugged. "What can I say? It's the first number that popped into my brain."

"You definitely are an enigma. I'll be right back." The nurse fled down a hallway and returned pushing a wheelchair. She wrapped a towel tightly around the bulging, bloody sweatshirt, urged him into the wheelchair, flipped the leg rest into position, and lifted his leg onto it.

When she whisked him through the crowd of patients waiting to be called in, several annoyed glances smacked him in the face. Sheesh! It wasn't like he'd purposely gotten a knife wound in order to jump the line. When Lily's eyes met his, her forehead wrinkled with worry. Immediately, she was at his side.

"May I accompany him?" Lily asked.

The nurse frowned. "Are you his wife?"

"Um, no, a good friend." Lily's eyes met Harrison's and the tenderness he saw temporarily sidelined his pain.

"We're very crowded back there. I'll let you know when you can join him."

"Thank you." Lily stepped back.

As the nurse scanned the locked door with her hospital ID, Lily reached for his hand and gave it a squeeze. "I'll be waiting right here for you. I'm not going anywhere."

His heart thumped loudly at her kind words and warm touch. "Hey nurse? Guess what? I'm now a flat six. Maybe I'm not such an enigma after all."

The nurse laughed as the door closed behind them. "The love of a good woman is the best medicine in all the world."

Harrison looked back at Lily who was staring through the window in the door, a perplexed look on her face. Hopefully she hadn't overheard the nurse, or she might scurry away like a rodent with a red-shouldered hawk after it.

Besides, Lily didn't love him. Not like that anyway. She'd told the nurse she was a good friend. And good friends were hard to find.

That should be good enough for him, right?

CHAPTER TWENTY-FOUR

Lily contemplated the waiting room as she awaited news on Harrison's condition. It was two o'clock in the morning and the room was just as busy as it had been when she arrived. Luckily, she'd been offered a seat about half an hour ago.

It had been almost three hours since Harrison had been wheeled through the locked doors. Her gut clenched with worry. What was taking so long? Perhaps his condition was more serious than she'd imagined.

An elderly lady shuffled out of the triage area on the arm of her aged husband. Lily jumped up and offered her seat. She might be tired, but the frail woman needed to sit far more than she did. Lily slipped into a corner by a vending machine and tried to occupy her thoughts by scrolling through old photos on her phone. But that soon became mundane.

God, please be with Harrison. Let his physical injuries be minimal. But more importantly, in his search for the meaning of life, may he truly find you.

Somehow, she felt responsible for Harrison's fall. If she hadn't scurried away in such a hurry, he wouldn't have come after her and taken a tumble down the steps.

Why did she leave in the first place? Oh. It had something to do with her rosy lips. A finger went up and touched her mouth. Honestly, her rosy lips were the last straw. It was the list of compliments from another man that her made her feel unsettled. The divorce had only been finalized a year ago and the wounds were still fresh and painful. Maybe she just wasn't ready to consider another man's interest in her. If that's what it truly was.

"Lily?" A pretty healthcare worker in green scrubs, hair pulled back in a long, silky black ponytail, called her name from the doorway. Phew! Saved from trying to figure it all out. First order of business was to make sure Harrison was okay.

She followed the nurse down a hallway and around a corner. The woman stopped outside a private room and motioned with her hand. "Mr. Somerville is in here."

Lily thanked her, pushed open the door, and had to step back to avoid running into a police officer who was leaving the room. What was going on? Had the nurse led her to the wrong patient? But when she saw Harrison sitting up in bed, a new concern charged through her. "How are you feeling? And why was there a police officer in your room?"

"I'm fine. Only thirty stitches and a bruised rib." Harrison shrugged.

Lily gasped. "Thirty stitches? And a bruised rib? Only? That's terrible. But you didn't answer my other question. Why was a policeman leaving your room?"

Harrison sighed. "Fine. I didn't want to tell you. It's possible that my injuries could have been caused by a knife. I had to file a police report."

Lily blanched. "You mean you were slashed? There was no one around. How could that possibly have happened?"

Harrison fidgeted with the neck of his hospital gown. "This thing is strangling me. They don't make them big enough." He grabbed a piece of paper off the metal trolley and studied it.

Lily felt like strangling him with her own two hands. "Harrison, answer me. What are you not telling me?"

Harrison held the paper up. "Doc gave me a prescription for some pain meds. And I already have some galloping through my system. Powerful stuff. I'm feeling mighty fine." He grinned.

"That's good, but I'm about to resort to torture to get an answer out of you, regardless of the trauma your body just experienced."

Harrison's grin flipped upside down. He shifted his weight and winced. "To be honest, I can't be sure what I saw. It was almost dark, and he was behind the staircase, half concealed in the tall dune grasses."

Lily's eyes narrowed. "*Who* was behind the staircase?"

"Your stalker."

A trembling hand covered her mouth.

"Maybe I was wrong. Try not to worry." Harrison rubbed the side of his hand over his forehead. "It was dark, and I really couldn't be sure."

"You think my stalker slashed you?" A shudder moved through her. "I should have listened to you and contacted the police earlier. I'm so sorry."

"Don't beat yourself up. You couldn't have known that the guy's actions would escalate to this degree."

"But if I had taken your advice, you might not be in emergency right now."

"Speaking of that, I'm allowed to go. Can you hand me my pants?" Harrison pointed to a pile of clothes on the chair in the corner.

"Seriously? You're free to go? What about your head? Did they rule out a concussion? And didn't I just see you wince when you moved?" Lily scooped up the pile of clothing and dropped it at the foot of his bed.

"Nah, must have been your imagination." Harrison smirked. "Besides, I need to get back to the campground. I have to report for work in the morning." He whipped back the white sheet and dangled his muscular bare legs over the edge of the bed. "And, the OPP are sending a police officer out first thing to search the area for clues. I need to show him where the assault occurred."

One sight of his legs and Lily took a step backward. "I'll just... um... wait outside in the hallway."

"No, don't go. Stay in the room in case I get dizzy or feel lightheaded." He pointed upward. "There is a privacy curtain."

"Fine. I'll wait right here." She pulled the curtain around the metal rod and waited on the other side, turning her back to the fabric regardless.

Seconds later, metal rings scraped the curtain rod and a slight breeze ruffled her hair as the curtain was whipped aside. "I'm ready to go." The voice next to her ear made her jump. When she turned, a full toothy grin had crossed the face that was only inches from hers. *Oh boy.*

Had the doc given him a little more medication than was necessary? A firm hand closed around her arm. "Let's fly this popsicle stand."

Lily followed him across the room. "What's the rush?"

"Hospitals are not my favourite place. I want out of here." He yanked open the door with his free hand.

Lily shook her head. "I'd take your time if I were you. You don't want to pass out, hit the floor, and spend several more hours here, do you?"

"I've got you to hang on to for support. You wouldn't let me fall, would you?" An arm with bulging biceps wrapped around her shoulders.

Her pulse jumped erratically when he smiled down at her. Harrison was flirting with her. And she kind of liked it. Shame on her. "Not if I can help it, but if you pass out, considering your size, I have a feeling it's more likely you'll take me down than that I'll hold you up."

Harrison laughed as they passed through the sliding glass emergency doors and walked across the parking lot toward his truck. Lily's hands shook as she searched her pockets for the key.

"At least you'd cushion my fall, making it a very pleasant experience indeed."

Oh my. Her cheeks were about to erupt into flames. Thankfully, it was dark, and he couldn't see. Lily opened his door and fled to the driver's side of the truck.

"Where are you going in such a hurry, Nurse Lily? Aren't you going to help me climb in?"

"You're perfectly capable," she said flatly. Harrison shuffled awkwardly inside, lifting his injured right leg with both hands and attempting to position himself before closing the door. Guilt pricked her chest. She should have helped. "Do you really have to work in the morning?"

"Yes, pretty lady, at eight o'clock."

Lily swallowed. He thought she was pretty? Probably just the drugs talking. She fiddled with the controls and blasted the air-conditioning. He may not be able to see her flaming cheeks, but he could probably feel the heat radiating from them. "How do you think you'll manage that? It's two-thirty in the morning. You won't get much sleep by the time I get you back to your place and you get settled. By the way, where do you live?"

"A cabin in the park. But, I have news for you. With that crazy dude on the loose, I'm parking myself in my truck right outside your tent."

His offer pleased her, but she couldn't let him know. "No way. Ross is camping with us now. You don't need to do that. Those pain-killers are skewing your thinking."

"Me? Skewed thinking? How can you say that?"

"Your bold flirting is a little out of character for you."

"I'm only telling the truth." His dastardly handsome smile acted like an oxidizer to her already flaming face. Yep, any minute now, she may totally catch fire.

After a few minutes, soft snoring met her ears. Lily breathed a sigh of relief as she navigated the dark empty roads back to the campground. With Harrison asleep, she had a few minutes to collect her thoughts and emotions which were all over the place tonight. Her mind flashed back to their walk on the beach. She'd enjoyed it tremendously. More than she liked to admit. Harrison was a kind man and oh-so-very handsome. When he looked at her and smiled, her insides did a funny flip. But there was more to a relationship than good looks. Ross had not only seared that fact in her heart, he'd burned a hole in it in the process.

And there was the matter of Harrison's faith—or lack of.

Deep in thought, Lily was surprised when her headlights lit up the sign to Piney Campground. "Okay, where do I take you?"

A muffled snort echoed around the truck's interior. "What? Oh, we're here already? I must have dozed off. I need to let security know about my accident. Then on to your campsite."

After Harrison informed the security guard at the main gate, she drove toward her campsite since he refused to tell her where his cabin was. It was an eerie ride through the dark campground.

It was even more disconcerting to find her ex-husband at the still-burning campfire waiting up for her. When he stormed toward the truck and flung open the passenger door, she swallowed the lump in her throat.

"Where were you two?" The angry expression on his face was alarming as he glared at Harrison. "If you've taken advantage of my wife, I'll make your smile resemble that of a hockey player."

"She's not your wife." Harrison straightened up. "And what we did or didn't do tonight is none of your business." He cocked his head toward Ross. "Do you have some sort of obsession with my teeth?"

Lily pressed her lips tightly together to squelch her amusement. Why was Harrison always talking about toothpaste and teeth?

"All right, that's it. I think it's time I set you straight." Ross rubbed a hand around a fist and shifted from one foot to the other.

Lily sighed. "Stop it, Ross. Harrison has experienced enough pain for one night. He had an accident at the beach. We've been in the Sarnia General Hospital emergency for the last several hours."

Ross's gaze was hooded as he peered inside the vehicle. "Were you swimming and almost drowned?"

Harrison frowned. "No."

"Then please enlighten me as to what kind of accident you could have at the beach? Did you get your toe pinched by a tiny crayfish? Were you attacked by a swarm of sand fleas?" Ross's grin was sarcastic. "Perhaps you tripped over a piece of driftwood."

"I fell down a flight of steps and required thirty stitches on my leg. And I bruised a rib."

"Really." Ross crossed his arms.

"Would you like me to remove the bandage and prove it?" Harrison angled his calf toward him.

Ross stared at the blood-soaked gauze and took a step back. "I guess that won't be necessary." He crooked a finger at Lily. "You. Come with me. It's time to call it a night. We'll let this clumsy park employee go home, get some sleep, and recover from his ... booboos."

"Are you sure you're okay to drive?" Lily turned off the engine but held the keys in her hand.

Harrison snatched the keys and dropped them into his shirt pocket. "Like I said before, I'm not going anywhere." He leaned his seat back in the reclining position and pulled his cap over his face. "Besides, I'm too drugged to drive."

Ross scowled. "You're a big boy. You can get yourself home. You are not parking at our campsite for the night. Absolutely not."

"Ross, leave him be. Good night, Harrison. Hope you feel better in the morning." Lily slid from the vehicle and moved to Ross's side.

"You should be more concerned about my scalding burn than his little tumble down the steps. I've developed a blister on my middle toe about the size of a dime. It could get infected, you know," Ross whined as they walked away.

"Be sure to take care of that injury, Ross. Did you know that marshmallow burns are particularly susceptible to flesh-eating disease?" Harrison hurled the comment out the truck door.

"You're ridiculous," Ross snarled back over his shoulder.

A few more steps away and he stopped and whispered in her ear, "I need more antibiotic cream on my foot. And pronto. Just in case the idiot knows what he's talking about." His voice carried alarm as he hurried away to the picnic table and grabbed the first-aid kit.

Lily rolled her eyes and glanced back at Harrison. With the passenger door still ajar, the truck's interior was lit up, and in the dim light, Harrison tipped his hat toward her and whispered the words, "Good night, pretty lady."

His message sent a tingle from the top of her head to the tips of her toes. Even if it was drug-induced and probably didn't mean a thing.

Just for tonight, she'd dare to believe the words were real.

CHAPTER TWENTY-FIVE

The morning weather conditions felt much like he did. Dreary and grey. A misty rain fell, and a thick layer of eerie fog hovered over the lake and shoreline.

Harrison had managed to grab about two hours of restless sleep in the truck, fighting against pain and a thunderstorm that whipped through the campground shortly before dawn. When he'd jerked awake a short time later, he was in a great deal of discomfort. He'd have to make a trip into Grand Beach and fill the prescription for pain meds the emergency doctor had given him. And soon.

Harrison limped through the damp sand, his lower right calf pulsating painfully, his rib cage aching with each step, leading the OPP officer to the place he'd seen the stalker. "So, this is the spot where I landed." Evidence of last night's brutal attack was indecipherable, washed away in the heavy downpour of the overnight storm.

"Tell me again what happened," Officer Brent Nichols prodded.

Harrison related the distressing incident to the best of his ability. Unfortunately, his mind grew as foggy as the weather once he got to the part where he began to fall. "I remember a sharp stabbing pain in my lower leg when I was about halfway down the steps. The rest was a blur until I landed at the bottom. It was then that I saw the figure of a man behind the staircase."

"You never got a look at his face?"

"Not a clear look. He was half-hidden in the tall grasses and the twilight made it difficult. But judging by his height and build and the fact that he was wearing a dark ball cap, I'm fairly certain I know who it was."

"Do you want to enlighten me?"

Harrison explained about Lily's stalker.

"Why would he attack you?"

"Maybe he thinks of me as a threat since I was with Lily at the time."

"Makes sense. Tell me everything you know about this dude and we'll check him out."

"From what Lily tells me, he's been calling himself Brad Pit, with only one t."

The officer smirked. "O ... kay."

"He told her he delivers bread to The Gardens Nursing Home where she works, although Lily admits she has never noticed him. And he is pressing Lily for a relationship."

Officer Nichols tapped his pen on the notepad he'd been writing in. "This guy sounds unstable. I'd be very careful, if I were you. Here's my cell number. Contact me anytime if you have concerns. And I'll keep you apprised of any information you need to be aware of."

The officer wandered around for a few minutes under the staircase making notes. Then Harrison led him back to the parking lot and said goodbye.

Next, Harrison stopped at the park office and notified his supervisor of last night's unsettling incident. Because of the discomfort from his wound and his lack of sleep, he wasn't about to argue when his boss suggested he take the day off.

Four hours later, bleary-eyed from lack of sleep and in a great deal of pain, Harrison finally caved and decided he'd better fill that prescription. He left his cabin in the campground and drove toward the pharmacy. He hated taking medication of any kind, but desperate times called for desperate measures. Relief from pain and a good sleep were top priorities. His body didn't tolerate meds well, though. In fact, last night's events were rather hazy.

As he drove, he couldn't stop thinking of Lily and Jasmine. Were they safe? Had Lily informed Ross about her stalker problem? If not, maybe she should.

He needed to see Lily again. That was another reason he couldn't sleep. She said she had the answer he'd been looking for. And it had something to do with God. Unfortunately, he had scared her off before she had a chance to enlighten him further. He had questions. Lots of questions.

How could she possibly have the solution to the turmoil running rampant in his soul? Could she understand the pain and regrets of his past? She mentioned something about God loving him. If God loved him, why had he allowed Harrison to suffer under the suspicion of murder for two years? Even worse than that, why had he allowed the murders in the first place? And why had every relationship ended in heartache and disappointment for Harrison? Perhaps he was truly unlovable.

Is that why Lily had fled? Had his compliments crossed the line of friendship? His grip on the steering wheel tightened. It was settled. He had to see her again. Ross would have to deal with it. Besides, being with Lily was getting to be kind of addictive.

After filling his prescription, his stomach growled audibly, and he slowed at the main intersection in Grand Beach. Of course, he was hungry. He hadn't had a thing to eat since dinner yesterday.

He flicked on his right-turn signal and headed to his favourite coffee shop for something to eat. Drained of energy, he limped across the parking lot and pushed open the door. A sharp screech assaulted his eardrums.

He'd know that sound anywhere. Jasmine Martin barrelled into his chest and wrapped her arms around his waist. Then she jumped back, her tiny features pinched with worry.

"What happened to your leg, Mr. Somerville? I saw you limping. Poor little lamb."

"Poor little lamb? He's more like an over-sized elephant who's blocking the doorway."

Harrison turned at the annoyed voice. An elderly, well-dressed woman drilled him with her gaze. It was Sunday and if she had just come from church, she certainly hadn't learned a thing about patience and kindness.

"I'm sorry. Excuse me." Harrison hobbled out of the way.

"Come with me, Mr. Somerville. Some people can be so rude." Jasmine grabbed his hand and dragged him toward a table in the corner where her parents were seated.

"Mom. Dad. Mr. Somerville is hurt. He was about to tell me what happened."

Harrison met Lily's gaze. The connection shook him to the core. And it was a very pleasant shaking indeed. He glanced at Ross. The disdain was almost tangible.

The young child dragged over a chair from a nearby table. "Please sit down, Mr. Somerville. You'll feel much better."

Harrison eased onto the seat, stretching out his sore leg. "Thank you, Jasmine. Are you sure you want to know what happened?"

"I don't care how bad it is. I'm tough. I can handle it." Jasmine sat up straight in her chair and folded her hands on the table, as if settling in for a long story.

Harrison's lips twitched. "What would you say if I told you that a pileated woodpecker mistakenly thought my leg was a tree and began pecking away for insects?" He held up one palm and hammered it with the fingers from his other hand for visual effect.

Her giggles thrilled him; they were exactly what he was hoping for when he fabricated the story.

Jasmine's nose scrunched up. "Try again, Mr. Somerville. We both know that's not likely."

Harrison blew out a breath. "All right, you've got me. As you know, I picked up your mother last night and we went for a walk on the beach. We climbed up a long flight of steps and were seated on a bench. The view was very beautiful."

Harrison smiled boldly at Lily. He was flirting again. But this time it was intentional. Her cheeks flushed red and remorse struck him. He didn't mean to embarrass her. She reached for her coffee mug and lifted it to her lips.

Ross grumbled something unintelligible, but the nasty tone was easy to discern.

When Harrison looked down at Jasmine, her wink surprised him. Had the little girl caught the implied meaning of his use of the word *beautiful*?

"When we were leaving I fell down the stairs. Clumsy me. And voila, the rest is history." He swept a hand over his leg.

"Oh, you poor little injured lamb." Jasmine stuck out her lower lip. "Does it hurt terribly?"

"Off and on. Could you do me a favour, Jasmine?" Harrison reached in his pocket and pulled out a ten-dollar bill. "Can you go up to the counter and order me a toasted bagel with cream cheese and a bottle of water? And get yourself a doughnut if it's okay with your parents."

She jumped to her feet. "I already ate, but I'd be glad to get your order." She crumpled up the money in her little hand and skipped to join the lineup at the counter.

Ross whirled on him. "What do you think you are doing? Flirting with my wife in front of Jasmine and me?"

Heat crept up Harrison's neck. Ross was right about one thing. "Okay, fine. Guilty as charged, but only on one count. I should have waited until Jasmine was out of earshot. But maybe it's time someone told Lily how beautiful she really is. And by the way, she's not your wife."

Ross opened his mouth then quickly closed it. He slouched in his chair. Perhaps the truth of Harrison's words had finally hit home.

"Thanks for watering down your injury to spare Jasmine from worrying. I appreciate it." Lily's hands were wrapped tightly around her mug.

"What do you mean, watering down his injury?" Ross tilted his head.

"I think you should tell him what really happened," Harrison suggested. "He needs to know for your protection and his daughter's."

Lily traced the edge of her mug with a shaking finger as she shared a condensed version of the troubling events.

The eyes of her ex bulged as he straightened, ramrod-like, in his chair. "Why didn't you tell me this before?"

"You haven't been involved in our lives for over a year. I didn't think you'd care."

Ross sprang to his feet. "Of course, I care. I care enough to get out of here, as far and as fast as I can. I'm not about to become this lunatic's next victim. Between that disturbed psychotic stalker and this player..." Ross waved a hand dismissively in Harrison's direction, "...you've become too high maintenance for me." He bolted across the coffee shop and disappeared through the glass doors.

Harrison's jaw dropped. Mortified, he risked a peek at Lily's stricken face. She looked as though she'd been slapped. He couldn't think of a single thing to say.

Was any of this his fault? He wished he'd avoided the coffee shop altogether, driven back to his cabin after he filled his prescription, and made himself a peanut butter sandwich.

But wait. He may have been guilty of a small amount of flirting to make Ross realize what he'd lost, but he wasn't guilty of the man's cowardly disappearance. Nope. Ross owned that all himself. And deep down, after knowing how Ross hurt his wife and daughter, Lily and Jasmine were much better off without him.

The spineless act was so reprehensible, it went beyond words. Did Ross really believe that Lily would ever take him back after that? Whatever happened to fighting for the woman you loved? As far as Harrison was concerned, Ross had just sealed his fate. Despite the fact that she was better off without her ex-husband, Harrison ached for her. "I'm so sorry." He covered her hand with his. Surprisingly, she let him.

Someone plunked a wrapper on the table in front of him, followed by a water bottle. "Here's your order."

"Thank you, Jasmine. That was very kind of you."

She held out her hand with the change clutched in it, but he shook his head. "You keep that for your favourite treat."

"Really? Can I, Mom?"

Lily nodded, her lips pressed in a thin line. Clearly, she was desperately trying to keep it together for her daughter.

"What's wrong, Mom?" Jasmine glanced around the shop. "Where's Dad?"

Harrison waited for Lily to answer. When it was apparent that she was unable to, he intervened. "Your dad left in a hurry. I'm not sure I understand why, but it was important to him."

Jasmine sighed and plunked onto her chair. "I suppose he got called into work and maybe that's a good thing. My dad always manages to make my mother upset. Now we'll need a ride back to the campground."

"Of course, I'll take you both back." His thumb massaged the backs of Lily's fingers.

She jerked her hand away. "We need to get our sleeping bags. They got wet last night because of the rain and they're in the Laundromat next door. And I need to stop for a few groceries on the way home. Is that okay?"

Harrison grabbed his food and drink and stood. "I'll eat this on the way. Let's go."

"Are you feeling better now, Mr. Somerville?" Jasmine nudged his side with her elbow as they walked through the parking lot.

"A lot better, my little rapscallion." He rested a hand on top of her head and smiled. "Thanks for taking such great care of me. This little lamb just needs some food." He rubbed his belly.

Jasmine covered her mouth and snickered. "You're welcome."

Harrison evaluated his condition. Physically, he felt better than he had before he entered the shop. The pain-killer he'd popped in the truck about fifteen minutes ago was starting to alleviate the intense throbbing in his lower leg. And as sad as he was for Lily and Jasmine, Cowardly Ross vacating the picture was good news for everyone involved. But had he played a role, even indirectly, in today's events?

Hobbling through the parking lot, an uneasiness about the future settled in his chest. Would Ross be back once he realized the mistake he'd made? Would the stalker try and attack him again? And, most importantly, were Lily and Jasmine safe?

CHAPTER TWENTY-SIX

When Lily discovered that Harrison had just taken a painkiller and his boss had given him the day off, she held out her hand. "Give me the keys."

"Okay, I won't argue with you." He dropped them in her outstretched palm.

After Lily had loaded the warm, dry sleeping bags into the back seat, Jasmine climbed in beside them and Harrison swung himself onto the front passenger seat. As Lily walked behind the truck she glanced into the back and her lower lip quivered.

She climbed into the driver's seat. "You fixed my bike? Are those two brand new tires?"

"Yes," Harrison mumbled through a mouthful of bagel.

"Thank you." The magnitude of his gift was touching. In her mind, the kind gesture only widened the gulf between the selfish actions of her ex and the altruism of the tender-hearted man beside her.

Despite Harrison's gift, Lily's heart was heavy. What kind of a man was Ross, to leave her at a time when her life could possibly be in jeopardy? And not just hers, but their daughter's? Lily sighed. She shouldn't be surprised. The only person he'd ever cared about was himself. But the adultery knife he'd stuck in her chest twice before twisted in a new direction. Not only had he not found her physically attractive, he didn't care about her at all—proven by his gutless actions just now.

Harrison must have sensed she needed some space, as he remained silent on the way back to the campground. Of course, he *was* downing his bagel as though he hadn't seen food in a week.

Jasmine squawked away in the back seat like an excited blue jay that had spotted a pile of peanuts. Extra money was scarce in their home, and Harrison's generous gift was an unexpected treasure. Deciding how to spend it was obviously causing some consternation. Oh, to be a kid again when your biggest dilemma was whether to buy bubble-gum ice cream in a waffle cone or a bag of M&M's. Lily repressed another sigh.

By the time they pulled into the grocery store parking lot, Harrison had nodded off. Lily rolled down the windows and shut off the engine. "Come on, Jasmine, let's let Mr. Somerville get some sleep while we get our groceries."

"Are you sure he'll be fine alone in the truck?" Jasmine sounded worried.

"Of course, he will. He's a grown man. No one will bother him. And we'll only be gone a few minutes."

Harrison hadn't even stirred when she and Jasmine returned to the vehicle. They loaded the groceries inside and drove to the campsite without disturbing him. However, the minute she shut off the engine, he bolted upright, words tumbling over his lips in a jumbled slur. "Oh, we're here."

"You fell asleep." Lily reached for the door handle. "How about I drive you back to your place after I unload the sleeping bags and groceries? Where do you live?"

"Aspen Ridge, Ontario."

She pursed her lips. "That's a long drive to work each day."

"What? Oh boy." Harrison raked his fingers through his hair. "I must be tired. My cabin is at the far end of the park. But if you drive me back, how will you get home? Walking back would take a few hours. And..." he waited until Jasmine had scrambled out of the truck and skipped out of earshot, "now that Ross is gone, I don't want you alone. It's much too dangerous."

A few days ago, Lily would have dismissed his worries, but after the vicious attack on Harrison, she had to agree. Because of the stranger's obsession with her, a completely innocent man had been injured.

Harrison glanced around the campsite. "I have a solution. If it's okay with you, can I park myself in your ex's tent until we apprehend this guy?"

Sadness intensified as she recalled Ross's panicked escape—so panicked that he had forgotten to pick up his camping supplies. "Suit yourself." She turned off the engine and began to unload the sleeping bags. She didn't mean to sound cold. And she really wasn't. She was just terribly sad.

"I won't stay if you don't want me to." Harrison reached into the back seat and loaded his arms with the two remaining sleeping bags. "It's totally your choice. Where do you want me to put these?"

"The picnic table is fine for now."

Harrison limped across the campsite and dropped one of the clean sleeping bags in the dirt. He stooped to pick it up and let out a groan. It was soft, but she heard it. And her heart faltered. An image of her bike with two new tires flashed through her mind. He'd been so kind to her and Jasmine. And his offer to stay on her campsite until the stranger was apprehended went way beyond the call of duty. Maybe it was time to give some of that kindness back.

Lily strode toward the picnic table and grabbed Ross's sleeping bag, which Harrison had just picked up. "Follow me." She crooked a finger at him as she headed toward the tent.

She opened the zipper and peeked inside. One positive note about Ross was that he was tidy. His backpack sat neatly in a corner beside a flashlight and a book he had been reading.

The stuffiness made it hard to breathe since the tent had been closed due to the earlier rain. "Give me a minute." She crawled inside, opened all the windows to allow a refreshing breeze to flow through, and unrolled the sleeping bag. Thankfully, the sun was now shining, and the oppressive heat and humidity had lessened somewhat.

She exited the tent and faced Harrison. The lines of exhaustion on his face worried her, but she cleared her throat. "Welcome to the Martin Inn. Your accommodations are ready, sir. I don't want to see you until supper time. Get a good rest." She held the flap door to the tent open.

Harrison smiled weakly. "Thank you."

He crouched down and sashayed his bulky frame through the small entrance. Before Lily had managed to zip up the tent, his eyes were closed. He really needed someone to take care of him right now. *And that someone has to be me.*

"Mom? Why is Mr. Somerville sleeping in Dad's tent? Isn't Dad joining us after work?" Jasmine walked toward her carrying a grocery bag.

Lily chewed on her bottom lip. How did she tell the truth without putting Ross in a bad light? "Your father left in a hurry. He didn't say when he'd be back. So, until then, I thought we'd take care of Mr. Somerville."

"Good plan." Jasmine lowered her voice. "I think he's in more pain than he's telling us."

"I'm glad you're okay with it." Lily blew out a breath. She hadn't really thought how her offer to help Harrison might confuse her daughter.

For the next few hours, Lily played several games of Monopoly with Jasmine then busied herself with preparing a meal.

While the steaks marinated in the cooler, she started a campfire, wrapped a few large potatoes in foil, and placed them on the rack above the fire to cook.

Then she made a salad with fresh greens, almond slivers, and mandarin orange slices to be topped with raspberry dressing just before the meal. At Jasmine's earlier insistence in the supermarket, she had picked up bakery-fresh cheddar breadsticks. They would go great with the salad.

While Jasmine perused one of her favourite science books, Lily set the table with her new blue-and-white-flowered tablecloth and blue plastic camp dishes. The only thing missing was a centrepiece of flowers. She'd love to grab a handful of Queen Anne's lace from the bush behind her site, but that idea wouldn't be received too well by a park naturalist. Wildflowers were meant to be enjoyed and left in their natural environment. Not to mention, the thought of wandering away from the campsite made her nerves a little jittery. Lily scrutinized the woods all around them but saw nothing out of the ordinary.

Finally, she plunked herself in her lawn chair and relaxed. Her daughter's description of Harrison as a 'poor little lamb' popped into her head and she smiled. What a paradox, considering his size.

Her thoughts fluttered to her walk on the beach with Harrison. Despite her quick exit, her heart did a little flip as she remembered his kind words. No man had ever said such wonderful things to her. Not even her own husband. She clasped her fingers in her lap. That thought could make her depressed. Instead, she would leave the past in the past and see what God had in store for her in the future.

Although... She bit her lip. If she hadn't hurried off, Harrison might not have been stabbed. Lily's chest tightened. *Wait one minute.* Just because she still suffered pain from Ross's actions and didn't know how to deal with Harrison's compliments, didn't mean she was responsible for a crazy man's violent actions. If her stalker had wanted to scare off Harrison, he'd have gotten to him eventually.

Thoughts of that demented man lingering around in the grasses below the staircase, probably listening in on their conversation, twisted her stomach into knots. Just how far would the crazy man go to get to her?

Prayer trumps crazy.

Lily smiled as the words a friend had once spoken to her flashed through her thoughts. They might not be Scripture, but she could latch on to those words and believe them in her heart. And that's exactly what she'd do.

CHAPTER TWENTY-SEVEN

A delicious aroma woke him. For an instant Harrison didn't recognize his surroundings. Then it dawned on him. He was in Ross Martin's tent. He didn't move for another moment, trying to force the grogginess from his mind. Were those tantalizing smells coming from Lily's campsite?

When he could no longer stand his gastric juices swirling with pleasure at the smell of barbecued steak, he sat up and awkwardly crawled toward the tent's opening.

Once outside he limped toward two amazing cuts of beef on a barbecue grill. But where was Lily? He called her name. He called Jasmine's name. No one answered.

Worry charged through him as he hurriedly scouted out the campsite and the surrounding area. What a fool he'd been to take a nap. What if Lily's stalker had abducted them both? The whole reason he'd offered to stay in Ross's tent was to protect them. If he'd failed, he'd never forgive himself.

Harrison continued to pace although each step shot discomfort through his calf. He forced himself to stop and think. They couldn't have been gone long, judging by the condition of the steaks.

He stared at his truck. Should he go and try to find them? Then he remembered. He had Lily's cell phone number. He'd give her a call. When a ringing noise emanated from her tent, he sighed and hung up.

Just then he heard voices approaching from around the bend in the road. Of course. Why hadn't he thought that maybe mother and daughter had paid a trip to the facilities?

Jasmine spotted him and flip-flopped toward him in her hot-pink sandals. "Mr. Somerville, you're up. Did you have a nice nap? We cooked supper for you. Do you like steak? Guess what I saw when you were sleeping? Two cedar waxwings were on a branch, working together to try and free some frayed rope, probably for nesting material."

Harrison laughed. "Yes, I had a nice nap. The meal smells absolutely fantastic and that's very exciting about the birds."

"Jasmine, will you get us all drinks from the cooler. I imagine the steaks are just about ready." Lily slipped past him and checked the grill.

Relieved that mother and daughter were safe and well, Harrison inched toward Lily. "You didn't need to do this for me. But I have to say that I'm glad you did. It smells fantastic and steak is my favourite meal."

"Someone had to take care of you and I'm happy to be that someone. You've gone out of your way to protect us; I appreciate all you've done." Lily removed the steaks from the grill and set them on a plate. "Besides, you're injured."

"It's not your fault that there's a disturbed man out there who attacked me. So, get that out of your head."

She didn't respond to that comment. "I'll just grab the potatoes from the fire and then we can eat."

A few minutes later the three were seated at the picnic table, Jasmine and Lily on one side and Harrison across from them.

"Do you mind if we give thanks for the meal before we eat?" Lily's eyes met his.

"Not at all." As he was about to bow his head, Jasmine reached for his hand. "It's a tradition. We always hold hands around the table when we pray."

As he clasped the young child's hand, his eyes shot toward Lily's. From the apprehensive look on her face, she had clearly been hoping Jasmine would forget the routine—just this once.

Their hands met halfway, and he liked the sensation. He could really get used to this. Out of respect, he forced his eyes to close, but it was hard to take them off the delicate flower whose petal he held.

As Lily's words, heartfelt and meaningful, poured out in reverence to her God, he was surprised at how personal they were. It was almost as if she was talking to a precious friend. He expected a rote prayer, like one that shot to mind from somewhere in his childhood, *God is great, God is good. And we thank him for our food.*

She thanked him for the food all right, and the weather, her job, her mom and dad, Jasmine and... he couldn't believe it. Did she really thank God for Ross? That loser?

How could that be? Didn't she hate the man? Harrison barely knew him and, even though hate was a strong word, he intensely disliked him. How could she now, after all Ross had put her through? What was going on here?

But the final straw—the one that almost broke him—she thanked God for him, for his kindness, helpfulness, and protection. Who was this man she talked about? He swallowed the lump in this throat. His emotions were taking a beating and he was thankful when it was over. She pulled her hand away and Jasmine did too.

"Let's eat. I'm feeling a tad peckish." Jasmine shoved a breadstick in her mouth and passed the bag, totally unaware of Harrison's rattled frame of mind. Jasmine's use of the English language continued to astound him.

A little while later Harrison sat back and patted his stomach. "That was the best meal I've had in a very long time. I usually eat take-out or have microwaveable dinners. The last home-cooked meal I had was with my mother when I visited last Easter. Thank you both so much. It was delicious." He pressed both hands to the picnic table and slowly stood. "Let me help with the cleanup."

"Absolutely not." Lily pointed. "Sit back down. Besides, you haven't had dessert yet."

"Dessert? You mean there's more to this fabulous meal? You ladies have gone all out."

"I'm making it," Jasmine boasted, poking a thumb at her own chest. She hurried to the cooler, retrieved a large bowl of vanilla pudding, and scooped it into three individual blue plastic bowls. While he watched, she opened a bag of M&M's and made a smiley face on the top of his dessert.

"There you go. I hope you like it." She nudged one of the bowls closer to him.

Harrison tilted his head. "When did you have time to do all this?"

"I bought the M&M's and pudding with the money you gave me, when my mom stopped at the store. While you slept Mom and I made the entire meal."

Harrison blinked as his eyes grew moist. The young child had taken the gift he'd given her and heaped it back on him. What was happening? Being around these two special people was turning him into a sentimental fool. If he wasn't careful, his insides would turn as soft and mushy as the pudding.

Harrison took a huge spoonful and gave her the thumbs up. "I've been treated royally by the two of you—so royally, you may have to roll me off the seat afterwards."

Mother and daughter giggled together. He loved the harmonic sound. Despite his concerns for their safety and the nagging discomfort from his knife attack, this was one of the best days he had experienced in a very long time.

CHAPTER TWENTY-EIGHT

Harrison glanced at the women as they cleaned up the dishes. How much time did he have left? Jasmine had plunked a book in front of him and warned him there would be a test when she was finished helping her mom with the cleanup. Jasmine amused him.

Even with his Masters in Ornithology, the review of birds was stimulating and informative. His quiz would involve being able to recognize the species of bird by an outline of its shape. Some, like the mourning dove, were easy to remember, others were not.

Jasmine tossed her tea towel up onto the rope clothesline and skipped to his side. "Are you ready for your quiz, Mr. Somerville?"

Harrison crossed his arms and grinned. "You are much too excited about this. I think you're secretly hoping I'll fail."

"Me? Never. Review is always good to keep the brain sharp."

"Right you are." He chuckled. "I'm as ready as I'll ever be."

It soon became apparent that she was a tough taskmaster. If he faltered even for a second, she made him move on to the next. He found himself breaking out in a sweat, but in the end only missed one... the tufted titmouse. For the life of him, his mind had drawn a blank on the name of that species, even though he knew it well as there were many in the park. Must be the medication skewing up his thinking, as Lily had informed him yesterday.

"Not bad, Mr. Somerville, you passed the test with flying colours." Suddenly, she snorted. "Did you catch the pun? Flying colours?" Her arms flapped like a bird in flight. "But, I'm disappointed that you missed the titmouse." She put a finger to her chin and tapped it. "Considering you're old, and your brain might be addlepated from time to time, I can throw you some slack."

"Old and addlepated?" Harrison pressed a hand to his chest. "I'm deeply wounded."

Jasmine parked her hands on her hips. "You're so funny. I wasn't insulting you. It's a biological fact that the human brain slows down as we age. Unless, of course, we keep it stimulated."

Harrison cast a glance at Lily who had her lips pressed together tightly while her eyes twinkled.

"Okay Jasmine, it's time to take your shower. Get your towel, pyjamas, and toiletries."

"Can we have a campfire later?" Jasmine jumped up and down, her ponytail whipping back and forth.

"Sure thing, but you're not staying up late. You've had a busy day."

Jasmine grabbed her book and skipped toward the tent. Why did little girls skip so much? *One of those mysteries of life, I guess.*

"I think I'll join Jasmine," Lily added. "I missed my shower this morning since Ross was in a hurry to get into town and dry the sleeping bags."

Harrison practically expected Lily to skip away too. His cell phone rang. "Excuse me a moment while I take this call." He walked to the far side of the campsite.

After Lily disappeared inside the tent with Jasmine, he spoke with the officer. As he listened, his steak sank to the bottom of his stomach, as heavy as if he'd eaten an entire cow. How much should he relay to Lily and how much should he keep to himself?

He ended the call as mother and daughter emerged from the tent. "I'm coming with you." He hobbled toward them.

"That's not necessary. It's obvious you're still in pain. I saw that face you just pulled, so don't try to deny it. We'll be fine."

"No. I insist."

"Fine." Lily sighed as she tossed her flowery bag over her shoulder. "Shall we take your truck or are you up to walking?"

"Let's walk. Exercise will be good for my leg."

"You are either one tough cookie or a foolish one." Lily shook her head and fell into step beside him on the gravel road.

"And just what would a foolish cookie look like?" A smile played at the corners of Harrison's lips.

"Like you, Mr. Somerville. Just like you." Jasmine slipped her hand into his left one. She had to stop doing that or he'd melt into a puddle onto the road.

"I've got broad shoulders. I can take it. There are worse things in life than being referred to as a foolish cookie," Harrison quipped.

"Like being called addlepated?" Lily nudged him in the elbow. When Jasmine giggled, Harrison found himself laughing along.

While the Martin girls had their showers, Harrison eased the discomfort in his calf by sitting on a nearby bench. The unsettling information he had just learned about Lily's worrisome stranger was eating away at him. How dangerous was this stalker to Lily? Would his actions escalate to the point of physical harm or abduction? He shuddered at the thought.

What was the solution? Suggest Lily depart for home? Although a house was more secure than a tent, it was out of the realm of his protection. That last thought surprised him and illuminated the depths of his feelings for the Martin girls.

In a short time, he'd become very attached to those two. Just how had that happened? A little over a week ago, he didn't know them at all. That seemed impossible. He felt as though they'd been a part of his life forever.

One thing he knew for sure. He'd wait until Jasmine was in bed before he broached the topic of the stalker with Lily. No sense upsetting the young child. She'd been through enough with the divorce and her own personal challenges of being a *gifted* child.

The moment Lily emerged from the washroom, his chest felt like a trampoline for his bouncing heart. When she stopped in front of him, the light flowery fragrance of her shampoo swirled through his nostrils, entered his brain and left him feeling... addlepated.

"I'm waiting on Jasmine to finish brushing her teeth." Lily ran a comb through her hair.

He nodded, then sobered. "Listen, Lily, when we get Jasmine settled for the night I need to talk to you. It's very important and I don't want the little munchkin to overhear."

"Does it have something to do with that phone call?"

"Yes."

Lily frowned. "I don't imagine I'm going to like what you have to say."

A child's hysterical cry cut through the air. Lily and Harrison turned toward the sound. Jasmine squatted on the pathway leading away from the washrooms, a wailing toddler in front of her. The young child's mother stood nearby, bouncing a screaming baby in her arms.

"What happened?" Lily hurried over and crouched down beside Jasmine.

"I opened the door and accidentally knocked him down." Jasmine's lower lip quivered.

The toddler crawled to his feet, stumbled to his mother's leg, and grabbed on tightly.

"You're fine, Owen." His mother patted his head, still bouncing the baby girl on her hip to try and settle her.

"I'm really sorry, ma'am. I didn't see your little boy." Jasmine scuffed the top of her sandal in the dirt.

"Not to worry. He'll be fine." The mother smiled and rubbed his blond curls.

In the middle of baby bedlam, a cyclist rode past on the main road and caught Harrison's eye. Harrison's chest tightened. The man wore a dark ball cap and black shorts. Beneath his shades, Harrison felt the man's threatening gaze drill him from the road. Was that Lily's stalker? Perhaps he was wrong, and his mind was playing tricks on him, especially after receiving such troubling information from the police.

Just in case, Harrison took note of the man's size, clothing, colour of his bike—every detail he could memorize before the guy disappeared past the building and out of view.

Harrison lumbered stiffly toward the scene of the calamity, which by now had calmed down considerably. The mother thanked Lily for her help and assured Jasmine that all was well.

On the trek back to the campsite, Jasmine twirled a strand of her hair around and around her finger. "I feel terrible. I didn't know that little boy was on the other side of the door."

"How could you? You are a kind, caring young lady. Accidents happen sometimes. That's why they are called accidents," Harrison reassured her.

Lily's gaze, angled in his direction, was so tender it made his insides flip flop like a fish on the dock. "It's wonderful when people take an opportunity and use it to build others up rather than tear them down."

Harrison's spirit was bolstered in a way he hadn't experienced in a very long time. Lily's words dove straight for his heart and made him feel valued. That he mattered in this world—to someone. He'd never, ever felt that way before. With anyone. Except maybe his mother.

His heart felt too large for his chest. Unbidden, the words of one of his favourite Christmas movies flashed through his brain and he had to bite his tongue from saying them aloud. *The Grinch's small heart grew three sizes that day. And the true meaning of Christmas came through, and the Grinch found the strength of ten grinches, plus two.*

Not that Harrison had ever thought of himself as the Grinch but being with Lily made his heart swell to astronomical proportions. And he knew without a doubt that he'd go to any length to protect Lily and Jasmine, even if he had to find the strength of ten Harrisons plus two.

CHAPTER TWENTY-NINE

Lily tucked her daughter in her sleeping bag and kissed her cheek. "Good night, sweetie, I'll be in soon."

"Wait, Mom, I can't find Cinnamon."

Despite a thorough search of the tent by flashlight, Jasmine's stuffed monkey was nowhere to be found.

"Perhaps it got caught up inside the sleeping bag and left in the dryer at the Laundromat," Lily suggested. "Or maybe you took it outside."

"No, I distinctly remember leaving him in the tent when we left this morning. He sleeps by my pillow in the daytime and then keeps me awake all night with his tomfoolery. He's nocturnal, you know."

Lily cocked her head. "Monkeys aren't nocturnal, are they?"

"Most aren't, but Cinnamon's species is. He's an owl monkey or douroucoulis and he comes from Panama."

Lily pursed her lips. "I see. Well, as soon as he comes out from his hiding spot, I'm going to have a talk with that furry character."

Jasmine pulled her sleeping bag up to her neck. "It's okay. I think I'm getting a little too big for stuffed animals anyway." Her voice faltered.

"Are you sure?"

"Yes." Jasmine yawned. "I'm sleepy."

"I'll be in soon. I'm tired too."

Lily slipped from the tent and joined Harrison at the campfire.

"That's odd." She zipped up her hooded sweatshirt against the cooler night air as she settled on to a lawn chair. "Jasmine has misplaced her stuffed animal. I can't imagine what she would have done with it." She stared at the dancing flames.

"Kids lose things all the time. I'm sure it will show up."

"You're probably right. How are you so wise for someone who has no children?" Lily flipped her gaze in his direction.

Harrison lifted a shoulder. "I was the most forgetful kid on the planet, as my mother still likes to remind me. My reputation was well-known in my family. Because of it, my father used to call me a noodlehead."

"Interesting." Lily smirked. "That nickname resonates with Jasmine's description of you earlier today when you forgot the tufted titmouse's name. What was that word she used again?"

Harrison lips twitched. "You know what it was. I believe she called me addlepated. And before that I was referred to as a foolish cookie by you. Maybe I haven't changed much, after all."

Lily's smile slid downward. "Okay, out with it."

"Pardon?"

"Unload the horrible news from that phone call you mentioned you wanted to talk to me about, once Jasmine was in bed. How sick is Brad Pit?"

Harrison reached down, picked up a handful of kindling, and tossed it into the fire. "Believe it or not, that *is* his real name."

Lily took a deep breath. "Really?"

"Harvester Breads fired a man named Brad Pit several weeks ago."

Her stomach swirled with apprehension. A large pop cracked the air and a sizzling spark flew toward her. She swung her leg wildly to avoid being burned. "Why did they terminate him?"

"They had several concerns. A belligerent attitude, late deliveries, and complaints of rude treatment by his customers were of the less alarming variety. But by far the most worrisome, and the main reason for his dismissal, was a report of harassment filed by a female employee from an unnamed business. It ended in a restraining order against him."

"Go on." Lily circled one hand.

"His harassment of this woman grew into obsession. When she refused his advances, he left her a death threat. She came into work one day and found the severed head of a bird by her computer.

Accompanying it was a note that warned her she could end up like the decapitated bird."

Lily's hand landed on her stomach. "Oh my. What happened after that?"

"The young woman quit her job, changed her name, and moved away. And Brad Pit has lain low since then. Definitely off police radar."

"Thank God he didn't hurt her."

Harrison nodded. "Unfortunately, you seem to be his next target."

"What do you think I should do?" Lily sat up straight and gripped the arms of her lawn chair.

Harrison scratched the stubble on his face. "I don't know. I would suggest you go home, but I'm sure this man knows where you live or could easily find out. He already knows where you work. I'm hoping he'll slip up in the park and we can nab him over the next few days. The police have been in contact with my park superintendent. They would like you to meet with a police sketch artist first thing in the morning, so they can post a drawing of his face in the campground. That would alert campers to not only watch for him but to be aware. The more eyes the better. It's a huge park and security can only do so much."

"That sounds like a plan. I'll agree to do that."

"Good. Considering the circumstances, would you allow me to stay on your campsite tonight? I don't feel right leaving you alone."

Lily touched his arm. "I would like that. Again, I want to thank you. I can't explain how much your help means to me. Ever since your assault, I've been very concerned. Add the maiming of the turtle and there has to be something seriously wrong with this man."

"I agree."

"I suppose I should file an official restraining order at the same time."

"Wise move." Harrison cleared his throat. "On another note, I can't stop thinking about our date last night."

Lily's insides somersaulted with his unexpected remark that seemed to materialize out of thin air, just like the spark had. When she realized her hand still rested on his arm, she pulled it back.

Harrison shifted on his chair to face her. "There are a couple of things I'd like to discuss with you. I want to know why you left in such a hurry. And I need some clarification over your answer to my question about the meaning of my life."

"Which one do you want first?" Lily clasped her hands together in her lap.

"Why did you run? I apologize if I offended you in any way."

Lily blew out a breath. "I didn't know what to do with your... compliments. Not only that, I felt guilty."

"Guilty? Why?"

"Like somehow I was being unfaithful to Ross." Lily watched the flames increase in size as they devoured the added fuel.

Harrison frowned. "You are no longer married to Ross. How could you be unfaithful? And because I mentioned you have rosy lips you were riddled with shame? I'm totally lost."

Lily skittered her gaze toward Harrison. "Do I have to spell it out for you?"

Harrison's forehead crinkled. "I think so."

"I... um... I fled because..."

"Yes?"

"Oh, I can't even say it." Both hands flew up to her cheeks, which felt hot to the touch. "I think you put too much wood on the fire. You've built a towering inferno." Lily got up, slid her chair back, and sat down. Then she jumped at the dark figure in front of her. How had he gotten up that fast? Harrison's bulky frame blocked the heat and light from the campfire. He extended both hands toward her and left them there until she clasped them. He pulled her to her feet.

When she made eye contact, her breath caught in her throat.

"I think I get it." His voice was husky.

"You do?" Lily bit her bottom lip.

"You are beginning to feel what I am, and it scares you."

Lily's pulse jack-hammered. Her heart felt as though it was clawing its way up her esophagus and trying to climb out her throat. "I don't exactly know what I'm feeling. I..."

A finger touched her lips. "It's okay. You don't have to say anything. You're confused and terrified, all at the same time."

She blinked then grasped his finger and pulled it away from her mouth. "How did you know?"

"Because I'm feeling the same way."

"You are?" Lily whispered the words as she tightly clasped his finger.

"I am."

"That fire is throwing out way too much heat." Lily let go of him and took a step backward. The lawn chair behind her tipped and fell onto its side.

When she stumbled, Harrison wrapped an arm around her waist, keeping her upright.

"Thanks. I'm so clumsy lately," Lily babbled.

Harrison grinned down at her. His gaze was so powerful she thought she might burst into flames. Perhaps she'd been hit by a flying spark after all. That must be it.

"To be honest, it's all a crazy kerfuffle." His hands slid down to rest on her hips, burning imprints right through her sweatshirt.

A nervous giggle escaped her. "What's a crazy kerfuffle?"

"Us."

Lily's knees weakened at his use of that personal pronoun.

"You emit some kind of addictive aura that is almost impossible to avoid."

Lily chortled. "What are you talking about?"

"I made this move to Piney Campground in a desperate attempt to start over and try to figure out why I was born in the first place. That's all I was looking for. But you fell into my life, literally, when you hit the back fender of my truck. Since then, everywhere I turn, there you are. There's a brightness about you that draws me and, so help me, the more I'm with you, the more I want to be. You are kind of addictive, even more so than my morning coffee."

Lily scrunched up her nose. "Me? Addictive? That's the craziest thing I've ever heard. Are you taking too many pain meds?"

"I've never seen things so clearly before."

"I'm not ready for any of this."

"Neither am I." Harrison shrugged, but he had an enormous smile on his face.

"Stop smiling. You're making this more difficult than it has to be. Let me go, you big lug." Lily placed her palms on his chest. But she didn't push.

"You don't mean it."

"If we stay in each other's arms, we may do something neither of us is ready for."

"I don't think I'd ever regret kissing you." Serious and impactful, his words reached deep inside and left her feeling very... kerfuffled.

"Please don't talk like that." Lily's voice trembled.

Harrison tapped the tip of her nose with a finger. "I do take exception with you calling me a big lug. I'm going to get a complex with this growing list of nicknames I seem to be acquiring."

Lily relaxed a little in his arms. "The noodlehead name was all your own."

"Your laugh is the most musical sound in the entire world. It reminds me of wind chimes tinkling softly in the breeze." He played with a curl that had coiled on her forehead.

"No one has ever told me that before." As much as she tried to deny it, being in Harrison's arms was like finding safe harbour, or a port in a storm. The connection between them defied logic. How could that be? She barely knew him.

"I think we should call it a night." He let go of her and took a step back.

"I concur."

"You concur? Now I understand why Jasmine is so articulate." He reached for her hand and led her toward her tent. "Goodnight, Lily. Keep your cell phone nearby and I'll do the same. Call me the moment you have any concerns. I'm just a few feet away."

"That's comforting. Thank you." She didn't want to let go of his hand. She was starting to understand the addiction thing.

"No need to thank me. It's my pleasure to keep you safe."

"Even after you got stabbed on my account?" Why was it so hard to separate from him? She'd never felt so conflicted in her life.

"Don't worry. It's just a scratch." He lingered too.

"Hardly." Her eyes travelled to his lips.

Harrison let go of her hand and crossed the campsite, heading for his tent. "See you in the morning, Lily. Sweet dreams."

"Good night," Lily replied, the words trailing after him softly.

For a moment, she didn't move. Maybe she'd really and truly melted to the spot. Her emotions were in turmoil. How in the world had she gone from her mad dash at the beach when Harrison mentioned her rosy lips, to an overwhelming desire to kiss the man?

That transformation in a few short hours was a conundrum for sure. Was she truly falling for Harrison? Or was she lonely and confused, vulnerable from the heartache of her failed marriage. Maybe it was the threat from a very scary stalker that had her clinging to this kind park employee.

Perhaps it was a combination of the three. That would explain why she had trouble sorting out her feelings.

Lily slipped into the tent and a few minutes later into her sleeping bag. The minute her head hit the pillow and her eyes closed, the entire last few minutes stuck in her head like a video on replay.

But this was one she could watch over and over again.

CHAPTER THIRTY

Harrison tossed and turned. His leg throbbed, his head ached, and for the life of him, he couldn't get comfortable. He really needed to take another painkiller but was afraid if he did he'd sleep too soundly and possibly miss a distress call from Lily. If her stalker re-appeared, he needed to be ready. If anything happened to Lily or her daughter, he'd never forgive himself. He grimaced. Such strong feelings for a mother and daughter he didn't even know a week ago.

Another reason for his sleeplessness was the undeniable attraction he felt for Lily. He'd been almost blind-sided by the arrival of the lovely brunette in his life. It was remarkable when he thought about it. It was as if she had just dropped into his path. Of course, she did do exactly that. Or crashed in front of him, at least.

Usually when he met a woman he was interested in, he'd been searching for someone. This time was different. He'd sworn off relationships in the hopes of solving the distressing dilemma of whether or not his life had meaning and purpose.

When Lily fell off her bike that first day, he'd found her intriguing. Then it seemed as if some hand of fate *kept* dropping her and her daughter in his path. And he liked it. No matter where he turned, there they were. Maybe there was some truth to Jasmine's words on the canoe dock. Was God arranging this? Was he in control? Such deep thoughts for his addlepated, noodlehead of a brain.

Harrison smacked his forehead. It had happened again. He still didn't have that answer from Lily to his lunar-trek for truth. His first question about the reason for her hasty departure on the beach had not only consumed their evening but led to some interesting developments between them.

Oh well, that was another excuse for him to spend more time with her—not that he needed an excuse. But he desperately wanted that answer she confessed she had, to judge its validity. The little bit she had shared about God left him with more questions than answers.

Terribly uncomfortable, he wrestled around on top of his sleeping bag. It was too warm a night for him to crawl inside. Besides, he always ran a tad warmer than most people. He often joked with friends that he must have ancestry from Siberia.

He turned onto his side and felt a lump beneath him. What was that? Probably a clump of uneven earth below the tent. But the lump shifted with his movement. Had Ross left an article of clothing inside the bag? Assuming he'd find a pair of scrunched up stinky socks, he dug between the layers of fabric and pulled out a...

His forehead furrowing, he reached for the flashlight. No. It couldn't be. A chill settled over him as he stared at what could only be... Jasmine's lost monkey. Missing its head.

CHAPTER THIRTY-ONE

"Good morning, Mr. Somerville. You don't look very well today. Is your leg continuing to hurt?" Still in her pyjamas, Jasmine skipped toward Harrison, her long hair flying helter-skelter around her shoulders.

"It's better than yesterday. Thanks for asking." He smiled down at the spunky sprite.

"Time for breakfast." Lily juggled bowls, cereal, and milk as she approached the picnic table. "Can you grab the spoons, Jasmine? I forgot them."

As the young child hurried off, images of her decapitated monkey haunted Harrison. "I don't think Jasmine should come with us to the police station this morning."

"My thoughts exactly, but do you have a solution? What should I do with her?"

"I have an idea. My co-worker, Megan, loves kids. In fact, she runs a kid's nature program in the park. I think she'd be fine with us dropping Jasmine off to visit with her for a couple of hours."

"I'm good with that, as long as Jasmine doesn't object." Lily set the items on the table and passed the bowls around.

"Object to what?" The young child plunked herself down on the bench beside him, her eyes wide with curiosity.

"Mr. Somerville and I have an appointment today. Would you mind spending time with a co-worker of his?" Lily opened the lid of the cereal box.

"Not at all. Unless it's 'Old Cranky pants'." Jasmine snorted while passing out the spoons.

Harrison cleared his throat. "Actually, it *is* with Megan and I was hoping you could do me a favour and forget that I called her by that name." As he poured cereal into his bowl, he could feel the heat of Lily's gaze, but couldn't decipher if she was annoyed or amused. Maybe a bit of both, if that was possible, since he figured she was unaware of the nickname he'd saddled on his co-worker.

"I'll do it for you, Mr. Somerville, but I'm not sure I'm going to like it. She can't even tell her bird species apart."

Harrison clamped his lips together tightly. Laughing would only encourage her. He reached for the jug that Lily passed him. She was biting her bottom lip. He turned back to Jasmine. "I don't think we should judge a person's worth based on that criteria."

"I guess I can give her another chance. But only one more. There's a limit to my endurance." Jasmine dipped her spoon into her bowl and brought it to her lips then paused.

"Hurry and finish your cereal," Lily prodded her daughter. "We're running late."

Harrison could almost feel the tension emanating from Lily and he didn't blame her. Most likely, it was over their morning appointment. And he couldn't imagine it would get any better once he broke the news of the disturbing discovery that he'd found in his sleeping bag.

"I'm almost done, but I just thought of something. I need to run inside and get my book. I'm going to give old cranky... I mean Megan, the same test I gave Mr. Somerville and see how well she does." Jasmine dropped her spoon into her bowl, splashing cereal and milk on the tablecloth, and raced toward the tent.

Lily rolled her eyes. "Jasmine Martin. Did you not just hear what Mr. Somerville said?"

Harrison waited until Jasmine was inside the tent and out of earshot. "Ah, leave her be. Besides, I'd love to know how Megan scores."

Lily ripped a banana from the bunch and held one out to Harrison. "Only if you stop encouraging her. She can be downright rude to people who don't think as she does."

"No thanks." Harrison raised a palm toward the banana. "Megan will be fine. Besides, she *was* very cranky on the birding excursion the other morning. She deserves a little payback."

"Suit yourself, but bananas are high in potassium. They're excellent for you." Lily peeled back the skin.

"That's nice." Harrison swallowed his last bite of cereal. "But, I prefer getting my potassium other ways."

"Such as?"

"Chocolate chip cookies."

"Nice try. I think you need a lesson in nutrition." Lily smirked.

Mission accomplished. She faced a tough day ahead and if he could make it a little brighter with his crazy humour, so be it.

Lily wiped the tablecloth where Jasmine had been sitting then flung the cloth in his direction, sending a lone Cheerio at him. Harrison picked off the sticky oat that had glued itself to his park shirt and flicked it back at Lily.

"Don't be throwing food around, you two. It's not only wasteful, but immature behaviour." Jasmine glared at them, hands on hips.

Harrison cocked an eyebrow at Lily. He'd never seen this playful, mischievous side before. Perhaps his attempt at humour was wearing off after all. If it helped her relax and smile a little, he'd clown around even more. "She started it." He pointed at Lily.

"Guilty as charged." Lily continued wiping the tablecloth, but not before skittering him a gaze that spiked his pulse.

A sizzling spark passed between them, reigniting the passionate flicker from last night. At least he felt it. Did she? Or was this growing attraction all a flickering of his own imagination?

⚜

A few minutes later, Harrison and Lily dropped Jasmine at the park office. Harrison knew Megan well enough to decipher that her enthusiasm for being saddled with Jasmine was phony. But it was important that Lily meet with the police sketch artist and file her restraining order. And it was crucial to shield Jasmine from the distressing circumstances as much as possible, especially the condition of her favourite stuffed animal. A shudder raced through Harrison. He was not looking forward to breaking the news to Lily. Better now than in front of the police, though. He waited until they climbed into his park truck. "I have something to tell you and you're not going to like it."

"That sounds ominous. Go ahead, I'm listening." Lily fastened her seatbelt and dropped her purse at her feet.

"I found Jasmine's monkey."

"That's good news ... isn't it?" Lily's gaze was hooded.

"Not exactly." His hand paused on the key in the ignition.

"Why?"

"It was missing its head."

Lily gasped. "Where did you find it?"

"It was stuffed inside my sleeping bag."

"Where is it now?"

"I brought it along. It's in my backpack. We'll need to show it to the police." Harrison turned the key and the engine rumbled to life.

Lily stared straight ahead as they drove through the campground, almost as if the news had sent her into shock. "There's no doubt in my mind that I'm filing that restraining order, especially now that my daughter may be targeted. I wonder when he could have done that."

"Those few minutes when I accompanied you and Jasmine to the showers is the only opportunity he would have had."

Lily nodded. "Makes sense."

She remained extremely quiet for the rest of the drive, until they arrived at the OPP station in Grand Beach.

Harrison was pleased to see Brent Nichols again as he liked this law enforcement officer. Besides, he was familiar with their case.

Lily did her best to describe the perpetrator's face to the young artist named Marcel, who sketched as she supplied him with a description of her stalker's features.

Harrison grimaced at the look on Lily's face as she considered the sketch in her hands. "Yes, that's a very good likeness of him." She dropped the paper as though it carried bubonic plague.

After the sketch artist disappeared from the room, Harrison broke the news he was dreading to the officer. When he pulled out the headless monkey, Lily covered her mouth with a hand. "I think I'm going to be sick."

Officer Brent pointed down the hallway. "First door on your right."

Harrison jumped up to accompany her, but she shoved him out of the way and sprinted past him. His heart felt heavy as he slumped back onto his chair.

The officer steepled his fingers. "This tells me that you are still his prime target."

"*I* am?"

"The fact that the monkey was found in your sleeping bag was a direct threat against you. If he had wanted to scare Lily or Jasmine, it would have been in their tent."

"Sensible deduction." Harrison kept his eyes glued down the hall.

When the door to the ladies' room opened and Lily's face, although pale, carried fresh determination, he marveled at her stamina.

"Once the sketch is posted in several locations around the campground, I hope it will panic your stalker enough that he will either flee or slip-up, so we can catch him." Brent tapped his pen on the table.

Harrison nodded. "Let's hope you're correct."

"If the posters are ready before day's end, I'll bring them by the park office." The officer's chair scraped along the floor as he stood. "In the meantime, I'd caution both of you to be vigilant and not go anywhere alone, especially you, Lily."

As Harrison and Lily left the station and walked through the parking lot, he reached for her hand. "Are you okay?"

"I'm scared."

"I'm not going to let anything happen to you or Jasmine." He squeezed her hand tightly and her eyes misted.

Lily blew her nose a few times on the way back to the campground, clearly struggling with her emotions. Harrison remained silent. What else could he say? There really were no more words to soften the crisis she was going through.

About twenty minutes later, they entered the park office building. Harrison stopped outside a small room. "I need to talk to my supervisor for a minute while you get Jasmine."

While Lily slipped down the hall in search of her daughter, he hobbled inside and met with his boss, Randy. "I'm in need of a few more days off. Will you operate okay without my help?"

"That leg still giving you grief?" Randy reclined in his chair, feet propped on his desk, arms behind his neck.

"Yes, but the request for time off is more of a personal nature."

"Does this have anything to do with the situation with Lily Martin and her daughter?"

Harrison looked down at his feet. "I'm really sorry to ask, but I fear their lives are in danger and..."

Randy dropped his feet to the floor with a loud thud and sat up straight. "No need to apologize. Take all the time you need and keep us posted on any new developments."

Harrison reached across the desk and shook his hand. "Thank you, sir. By the way, the police will hopefully be stopping by later today with sketches of the stalker to post around the campground."

Randy Wilson sighed. "Yes, they've been in contact with me about the flyers. Let's hope they help and this all gets resolved quickly."

As soon as Harrison stepped from his supervisor's office, he recognized Jasmine's jingling giggle trickling down the hallway. He blew out a breath. He had to admit he'd been a tad nervous about leaving the young child alone with Megan.

His relief was short-lived. The moment he entered the room, tension emanated from his co-worker like steam from the spout of a boiling kettle.

"Well, there he is, my wonderful co-worker and friend. Now it's your turn." Her demented grin made Harrison uneasy, like a bird about to be pounced upon by a ravenous cat.

"My turn?" Harrison's forehead wrinkled. "I already had my test yesterday."

"Megan didn't do quite as well as you did, Mr. Somerville." Jasmine snickered. "But I'm sure with a little practice she'll improve. The potential is there."

"Let's see how you do with test number two." Megan cackled like a lunatic. "Quick, name the bird that makes a sewing-machine-like sound."

"The marsh wren," Harrison replied.

"What bird tells you to drink your tea?"

Harrison crossed his arms. These questions were not that difficult. "A towhee."

Megan growled, obviously displeased that she hadn't tripped him up. "What bird makes the sound of his name?"

"A chickadee."

"Wrong," Megan belted loudly. Harrison stared at her. Was she losing her mind? "It's a whip-poor-will."

"Technically I'm not wrong. Chickadees do say their own name too."

"But that's not the answer I was looking for, so you get two out of three." Her smile was as phony as his Grandma Esther's teeth. "Apparently it's better than I did." Megan tossed the book onto the table.

"Megan *flunked*, but I offered to come tomorrow and give her another lesson."

Harrison cringed at Jasmine's over-emphasis on the *flunked* word. He was definitely going to get an earful from Megan the minute she had him alone.

"That's a generous offer, Jasmine, but I'm busy tomorrow and the next day and the next day. In fact, the rest of my week is tied up."

"Thank you for spending time with my daughter today. It was greatly appreciated. I had a very important appointment that I couldn't have kept without your help." Lily's soft words seemed to whoosh the annoyance from his partner.

Megan's gaze dropped to a pile of colouring sheets with nature scenes and a box of pencil crayons. "Glad I could be of help." She stood, grabbed the supplies, walked to the far corner of the room, and placed them in a tall cabinet.

Harrison watched her. "It's time for lunch. Would you like to join us, Megan?"

His co-worker kept her back to them. "I'll pass, thank you."

"Suit yourself. Come ladies, this poor little lamb is really hungry." Harrison patted his stomach.

Jasmine giggled. Even Lily managed a crooked smile. Which was what he lived for. That realization slammed him full in his unsuspecting heart.

CHAPTER THIRTY-TWO

Lily sat sipping coffee in her lawn chair under the shade of two large trees, beside the lightly swaying hammock. She surreptitiously stole a peek at Harrison over the top of her mug as he fixed himself a peanut butter sandwich. That man had her puzzled. Did men like him truly exist? His kindness was, at times, so over the top that she didn't know what to do with it. Lily traced circles in the dirt with the tip of her sandal. Her thoughts were a jumbled, muddied mess.

It had been very generous of Harrison to offer to treat them all for lunch at the park restaurant, but ever since she had taken one look at her child's decapitated stuffy, she'd felt ill. And she had the start of a headache. The seclusion of her campsite was far more appealing than sitting in a restaurant.

Lily bit the inside of her cheek. She had a decision to make. As much as she didn't want to give up her hard-earned and long-awaited vacation, she was seriously thinking of packing up and going home. It wasn't what she wanted to do but, considering the circumstances, it felt as though it was the safest option for everyone involved.

Jasmine would not be thrilled at cutting short their camping trip, but it was for the best. With a stalker after them, home would be a lot more secure than a tent. Still, she couldn't make that final decision just yet. Jasmine not only thrived but blossomed in nature.

"I still haven't found my monkey. Have you seen him, Mr. Somerville?"

Lily's stomach swirled in turmoil. Her eyes darted toward Harrison's as she brought her mug to her lips then lowered it again. She couldn't seem to take another swallow. How would he answer that question truthfully?

Harrison screwed the lid on the peanut butter jar and snapped his fingers. "I have an idea. How would you like to go shopping today?"

"Are you serious?" Jasmine clapped her hands together and jumped up and down on the spot. "Mom and I love shopping."

Harrison rubbed the top of her head with his hand. "I heard the weather forecast earlier and they're calling for more thunderstorms, so I thought we could spend the day away from the campground."

Jasmine dashed to Lily's side and yanked on her arm, almost spilling her drink. "Come on. We need to get ready."

Lily laughed. "Okay, honey. I'm coming. Just give me a minute to finish my coffee."

"Hurry up, Mom. We don't want to make Mr. Somerville wait. I'm going to change into my purple sundress."

Lily watched Jasmine slip inside the tent and nixed her plans to go home—for the moment. Maybe she'd reconsider when they got back from their shopping trip. She didn't know what Harrison had in mind, but at least it was a great diversion from the question Jasmine had thrown at him about her stuffed animal. And it would hopefully get them far away from Brad Pit's dangerous clutches.

Lily tipped the remnants of her coffee into the bush beside her and walked toward Harrison. Why did her legs feel like sloppy noodles? "Thank you. I don't know how you came up with that idea so quickly."

"Oh, the plan's been brewing in my mind for a little bit now." His roguish grin weakened her knees even further.

"Really?" Her chest felt funny. In fact, she didn't feel well at all. She had to stop drinking so much coffee. Her heart was racing so fast, she felt light-headed. A fresh wave of nausea rolled through her. She broke out in a cold sweat. If they were going shopping, she'd better clean up. She reached for the jar of peanut butter, but it moved on her. Why was the picnic table tipping onto its side?

Then everything went black.

Who keeps yelling about a cloth? Nothing made sense. Lily tried to focus, but everything swirled around her, like when she was a kid spinning on a merry-go-round. Where was she? Something pounded loudly in her right ear as she was being jostled about. *Is that a heartbeat?* Slowly her vision cleared. She was in Harrison's arms, her head leaning against his chest. He lowered her onto the hammock and wiped her face with a cool cloth. It felt so refreshing. The longer he wiped, the clearer her vision became.

"What happened?" Lily stared up into two very concerned faces, Jasmine on one side of her and Harrison kneeling on the other.

"That's what I'd like to know, Mom." Jasmine stroked her arm. "You've got me quite distressed."

"I have no idea." Lily placed the back of a hand on her throbbing forehead. She licked her lips. "Can I please have a drink of water?"

"I'll get it." Jasmine raced off.

"What happened to me?" Lily whispered. "I'm as weak as a kitten."

"You reached for the jar of peanut butter and the next thing I knew, you were falling. I grabbed onto you just before you hit the dirt."

"I fainted? That has never happened to me before. But, I haven't felt well since..." Lily lowered her voice, "... you brought out what was left of Cinnamon at the police station.

Harrison nodded, a tender look in his eyes. "I'm so sorry. I wish you didn't have to see that. But I think I know what might be going on here. Did you vomit at the police station?"

Lily bit her bottom lip. "Yes."

"And you haven't eaten anything since."

"No. I wasn't hungry."

"I think your sugar took a nosedive. Add the stress of everything else you've been going through, and this is how your body reacted. Do you suffer from hypoglycemia?"

Lily shrugged. "Not that I'm aware of. I've never passed out before."

"Make a doctor's appointment when you get home and have your glucose levels checked."

"Okay, Dr. Somerville." She smiled weakly.

Harrison reached for her hand and pulled it toward him, entwining his fingers through hers. "Seriously, Lily, you scared the life out of me."

Jasmine thrust a water bottle in front of her face. "Here you go, Mom."

Lily reached for the bottle and was surprised at how her hand shook. She uncapped it, but because of her reclining position, wasn't able to take a drink. She looked at Harrison. "Can you help me sit up?"

He slid a hand under her neck, another under her legs, and scooped her up into his arms. A small amount of water slopped over the edge of the bottle and onto her face. Lily inhaled sharply at the cold shock.

He carried her to a lawn chair and lowered her carefully into it, as though she might break or something. "Did you pack orange juice with you this camping trip?" Harrison stared down at her, his eyes thoughtful.

"Yes, why?" Lily swiped at a dribble of water on her chin.

"I'm thinking it would be good for you to drink. It will raise your blood sugar."

"I'll get some." Jasmine scurried off before being asked.

"Then you should try having something to eat."

Lily recapped the water bottle. "Thanks for the suggestion, but I don't have any appetite and I'm not sure food will stay down."

"Will you at least try? How about some crackers and cheese? Do you have those with you? If not, I could run up to the camp store."

Lily's heart warmed at his caring offer. "I have crackers and cheese. And I'll try to eat some... for you." She smiled up at him.

"Good."

"Are we still going shopping?" Jasmine held out a small cup of orange juice.

"If your mom feels up to it." Harrison tugged gently on Jasmine's ponytail. His attempt to reassure her daughter was heart-warming. In fact, the way he'd just cared for her left her feeling rather discombobulated.

Lily forced down the orange juice, and a few minutes later finished the last bite of her aged cheddar.

"How are you feeling now?" Harrison asked.

"Like I could shop until I drop." Lily got up from her chair. "Let's go. Time's a wasting."

He studied her. "Are you sure you're up to this? There will be no more dropping on my watch or we'll be paying the ER another visit. This time for you."

"I feel fine. Really, I do." Lily walked toward the tent. Harrison didn't leave her side. In fact, he kept a hand on the small of her back. "Um... I would like to change my clothes. I spilled some water down my shirt."

"I'll be right outside. No sudden moves. If you get dizzy just yell." Harrison's face reddened slightly. "Of course, it wouldn't be proper of me to enter your..."

Jasmine slipped in front of them and released the zipper. Then she pointed a finger at Harrison. "I'll take care of Mom. You go rest your injured leg, since it's common knowledge that rest promotes healing. Not to mention, I've heard woodpecker wounds are slow to heal."

Harrison guffawed and stuck a finger in the air. "Touché. Chalk one up for Jasmine." He lumbered to the picnic table bench and plunked down on the seat.

Biting her lip to stifle a laugh, Lily ducked her head to enter the tent. From a crouched position, she turned back to close the zipper. When her eyes met Harrison's smiling ones, a tingle zipped through her entire body.

Lily blew out a breath and tugged the zipper closed. How much could a girl take in one day?

CHAPTER THIRTY-THREE

Lily chose a soft peach and sage-green, floral cap-sleeved top, with tan knee-length shorts. She took extra care with her rebellious locks and applied fruity coral lip gloss and a light fragrance.

"You look really nice, Mom."

"Thanks, honey. You do too. I love that sundress on you."

"And you smell nice too." Her daughter crossed her arms and stared at her. "I know what's going on here. I told you Mr. Somerville was interested in you." Jasmine tapped a finger to her chin. "Let me think, about a week ago."

"This topic is not up for discussion, Jasmine." Did her voice sound as shaky to her daughter as it did to her?

"Whatever you say, but I saw him holding your hand at the coffee shop yesterday when Dad left in a hurry."

"That was a friendly gesture."

"If you say so. When is Daddy coming back anyway? Have you heard from him?"

Lily's stomach rolled and pitched. "No, sweetie, I haven't heard a thing."

Jasmine shrugged. "He must really be tied up at work. Oh well. I'm ready to do some serious shopping."

"With what money?"

Jasmine sighed. "Oh right. That could be a problem."

Lily smiled and adjusted the ponytail on Jasmine's hair. "Let's go."

When she ducked from the tent and caught Harrison's eye, she knew the extra time she'd spent getting ready was worth it. The guilt returned—unwelcome and unwanted. But it came back just the same.

"You ladies look absolutely stunning."

Although he was careful to include Jasmine, his eyes remained locked on hers.

"Thank you, Mr. Somerville. You don't look so bad yourself."

"I appreciate that, lovely Miss Jasmine," he answered, as they climbed in his truck.

"Didn't you just go the wrong direction?" Lily asked after they left the park entrance.

"No."

"We're not going to Sarnia?"

"I thought an afternoon of shopping and dinner in London would be fun."

The squeal, even though she was used to it, still managed to hurt Lily's ears. "London? Wow! Mom and I haven't shopped there since last Christmas."

"I'm glad you're excited." Harrison covered one ear with his hand. "But you've got to work on that screech, Jasmine. It terrifies the life out of me."

"I'm sorry, Mr. Somerville. I'll try hard not to do that again."

Lily was flabbergasted that Jasmine was even admitting that she would try. In all the years she'd been attempting to rid Jasmine of that horrible habit, she'd never been successful. Would Harrison's influence finally cure her?

An hour later they ambled slowly through Masonville Mall, gazing at whatever caught their fancy. When Harrison pulled them into a 'Create Your Own Stuffy' shop, she turned to him, one eyebrow raised.

"Since Cinnamon is missing, I thought you'd like to find a replacement. I know it won't be the same, but I'd like to buy a new stuffed animal for you." Harrison's voice faltered as he stared down at Jasmine.

"Seriously?" Jasmine's screech caused the cashier to look up from her computer.

Harrison put a finger over his lips. "Remember what we talked about in the car about those outbursts?"

Jasmine clapped a hand over her mouth. "I'm sorry. It snuck out without my permission."

Harrison grinned. "Fine. I'll let you off the hook this time." He waved a hand around the store. "You'd better start looking. There are lots of fine-looking characters to choose from. Besides, we have other shopping to do today."

When Harrison looked in Lily's direction, she hoped he didn't see the moisture in her eyes. His unbelievable kindness was about to knock her to her knees... or to the floor again. Lily took a deep, wavering breath and stuffed her emotions in a dusty corner of her heart to be considered later.

"Look, Mom. Isn't Homicide Detective Harry cute?" Jasmine shoved a monkey in front of her face.

Lily reached for the monkey and studied it. "That didn't take you long to decide. Your monkey is a Homicide Detective? Why Harry?"

"I named him after Mr. Somerville, since he was so kind to replace my missing Cinnamon." Jasmine shoved the stuffy under her arm, whirled around, and clasped Harrison tightly around the waist with her free arm. "Thank you. Your kindness will be forever remembered."

"You're welcome. Take good care of Harry."

Did Harrison's eyes gloss over just now? Between the three of them, there was no shortage of emotions in the 'Create Your Own Stuffy' shop.

"Oh, I will. He's not leaving my sight. Not like Cinnamon. He was always misbehaving."

"Is that right?" Harrison smirked.

"And I just handed him his first assignment. He's to keep alert for that stalker that's been harassing my mom."

"Great idea." Harrison stepped toward the cashier. "Let's pay for Harry and then it's time for Mommy's gift."

"My gift?" Lily blinked. "I don't need a gift."

"Yes, you do."

After Harrison paid for Detective Harry, he rested a hand on Lily's upper back and steered her directly across from the toy store and into a sporting goods shop. "I'm replacing your hooded sweatshirt. Remember you wrapped it around my injury and it got destroyed?"

"What? Oh, I had totally forgotten about that. Believe me, it was old. You don't need to worry about it."

"I insist on buying you a new one."

The look Harrison gave her sent an electrically-charged current to the tips of her tingling toes. It was difficult choosing a new sweatshirt after that. But a few minutes later, she left the store with a navy brand-name hoodie, the nicest one she had ever owned. Lily could barely contain the emotions whirling inside.

"Who's hungry?" Harrison patted his belly. "This little lamb is."

"Me," Jasmine squealed.

Lily shook her head. "I didn't realize lambs ate so much."

"This one does. Shall we eat at the Orange Duck?" Harrison stepped behind her to make room for a young mother with a stroller who was approaching them.

Lily waited until he was back at her side. "The Orange Duck?"

"Is that not to your liking?"

"Are you kidding? I've heard so much about it, but never had the privilege of dining there."

"Then it will be my pleasure to take you both."

A half an hour later, Lily was flabbergasted at the extensive buffet and friendly service. The Orange Duck offered everything from a soup and salad bar, grill tables, Sushi corner, a prime rib station, and a large variety of foods that showcased the best in Canadian Chinese.

Lily picked at her food. It all looked and smelled amazing, but there was one problem. Her stomach still did not feel right. Probably a case of nerves. Jasmine and Harrison seemed to have no problem making several trips back and forth to the buffet.

"What's wrong? Are the foods not to your liking? Or are you still feeling unwell?" Harrison's brow wrinkled as he shoved the last sweet and sour chicken ball into his mouth.

"No, everything is delicious." How did she explain that the magnitude of emotions coursing through her had her stomach twisted into knots? Worry about the stalker intermingled with her growing attraction for the man across the table from her. All in all, she was a mess.

"I guess I'm not as hungry as I thought, but I will definitely make room for dessert." Lily rose. "Is anyone coming with me?"

"You bet I am. I hope that last piece of chocolate cake is still there." Jasmine hurried off toward the dessert table.

Harrison's lips tugged to one side. His eyes twinkled.

Lily shrugged. "What?"

"How is it that you don't have an appetite for main course, but you do for dessert? And to think you gave me a lecture about my choice of chocolate chip cookies over bananas to get potassium in me."

Lily threw her palms up toward him. "Guilty as charged. You found one of my weaknesses."

"Uh huh." Harrison grinned.

He accompanied her to the vast array of desserts, but as she studied the decadent display, he disappeared. Lily loaded her plate with some kind of square with butter tart filling, a sliver of caramel cheesecake drizzled in chocolate sauce, and a mint iced brownie.

Unable to find either Jasmine or Harrison in the crowd, she made her way back to their table where she found them both immersed in their desserts. Harrison had a lone chocolate chip cookie on his plate and was munching on another one.

"I got the last piece of chocolate cake. Yum. It's delicious." Jasmine stabbed her fork into her cake.

"I notice that you are making a valiant attempt to raise that glucose value," Harrison teased as he contemplated her plate.

"And you are getting your extra potassium, I see." Lily bit into her brownie.

She finished her last bite of dessert and slipped to the restroom. As she washed her hands and glanced up into the mirror, a surge of joy raced through her. Did it have anything to do with her growing feelings for Harrison? Or was it her body's wild reaction to the mountain of sugar she had just fed it?

Either way, she didn't have a care in the world. At least for the time being. And she'd enjoy every minute while it lasted.

CHAPTER THIRTY-FOUR

"That sky is freaky," Jasmine piped up from the back seat of the truck as the three headed back to the campground.

Harrison had already been studying the strange sky, but he hadn't wanted to alarm the child. "Lily, can you check the weather forecast?"

Lily opened the weather app on her phone while he drove. "The entire Southwestern Ontario region is under a Severe Thunderstorm Watch."

Harrison wasn't surprised. Although the sun still shone over the city of London, a line of menacing clouds approached in the shape of an anvil with an indigo-coloured base. He'd seen these types of cloud formations before and they usually signified trouble. They were capable of high winds, heavy downpours, intense lightning, hail, and even tornadoes.

"Do you think we'll make it back to the campground before the storm hits?" Jasmine squawked.

A quick glance in the rear-view mirror and the young child's face confirmed his suspicions. She was afraid. "We'll be fine, Jasmine. It may not even affect our area. It could head out over the lake."

"That's right, honey," Lily added. "How many times have we seen storms approaching at home, but they miss our area?"

"It's obvious what you guys are trying to do, but I think you're both wrong this time. I just finished studying a book entitled *Wild Weather*, and that storm front appears not only dangerous but imminent."

Harrison shook his head, still flabbergasted at the young child's thirst for knowledge. He looked at Lily, who shrugged. He just hoped they made it back to the campground in time.

Another look at the woman beside him and his insides became even more troubled than the sky. Lily had been talking a mile a minute during the first part of their drive. Now she had grown extremely quiet. Did thunderstorms cause her anxiety? Had her sugar taken another nosedive? He'd have to watch her for signs of fainting again. Or was something else troubling her? Although he didn't know her well, something didn't feel right. Was his growing attraction for the pretty woman one-sided? Perhaps he had read more into things than he should have.

She caught him staring. He averted his gaze in the pretense of studying the impending storm. Words he'd spoken last night came back to haunt him. He had told her he was confused, terrified, and not ready. Is that how she was feeling?

The rest of the drive was awkward. While Jasmine hugged her monkey, Homicide Detective Harry, a name that amused and alarmed him all at the same time, Lily stared out the window at the portentous weather front.

Just as they reached the Piney Campground main gate, the song Carrie Underwood had been belting out on the radio in his truck was abruptly interrupted by a weather bulletin from Emergency Management Ontario. The dire warning was almost too phenomenal to believe—in fact, Harrison had never heard such a message in Ontario.

Tornadoes had been spotted in Mitchell, Arthur, Kettle Point, and Bayfield. The announcer urged all persons in the above-mentioned areas to take cover immediately.

A chill descended over Harrison. Piney Campground was not far from Kettle Point. Should the ferocious funnel head in their direction, many lives could be jeopardized.

"I told you that storm was imminent, didn't I? Now what are we supposed to do?" Jasmine wailed from the backseat.

"One thing is for sure," Lily turned in her seat to reassure her. "We're not going to panic."

"I agree." Harrison nodded. As he drove the winding camp road alongside the Placid River, Jasmine screeched. "Stop the car right now. We need to get to a low-lying area and climb down the riverbank for protection."

Instantly, the gravity of the situation struck him; the lives of the mother and daughter in his vehicle were in his hands. If he made the wrong decision, he could be responsible for the outcome.

"Calm down, Jasmine. Mr. Somerville is trained in these types of scenarios. He will do what is best."

Fuelled by Lily's confidence, he drove by the main washrooms. Scores of campers filed into the small brick building. Normally, he'd agree that was their safest option as well, but for some reason he felt compelled to drive toward the Sandy Dunes Beach, even though it made absolutely no sense.

Due to the time of night and the approaching storm, darkness descended swiftly, blanketing the forest with an eerie black-green hue. Trees loomed over the road like monsters waiting for the right moment to snatch their unsuspecting prey. A blinding bright blue flash of lightning illuminated the red eyes of a raccoon lurking in dense bush at the side of the road.

A whimper from the backseat tugged at his heartstrings.

"I won't let anything happen to you, sweetie." He bit his lip. Had he just made a promise he couldn't keep?

Lily remained silent. Was she praying? The thought crossed his mind to join her, but he dismissed it. For one thing, he didn't know how. For another, he figured God wouldn't know who he was.

As they inched along the deserted Sandy Dunes Beach road, Harrison gripped the steering wheel. Whatever had made him do such a hare-brained thing? Here they would be completely at the mercy of the perilous elements.

Another flash of lightning revealed a serene lake, devoid of waves. Not a drop of rain had fallen. The calmness of the wind was troubling, almost oppressive, as if nature was waiting for just the exact moment to pounce.

"What do we do now?" Lily asked as he pulled into the pitch-black parking spot on the cliff facing the lake and shut off the engine.

"I don't know. I can't really explain why I drove here."

"Mom, can we pray? I'm scared." Jasmine climbed over the seat and landed between them.

"Yes, honey, we can pray. Would you like to join us, Mr. Somerville?"

"Um... I'll just listen if you don't mind."

Lily let loose with a petition that astounded him. She not only pleaded for their protection, she prayed for the safety of the entire campground. She asked God, who she said commanded the wind and the waves, to dissipate the violent weather and spare the lives of every camper.

Harrison opened his eyes. He blinked several times as he stared through the front windshield. What in the world was happening? He opened his door, put one foot outside, and half-stood, scanning the lake. His eyes were *not* playing tricks on him.

"Lily! Jasmine! Get out of the truck. You have to see this."

Lily opened her door, but Jasmine wouldn't budge. The first words out of Lily's mouth carried a whispered mixture of reverence and shock. "Absolutely incredible!"

Harrison left his door open and hurried to the front of his truck. Lily joined him. Together, they leaned against the hood and stared at a powerful explosion of shimmering, twinkling stars appearing over the lake and above their heads as they watched. On every side lightning flashed, but the clearing grew larger by the second, scattering the storm in all directions away from them.

Harrison picked Lily up by the waist and twirled her in a circle. "I've never seen anything like that." They laughed together at the amazing spectacle.

Lily slipped from his embrace, ran to the open passenger door, and leaned inside. "Jasmine, you've got to come and see this."

"No, it's still lightning out there. I don't feel like getting fried."

"Fine, stay inside, but you're missing a miracle."

"I am?" Jasmine slid across the bench seat and peered into the dark, hugging her monkey for dear life.

When she still seemed reluctant to exit the vehicle, Harrison reached his hand inside. "Trust me. You'll be safe."

Jasmine's tiny fingers grasped his and he guided her gently from the truck. Leaning down, he picked up her trembling body and held her close. Despite the fact her intelligence went beyond most, she was still a vulnerable child with worries and fears.

"Your mommy's prayers are powerful. Look what they did." Harrison pointed at the starry expanse.

Her wide-eyed gaze almost consumed her face. "Inconceivable."

"I think your mother has a direct line to God," Harrison exclaimed.

"Thank you, God, for answering our prayers and keeping us safe." Lily's adoration was unpretentious, furthering Harrison's intrigue. Was this whole unbelievable weather occurrence a whopping coincidence? Or was it possible to have such a relationship with the God of the universe that he would alter his plans as a direct result of a prayer?

Now he understood what had compelled him to drive to the beach in such dire conditions. Under the dense canopy of trees, he would never have witnessed the miracle—a dangerous and imminent storm dissipating in front of his eyes.

Suddenly, Jasmine broke into song.

It was an unfamiliar song about God directing lightning bolts. Is that what God had just done? Harrison contemplated the question until Jasmine hit the chorus.

It was as if he heard the voice of an angel as the words tumbled over Jasmine's lips in a perfect, sweet pitch. Her song claimed incredible things. That God had placed the stars in the sky and even knew them by name. Harrison stared up at the glimmering expanse.

"You are an amazing God." Jasmine ended the song.

Chills ran up his spine.

Strength ebbed from his body as her crystal-clear words walloped him with tremendous impact. Gently he placed the young child on her feet just as his knees gave way.

Dropping to the sand at the cliff top, truth slammed him full in the heart. Suddenly, he was transported back in time, to the beach at Shadow Lake, witnessing the silhouette of the cross upon the water and feeling a divine holiness surrounding him. The same holiness that had compelled him to remove his sandals then. And it enveloped him now.

"He tried to reach me, but I didn't get it. Now I do." Harrison covered his face with his hands.

He felt Lily's kneeling presence beside him, her softly-spoken words reaching deep inside. "God says that you will find him when you search for him with all your heart. And that is what you have done over the last several months. This is the answer you've been looking for. God is who you've been looking for."

His throat tightened until he couldn't speak. His life flashed before him, speeding through his mind like a video on fast forward. And he hated what he saw, that he had lived a life that was sinful and empty and apart from God.

A fiery sensation began in his chest and radiated throughout his entire being as God's supernatural presence surrounded him and filled him. Words of adoration poured from his lips. "Thank you, God, for revealing yourself to me. Thank you for the cross and what Jesus did for me. Thank you for not giving up on me all these months. Thank you for Lily and Jasmine." Lily's arm wrapped around his waist and Jasmine snuggled into his side.

A gentle breeze refreshed and revived him. He leapt to his feet—feeling absolutely no pain from his injury—jubilant and carefree, and wrapped his arms around two very special people as he continued to stare in awe at the incredible sky.

The words of Jasmine's song still echoed through his mind. Was it true? Did each star up there in the universe have its own name?

His mind could scarcely take it all in.

As his wide-eyed gaze continued to absorb the ever-expanding starry heavens, it occurred to him that, even if he lived to be a hundred, never again would he gaze at a clear night sky without remembering this night.

CHAPTER THIRTY-FIVE

The joy that filled him over the next several hours was unlike anything Harrison had ever experienced his entire life, going beyond the scope and description of mere words. As he basked in that supernatural and divine rapture, he felt different. Brand new.

Before retiring in Ross's tent, the night of the storm, he'd spent the better part of an hour talking with Lily, who shared his excitement as much as if it were her very own. She stressed the necessity of growing as a Christian, of developing deep roots by attending a Bible-believing church and studying God's Word.

She loaned him her Bible, suggesting that he begin reading the Book of John in the New Testament. So that's exactly what he did. All night long. He couldn't put the book down. Who would have thought the Bible was so interesting and filled with such inspiration and hope? Hope that the world desperately needed and lacked.

The silhouetted cross on Shadow Lake now made sense. Jesus was the way, the truth, and the life. No man could come to God without believing in the death of Jesus on the cross. Like blinders had been removed from his eyes, it was starkly clear. All religions didn't lead to God. He now could dispel the modern theological thinking that was so prevalent in the world today. There was only one path and that was Jesus. The words of "Amazing Grace" impacted him like they never had before.

Amazing Grace, how sweet the sound,
That saved a wretch like me,
I once was lost but now I'm found
Was blind but now, I see!

Once he was lost and now he was found. He could explode in excitement.

As he closed Lily's Bible and rolled over, he heard robins singing their early-morning wake-up song. Soon it would be dawn. Unbelievably, he'd spent the entire night reading God's Word and basking in his love.

He could spend the rest of his life doing that and be completely content. But then reality sunk in. He did have to work for a living. He chuckled to himself and closed his eyes.

CHAPTER THIRTY-SIX

As Lily snuggled inside her sleeping bag, her mind replayed the events of the entire, incredible day. It started with a tender-hearted man replacing her daughter's stuffed animal. If that was the only thing that had happened, it would have been amazing enough. But no. The miracles were only starting. God appeared on the scene in a spectacular way, not only diverting a powerful storm, but revealing his love to Harrison. She'd never seen someone knocked to their knees by God's truth as Harrison had been. Her heart was filled to overflowing with the knowledge that he had finally come to peace with his search for the meaning of life.

Jasmine's soft purring tickled her ears as Lily yawned and turned on her side in the sleeping bag, wrestling with her perplexing dilemma. What should she do with the growing attraction she felt for the handsome park naturalist? Her earlier idea to pack up the tent and go home didn't hold much appeal now. She couldn't imagine what it would feel like without Harrison nearby. That thought shocked and astounded her. Being around Harrison had become a habit she didn't ever want to kick—a very good habit.

But was she truly thinking clearly? For her own safety and that of Jasmine's and even Harrison's, perhaps she should reconsider leaving in the morning. Besides, the last thing she needed was to fall into another heart-breaking relationship—not that she'd seen any warning flags with Harrison. But really, how well could she have gotten to know him in a little over a week? Her thoughts grew hazier as sleep threatened to overtake her. Maybe things would be clearer in the morning.

Lily couldn't breathe. Down and down she sank. Deeper into the murky depths of the turbulent lake. Why couldn't she kick her way upward? Had her legs become tangled in seaweed or fishing line? Her vision grew dim. Panic set in. A tingling charged through her appendages, followed by numbness. Horrified, reality set in. She was going to drown.

"Don't make a sound. I'll let you breathe if you promise not to scream."

Desperate, Lily nodded. Her head popped above the water and she gasped in sweet precious oxygen; slowly her vision cleared. She frowned. Was that a man in the water with her? "Harrison?" she whispered.

"No, I'm not that idiot park dude. I'm Brad Pit, remember? Not a sound. Now get up and come with me."

Brad Pit? Get up? Awareness rushed in and with it came stark-raving horror. She wasn't in the lake but in her own tent. And her stalker had finally gotten to her. Jasmine! Where was Jasmine? A movement beside her confirmed her daughter's presence. *Please, God, don't let him hurt her.*

"I said get up." A firm yank on her arm ripped her from her sleeping bag and onto her feet. The pain was so intense, she gasped. It felt as if he'd almost wrenched her arm from its socket.

"What are you doing with my mom?" Jasmine bolted upright, obviously jarred awake by the commotion.

"Listen here, kid. I have a knife and I won't hesitate to use it. Get up and don't make a sound. You're coming with us."

As soon as Jasmine crawled from her sleeping bag, the man grabbed her and pulled her toward the tent's opening. "If either of you makes a sound, this knife will silence your daughter in an instant. So, don't be thinking of waking up your knight in shining armour."

Soft cries came from Jasmine as they slipped outside into the pre-dawn darkness. Lily shot a look at Harrison's tent. One scream from her and he would fly out to their rescue. But with the knife in the demented man's hands, she couldn't take the chance with her daughter's life. Her heart ached as Jasmine's whimpers reached her ears.

The stalker dragged them across the campsite and up the hill behind the tent. Once they reached the top of the hill and began their descent down the other side, the man spoke. "Shut up, you big baby. If you'd stayed asleep you would have been far better off. I only wanted your mother. Now I'm stuck with a snot-nosed kid."

"We'll be okay, Jasmine. God is with us." Lily spoke in as soothing a voice as she could muster.

"Good luck with that," her stalker snarled.

Lily winced when a branch dug into her upper thigh as they were forced deeper into the woods.

She had no idea how much time had passed before they came to a road. Instead of crossing it, they followed its downhill descent as the first rays of the sun peeked through the trees. Lily could hear running water ahead. Was that the Placid River?

A glimmer of hope raced through her as she recognized her surroundings. From years of camping with her family, the Burkley Bridge was a very familiar landmark.

As a child, her family had often hiked to the bridge that ran over the Placid River. Understanding her position in the park might be important in aiding her escape. But she'd keep that bit of information to herself.

They crossed the bridge and entered a path with a sign saying, *No Entry Beyond this Point.* She remembered that sign. As a child she had often bugged her parents to explore this forbidden zone, but they continually refused. Then she would invariably receive a lecture on the dangers of not following rules. Ironically, she would now get to explore the area, but not under the conditions she would have wished.

The trail was overgrown and difficult to navigate. After another thirty minutes or so, they finally arrived in a clearing where the scent of a dying campfire filled the air.

"Sit down," the kidnapper barked. He used his knife to point to an old decaying tree trunk that bordered one edge of the small space.

Lily reached for Jasmine's hand and the mother-daughter pair dropped to the rotting log. An angry scratch made a diagonal path across Jasmine's cheek and blood trickled down her face. Lily swiped at the crimson trail with her fingers and attempted to dry them off in the sparse grass at her feet.

She scanned her surroundings. So, this is where her stalker had been living. No wonder park security hadn't been able to find him. The demented man had created a lair with fallen branches and a camouflaged tarp deep among brambles and bush. A sleeping bag was spread out underneath the overhanging tarp along with a backpack, cooler, and a few cooking supplies. His bicycle leaned up against a nearby tree and a dilapidated brown canoe had been turned upside down in the tall grasses.

How long had he been here? And, more importantly, how long was he planning on keeping them here? What was he going to do with them? Were they even on park property? A niggling of guilt settled in her chest. Why hadn't she gone home yesterday?

As her stalker rummaged through his backpack, she shuddered. Was she chilled from being out in the early-morning dampness clad only in her light cotton sleep shorts and a T-shirt? Or was it fear?

She reached for Jasmine's hand and whispered an urgent prayer. *God, please help us. Save us from this man and his evil intentions. Please give Harrison and the park security wisdom to know what to do and how to find us.*

Please, God, please. We need you.

CHAPTER THIRTY-SEVEN

The squawking of blue jays outside his tent caused Harrison's eyes to flutter open. He knew exactly what they were squawking about. Probably fighting over the small pile of peanuts Jasmine had set out before she went to bed last night.

He yawned and glanced at his watch. Seven o'clock. He'd slept two or three hours at max but was wide awake and raring to go. He crawled from his sleeping bag, excited to see Lily and Jasmine again.

Outside the tent, the same breeze that had refreshed him last night cooled his cheeks and rustled his hair. And so, the incredible joy continued.

The campsite was quiet. The Martins, who were usually up early, must be sleeping in. Maybe he should surprise them and make breakfast. He chuckled. Who was he kidding? Perhaps a trip to his favourite coffee shop in Grand Beach to pick up doughnuts and coffee would suffice.

As he climbed into his truck, he smacked his forehead with the palm of his hand. Duh! What was he thinking? He couldn't leave them alone with the strange man lurking about.

Harrison plunked himself down at the picnic table and waited all of five minutes, rather impatiently. Perhaps he'd give them a little encouragement to get up. Pacing around their tent, he began whistling the first song that popped into his head. Oddly, it was "Happy Birthday".

When that didn't rouse them, he took off his sandals and clapped them loudly together. "Come on ladies, it's time to rise and shine. The day's a wasting."

Complete and utter silence. He punched in Lily's cell phone number and listened as it rang inside the tent. It went unanswered.

Uneasiness began in the pit of his stomach and clawed its way through his entire body. Something felt wrong—terribly wrong. He walked to the front of the tent and called Lily's name.

When total silence greeted his ears again, he reached for the zipper. Strangely, it was open. When he peered inside, his stomach flipped upside down. Mother and daughter were gone.

❖

Harrison attempted to run toward his truck, but it was more like a cockeyed hobble. Once inside, he made haste to the main washrooms, desperately hoping that Lily and Jasmine had risen early and chosen not to wake him.

He waited, playing the steering wheel like a set of drums. When an older couple arrived, he asked the lady to check the women's washroom for him. When the lady popped her head out the door and shook her head, he grew more anxious. To make matters worse, a flyer taped to the information board, with the sketch of Lily's stalker, flapped in the breeze, taunting him.

Had the twisted, demented little man won? Or was there a logical explanation for Lily and Jasmine's absence at this time of morning?

In a daze, he stumbled to his truck, picked up his radio, and arranged to meet security back at Lily's campsite. How could he have slept if danger was so close? Come to think of it, he was up most of the night. Wouldn't he have heard something?

He arrived at the campsite at the same time as Jason from security. A surge of hope galloped through him as he hurried towards the tent to check it once again. Perhaps he had missed them along the road and the pair was safely inside.

But that was not the case.

Desperately trying to control his mounting panic, he unloaded his fears to security. "Lily's stalker has to have them."

"Are you sure?" Jason scratched behind his ear. "Maybe they went for an early-morning hike."

"No way." Harrison shook his head. "Lily knew not to go off alone. Her stalker is the entire reason I spent the night in that tent. For her protection. He's got them. I know it. I feel it deep inside. According to my calculations, he had to have taken them sometime early this morning, after about four or five a.m. I was awake most of the night and only drifted off as dawn approached. Otherwise I would have heard something."

Jason placed a comforting hand on his shoulder. "Let me make a call to the night security guard and see if anyone left the park early this morning. In the meantime, contact the park superintendent. He'll need to get the police involved immediately."

Numbly, Harrison did as he was told. Perhaps he'd soon wake up and find himself in the throes of a horrendous nightmare.

Jason ended his call. "Hal was at the front gate all night until I relieved him at seven this morning and he said no one left the park on his shift. Not that he was aware of, anyway. It's now twenty past seven. Chances are, if they've been abducted, they're still in the park somewhere."

It was a torturous half hour before the park superintendent arrived, followed by two OPP cars carrying a total of four officers. When Officer Brent Nichols stepped from the squad car, Harrison blew out a breath. It was a small consolation that Brent was in charge. At this point, he'd take every bit of encouragement he could get.

The supernatural joy he'd felt last night was slipping away fast. He wasn't entirely sure how to pray, but the words poured over his lips as he paced the campsite, waiting for a search plan to take form. His plea was simple, to the point, and from his heart.

Please God, save Lily and Jasmine.

CHAPTER THIRTY-EIGHT

Lily and Jasmine were bound together, Lily's left ankle to Jasmine's right. Brad Pit had ordered them to stay on the log until he figured things out. Although this was the only restraint holding them from running, Lily knew they wouldn't get far. The bush was dense and the chain binding them was made of heavy iron links and would be very cumbersome.

As the pair shivered together in the dampness, Lily snuggled her daughter against her side. "Don't worry, sweetie. God will take care of us. And I bet that Harrison is out right now searching. He's a smart man and a park naturalist. He will look for signs."

Jasmine pulled her mother's ear down to her mouth. "I'm not worried. Homicide Detective Harry will help him too."

"He will?" Lily forced a smile. If it helped her daughter to imagine that her beloved stuffed animal detective monkey was going to aid in their rescue, then she'd play along.

Jasmine nodded. "He's perched in a vantage point, in reconnaissance mode, waiting for Harrison to arrive to show him the way."

"Is he? Well then, it's just a matter of time until we're rescued."

"Shut up over there. I can't concentrate," her stalker grumbled loudly.

Lily took a moment to study their abductor. He was a man of average height and scrawny build, still wearing the plain black ball cap on his head, a stained white T-shirt, and what appeared to be black swim shorts. His overall appearance reeked of unkemptness, as if he'd been hiding in the bush for a long time.

Occasionally, he removed his cap, exposing a high forehead with sparse, short, straw-coloured hair. As he wandered the small area, he seemed agitated and confused about the alteration of his plans, that being the presence of Jasmine.

"What to do, what to do?" he mumbled repeatedly. "This is not that complicated. She's only an annoying ankle-biter but trouble all the same. I didn't count on this, Frank."

"Mommy? Who's he talking to?" Jasmine whispered, her brow wrinkled.

His symptoms suggested mental illness to Lily. "Do you remember when you were young and had an imaginary friend?"

"Yes." Jasmine beamed. "Her name was Princess Pussy Willow."

"Sometimes adults can get an illness in their heads where they believe that they can see and talk to someone who isn't really there."

Jasmine's eyes grew large. "Is that what they call skits-o-something?"

"Close. It's called schizophrenia." Lily struggled to keep her emotions in check and stay strong and alert, especially as she watched their abductor converse with his imaginary friend.

"That makes sense, Frank. Until I can figure out what I'm going to do with the little brat, I'll cage them both."

The stalker picked up the knife that lay on the top of his backpack and approached.

"Come, ladies, I'm moving you to more *comfortable* accommodations until I can decide what to do with you. Just sashay yourselves down this little old path." He gave Lily a forceful shove, which sent her sprawling into the dirt. Because of their chained ankles, Jasmine couldn't help but land on top of her.

"Ow! My ankle hurts," Jasmine cried and grabbed her foot.

"Quit your belly-aching, kid. I should have left you in the tent. You're a pain where a pill can't reach."

"But I'm bleeding. Your stupid chain cut my ankle," Jasmine retorted.

"Cry me a river. Boohoo." The man rubbed his knuckles under his eyes in a crying motion. "See if I care."

"Just wait, you big creep. Soon justice will be served."

Jasmine's feistiness was worrying Lily.

"Shut your kid up or you'll regret it." Her abductor grabbed Lily's arm roughly, yanked her to her feet, and flashed the knife in her face.

"That's enough, Jasmine. Don't say another word." Lily feared her daughter didn't understand the gravity of the situation and her smart mouth was going to make matters worse.

Only a few steps through the bush and they reached what Lily judged to be a muddy, shallow area of the Placid River. The only way across was by stepping on a makeshift bridge of rickety, rotting fallen logs. "Over we go, ladies." The man pointed as he followed along behind them.

On the other side, they continued for another ten minutes until they reached a thick stand of trees. Beyond the stand was a squared-off area, about twelve feet on all sides, enclosed with metal fencing. An old worn sign on the fence displayed the words: *Deer Exclosure, Controlled Deer Vegetation Test Area.*

Brad Pit produced a key and inserted it into a padlock, releasing the gate. Within seconds they found themselves inside the cage of overgrown weeds, grasses, and small saplings.

"Enjoy your new accommodations, ladies." He snickered.

"I thought you said we'd be more comfortable. Liar. We'll probably get ticks in here. And I need to go pee." Jasmine crossed her legs at the ankles.

The demented man cackled and took a step backward.

"Wait! You can't leave us here without any food or water," Lily pleaded.

The kidnapper rubbed his chin and stared at them. He reached for something in his pocket, approached them, and inserted a key into the padlock around their ankles, freeing them from their restraint.

"Is that better? At least your daughter can pee without soaking your ankle in urine. Besides, you don't need to be chained in here. You're not going anywhere." He backed toward the gate, his eyes skittering back and forth between her and Jasmine. "I'll be back, beautiful lady. We're going to be together forever as soon as I figure out what to do with your pain-in-the-butt kid."

When he stuck his tongue out at Jasmine, Lily knew they were dealing with a very sick individual. One who maimed innocent animals, stalked women, suffered from mental illness, and was juvenile in his behaviour.

Lily studied the deer exclosure. Over her years as a camper at the park, she had noticed a few of these before, tucked away in remote locations. Oddly, this one was different. Most had a high-wire fence on all four sides but were open at the top. This one had been altered. A newer-looking wire zig-zagged across the top in haphazard directions. There would be no climbing out of this.

It appeared her abduction had been pre-meditated. Lily prayed harder than she'd ever prayed her entire life. *Please, God, save us!*

CHAPTER THIRTY-NINE

An hour later, the search was finally ready to begin. Harrison was distraught, to say the least. He understood these things took time, but time was of the essence. The longer they were gone, the deeper his despair grew, as his suspicions that Lily and Jasmine had been abducted became stronger.

An Amber Alert had been issued and was probably hitting the news about now. Scores of volunteers milled about in the office parking lot, assembling into groups of six, receiving their orange fluorescent vests, maps, bottled water, and photos of the missing Martin women and the sketch of their abductor.

At Harrison's insistence, he joined the group that would search the woods behind the Martin campsite. His members consisted of Hal and Jason, security guards employed by the campground, Officer Brent Nichols, and the older couple, the Rutledges, he'd seen earlier at the washrooms.

Finally, the six piled in two vehicles and made their way back to the scene of the abduction. Harrison bolted from the truck even before it fully stopped moving and headed for the bush behind the tents.

"Hold on, Harrison. There are a few things we need to discuss before you go running ahead of the pack." Brent waved him back to the group. "The first rule is 'No Lone Wolves'. We stick together in groups. Harrison, you take the Rutledges and I'll take Hal and Jason."

"Now, wait a minute." Harrison shook his head. "Your group is stacked in the brawn department. If we run into this dangerous abductor, I'm injured and they're..." He cleared his throat. He didn't want to call the couple old, but it was true. How could the three of them hope to overpower an able-bodied and possibly armed man?

George Rutledge held up both hands. "He's right. Unfortunately, I'm not as young as I used to be. It would be good to have someone stronger in this group."

"Okay, Jason, you join Harrison's group." Brent handed out walkie-talkies to the entire group. "Stay on frequency one and check in with the group every half hour, or sooner if you find anything. Report anything that appears out of the ordinary such as crushed vegetation, torn pieces of fabric, signs of a struggle..."

Elvira Rutledge gasped and covered her mouth.

"Are you sure you're up for this?" the OPP officer asked.

"I'm good." She took a deep breath.

"One more thing. Don't get lost," Brent added. "Let's meet at our rendezvous point in two hours or less, depending on what we find."

As soon as the words were out of the officer's mouth, Harrison nodded and charged up the steep, bushy incline leading the pack.

It didn't take long to discover large sections of crushed vegetation and fresh greenstick fractures of numerous small saplings. Ascertaining the direction that the kidnapper had taken, he promptly radioed Brent.

A bittersweet excitement coursed through him. Although he was happy that they'd discovered clues about the missing women, he was deathly afraid of what they might find at the end of the trail.

"According to the map, we'll hit the road leading into the Burkley Campground soon." Harrison spoke into the walkie talkie. "We'll wait for you there."

Within twenty minutes or so, the entire group had met and were discussing their next move. While Harrison paced the camp road, Brent placed a call to his police sergeant, relaying the latest information. At the end of his call, Brent announced they were bringing in search and rescue dogs.

Excellent news. Harrison rubbed his hands together. *Just get them here quickly.*

A movement caught his attention and he glanced over at Elvira, who stood beside her husband on the other side of the bridge. She waved frantically. "Come quick. I think I've found a clue."

Harrison bolted down the road as fast as his injured calf could carry him toward the couple who were staring into the bush. Despite his injury, he arrived ahead of Brent and Jason.

Unbelievable joy charged through him when he spotted the stuffed monkey in its uniform, perched on a tree stump in front of a *No Trespassing* sign.

He pulled Elvira into a large bear hug. "It's most definitely a clue. Meet Detective Harry! Thank you for finding him."

"What a smart thing to do," George remarked. "The youngster left us a clue."

"She's an exceptional child." Harrison bit his lip, fighting to keep his emotions in check. "I just hope we can find them before it's too late."

CHAPTER FORTY

For the next few hours, Lily waited, prayed and did her best to reassure Jasmine that everything would be okay. It was getting very warm and she was thirsty. She licked her dry lips. Worry for her daughter consumed her. Surely their abductor would come back soon and bring them water. Judging by the position of the sun and the growls of her stomach, Lily estimated the time to be around noon.

"Mommy, I think I hear something." Jasmine interrupted her thoughts.

Lily listened intently. Her daughter was correct. Crunching leaves signified someone's approach. Even though she expected it was the mentally ill man, hope flickered that Harrison had found them. When the kidnapper appeared from around the stand of tall cedars, hope extinguished like a campfire doused with water.

This time he carried a backpack. *Please, God, let him have water in there.* After unlocking the gate, he stepped inside and wiped the sweat from his brow with the back of his sleeve. "It sure is a hot one."

"We noticed," Jasmine sassed. "I hope you brought us water. It would be the humane thing to do."

"I brought water, but whether I let you have any is up to me." He dropped his bag on the ground, unzipped the main compartment, pulled out a water bottle, and held it toward Lily. "You can have some, pretty lady, but you can't share with her."

Lily shook her head. "Not if my daughter can't have any."

"You're passing on this life-giving liquid?" He smirked as he dropped it back in his bag. "How noble of you." He reached for a strand of her hair. "But then again, my woman would possess that quality. And you take the prize. Not only are you noble, but beautiful as well."

"I'm not your woman." Her kidnapper seemed not to hear the words she growled. Instead, he traced a path up and down her arm with a grimy finger. Lily thought she might vomit. A surge of anger mixed with panic charged through her. She had to find a way to get herself and Jasmine free.

But her daughter was one step ahead of her. Jasmine pounced toward his backpack like a lioness at her prey. Reaching inside, she grabbed the water bottle and hurled it at the man's head. The bottle burst open, spilling most of its contents when it hit the ground.

Brad Pit yelped as his sunglasses and ball cap were knocked askew. Blindsided, he spouted profanities at an alarming rate. "You little jerk. You're nothing but a pain. I've had it with you."

He chucked the sunglasses and ball cap into his backpack and reached behind Lily for Jasmine. Lily shoved him away from her precious daughter. Blood trickled down the kidnapper's nose and into one eye. For a few seconds, Lily revelled in a demented sort of pleasure. The blow from the water bottle must have shoved the sunglasses into his face and cut his eyebrow.

"I can't see a thing out of this eye. You better not have blinded me or broken my prescription glasses, you little brat," Brad yelled. He grabbed Lily's arms and yanked her forward so fast her head spun. Jasmine, who had latched onto the back of her T-shirt, fell to her knees from the sudden motion.

Brad Pit dragged Lily from the caged area and tossed her to the earth like a rag doll. Lily screamed as her abductor slammed the gate shut and locked her daughter inside.

"Take that, you trouble-maker. Let's see how long you can exist on your own without food and water. Your mother and I have business to attend to."

Jasmine wailed and ran to the front of the exclosure, winding her little fingers tightly around the chain fencing. "Mom! Help me!"

Lily scrambled to her feet and sprinted to the closed gate, her fingers touching Jasmine's. "Please, I beg you. Don't leave her here all alone. She'll die." Sobs rose in her throat.

"That's my plan," he barked. Cold metal pressed against the back of her neck. "Now, come with me and don't put up a fight. I've had a lot of practice with my knife-wielding skills lately, or haven't you noticed?"

An image of the bloody, severed turtle head flashed through Lily's mind and shocked her into compliance. She hoped Jasmine didn't understand the subliminal message in his veiled threat as she had protected Jasmine from the details of that incident.

Numb, Lily stumbled down the path and crossed over the makeshift bridge. Brad Pit shoved her from behind, driving her into his camouflaged hideout.

Her eyes widened. Was that barking dogs? Could a search and rescue team be coming for them?

"Hurry up and grab one end of the canoe," he ordered. "I don't like the sound of that. I think they're on to me."

Lily lifted the heavy canoe and trudged through tall weeds, her courage bolstered by the distant sound of barking. Her arms ached from the cumbersome weight as they travelled alongside the mucky, shallow river. How far would they have to go before the river grew deep enough to drop in the canoe? Would the dogs find them before they got too far out onto the river? Would their scent be lost when they entered the water? Maybe she could waste time. "I can't carry this any longer." Lily dropped her end of the canoe.

Howls from the dogs filled the air, louder now. Her spirit grew more hopeful.

"You can. And you will." The rays of the sun reflected off the steel blade in his hand, blinding her.

Chills ran up and down her spine. Her hands shook as she reached down and lifted the heavy beast again. A few minutes later, after rounding a small bend, the river widened and deepened, much to Lily's disappointment.

As they paddled away, her hope faded. She hadn't heard the dogs in a while. Would her scent be lost now?

Please God. I need you to help me. But more importantly, save Jasmine.

CHAPTER FORTY-ONE

The time Harrison and his group waited at the Burkley Bridge for the arrival of the canine search team felt like an eternity. It was only twenty minutes.

Jill and Gentry were formidable-looking German Shepherds. Mike their handler placed the stuffed monkey in front of their noses, as well as an article of Lily's clothing, and off they ran.

Harrison didn't know much about this type of rescue but was encouraged by the dogs' response. He sprinted behind Mike, followed closely by Brent, Jason, and Hal. The Rutledges decided to call it quits shortly after the discovery of Jasmine's monkey. Brent had been correct in his original assessment, that Elvira didn't have the nerves to continue. Still, the spotting of Jasmine's monkey had been invaluable to them.

Harrison gritted his teeth and ignored the painful throbbing in his lower calf. The grueling marathon he was subjecting his injury to wasn't wise. But he couldn't rest until the Martin girls were safe and sound. Sweat dripped down his forehead, stinging his eyes.

Thoughts of Lily and Jasmine tormented him. Were they safe? Thirsty? In pain? Afraid? Dead?

Shoving aside that last horrifyingly morbid thought, he prayed with every ounce of his being. Although he was new at this prayer thing, he poured out his heart in earnest.

Fifteen minutes later, the group caught up with the dogs, who had halted at the edge of a swampy area of the Placid River.

Harrison bent over and placed his hands on his knees. He was out of breath and parched. Footsteps pounded behind him as the rest of the group caught up to him and Mike.

Once his breathing returned to normal, Harrison slipped his bag from his shoulders and reached for a bottle of water. He poured it in so fast, it dribbled down his face and onto his shirt. He didn't care.

Mike rubbed Jill's head. The handler pulled out bowls from his bag and filled them with water for the dogs. Once their thirst abated, he produced a treat for each of them.

"We found where the kidnapper held the Martins. It's just a few feet deeper in the bush in that direction." Mike pointed. "But no one's there now, and the dogs led me here." He looked down fondly at his canine pair. "Good work. Do we head across those logs?" He spoke to the dogs as if he expected them to answer.

The pair barked furiously and strained to be let loose. One seemed in a hurry to cross the fallen logs over the muddy bed, while the other stared downriver.

"What does that mean?" Brent waved an arm at both dogs.

"I'm getting conflicting signals, but it means we're close." Mike tightened his grip on the leashes. "Let's cross the river first and see if we can pick up a trail. How far does the river go?" Mike fixed Harrison with his gaze.

"Port Hanks? Is that correct?" Harrison tilted his head in Jason and Hal's direction, knowing they'd been employed here much longer than he had and could verify his answer.

To Harrison's surprise, Brent spoke up. "Yes, it meets the manmade Placid Cut in Port Hanks before emptying into Lake Huron. I know this area well, having been stationed in Grand Beach for several years."

"Okay, let's go." Mike turned the Shepherds loose.

When the dogs took off running, a mixture of trepidation and excitement raced through Harrison. He wasn't sure what they would find, so he tried to mentally prepare himself.

When he heard the all-too-familiar screech from the tiny, dark-haired rapscallion not far ahead, it was the best sound in the world. Why had he ever told her to curtail that outburst?

Gasping for breath, he finally caught up with the dogs and men that had somehow managed to all get ahead of him. Like it or not, his leg was beginning to slow him down.

The sight of Jasmine behind an old fenced-off area brought bittersweet feelings. *Where is Lily?*

Jason pulled something like a paperclip or small piece of bent wire from his pocket and picked the padlock. Harrison didn't care when or how he had learned that trick. He was just glad he had.

The moment Jasmine was free, she leapt onto Harrison's chest with the agility of a monkey. He held her close, rubbing the back of her head as she sobbed against him. "It's okay, honey. You're safe now. Are you injured? Did that man hurt you?"

"No," she blubbered. "But he's got my mommy."

"Don't worry. We found you, didn't we? We'll find your mom."

She nodded but kept her head buried. It broke his heart to think of the trauma this child must have endured.

Jasmine looked up at him, her face wet with tears. "I'm hungry and thirsty."

"I bet you are. I've got water and granola bars. Will that do?"

Jasmine nodded and swiped the back of her hand on her nose.

Harrison looked at Jason. "Can you reach in my bag and get Jasmine a drink and snack?" His backpack still rested on his shoulders and he didn't have the heart to set Jasmine on her feet to get to it.

As Jasmine gulped water ravenously, Harrison reminded her to slow down or she'd get an upset stomach. Then he just had to ask the question that had been plaguing him since he found her. "Do you have any idea where your mom might be?"

"No." She frowned.

His heart sank.

"He got mad at me and took my mommy. It's all my fault." She took a large bite of her granola bar.

"None of this is your fault, Jasmine. Why did he get mad at you?"

"He brought us water but then wouldn't let us have any. So, I hit him over the head with his bottle of water because he was scaring Mommy. I think his sunglasses may have cut his nose. He was very, very mad. I probably gave him a headache too."

Harrison fought the incredulous desire to laugh. Must be stress. "Good for you. You are very brave. What happened after that?"

"He got furious with me and told me I could starve to death. Then he locked me in the cage and took Mommy with him."

"Can you remember which way they went?" Brent asked.

Jasmine pointed a trembling finger. "Back that way toward the river where we crossed on the logs in the muddy water."

"Just as I suspected," Mike replied. "The dogs were confused. Jill wanted to find you, Jasmine, and I think Gentry knew that your mother might be on the river."

Brent pursed his lips. "I wonder if he had a canoe."

Jasmine nodded. "Yes, he did. It was old and brown and had duct tape on it."

"You are a huge help, young lady." Brent smiled. "Is there anything else you can think of that will help us find your mom?"

"No, but please hurry, because he's sick in the mind." Jasmine chewed the last bite of her snack.

"Why do you say that?" Harrison's eyes narrowed.

"He was talking to Frank."

Harrison swallowed a large lump that had formed in his throat. What kind of chance did Lily have if there were two kidnappers? "Who's Frank?"

"His imaginary friend. Mommy said he suffers from... I think the word is schizophrenia?"

The entire group fell silent as the men exchanged worried looks.

"Are you sure?" Harrison shifted her in his arms.

"Yes, I heard him talking to an invisible man. There was definitely no one there. My mom took psychology courses, so she knows these things."

"What did he say to his imaginary friend?"

"He didn't know what to do with me. Apparently, I was an *unforeseen* complication." Jasmine reached down and scratched her leg. "His friend, Frank, told him to lock us in that metal cage. I think something bit me. If I got a tick or poison ivy because of him..."

Jasmine squirmed to get down from his arms, so Harrison set her on the ground. She soon forgot her itchy predicament.

"Can I pet the dogs? Which one is Jill?" Jasmine looked to Mike.

Harrison's heart warmed to see the little munchkin distracted from her terrifying ordeal. *Thank you, God, for dogs.*

"The one with the white markings on her throat." Mike rested a hand on her head. "You can pet them if you like, but then we'd better look for your mom."

Jason ended a phone call and waved a hand at Harrison. "Can I speak with you for a moment?"

The two men spoke quietly before Harrison slipped to Jasmine's side and squatted to her level. "Your grandparents are waiting for you at the main gate. Will you go with Hal? He'll take you back to meet them."

Her large dark eyes were caverns of worry. "But what about my mom? Maybe I should help look for her."

Harrison gently squeezed her shoulder. "No, honey, you will be much safer with your grandparents. I promise we'll find her." As soon as the words left his mouth, he wished he could take them back. What if he couldn't keep that promise? Would Jasmine hate him for the rest of her life?

Jasmine sighed. "Okay, I'll go. I understand a child can be a hindrance in such circumstances."

Her comment brought smirks to almost everyone's face in the group, except for Harrison's. Mike coughed to hide his chuckle. Harrison was encouraged to see that the carefree, intelligent child he'd come to love was putting up a brave front, despite her traumatic day.

Harrison stood as the entire group moved back down the trail in the direction they'd come. When Jasmine lifted her arms toward him, he picked up the vulnerable child. After crossing the riverbed, Harrison set Jasmine on her feet and pulled the uniformed monkey from his bag. "By the way, you were a very smart girl to leave Detective Harry on guard to point us in the right direction." He touched the tip of her nose.

She reached for her beloved stuffed animal and squished it against her little body. "I knew he would deliver. Now, if only he could help find my mom."

"He did his job for the day. You take him back and introduce him to your grandparents. I'm sure they'll be excited to meet him and learn about the hero that he is. And don't you worry. God knows exactly where Mommy is, and we will find her." Harrison let her hand go and she reached for Hal's outstretched one.

"Yes, he does." Jasmine looked back over her shoulder at him and nodded bravely. But the quivering in her voice shot arrows at his heart.

He blinked away the fluid obscuring his vision as Hal led Jasmine out of harm's way.

CHAPTER FORTY-TWO

For the next half hour, Harrison struggled along with the group of men and the canine team as they pressed through dense bush along the wildly overgrown trail. He knew they had left the campground by the wooden markers signifying the boundary line. Now they trudged through a long-abandoned former Boy Scout camp trail that ran parallel to the river, searching intently for clues.

By the time they reached the Placid Cut in Port Hanks, which ran at a ninety-degree angle to the Placid River, they stopped. The dogs appeared to have lost the scent a few minutes past the mucky makeshift log bridge that had led them to Jasmine.

Brent raised his palms. "Okay, men, the way I see it, there are three possibilities. Lily and her kidnapper either followed the cut east, which goes for several kilometres into the county until it reaches the Placid River again. Not much along the way except farmland. Or they followed it west to where it empties into Lake Huron at the town of Port Hanks. Or they exited the opposite side of the Placid River here, just before the cut, and doubled back down the other side. If they doubled back, we would have spotted a canoe on the opposite riverbank unless they are portaging. Personally, I think doubling back would be highly unlikely. I'll call in and request an aerial search of the area, which might help us find them."

"Good suggestion," Mike remarked. "While that is going on, we'll try to cross over the river and see if the dogs can pick up a scent on the other side."

"How do you propose we do that?" Jason slapped his hands on his hips as rivulets of sweat dripped down his face. "It's too deep and wide to get across, thanks to all the snow and rain we've had this winter and spring."

Harrison listened quietly. He removed his cap and ran a shaky hand through his hair. Sweat dripped from the tip of his nose. He was exhausted, extremely warm, and very worried. Fear for Lily's safety plagued him. Deep in thought, he jumped when chaos erupted behind him.

He turned at the hysterical, high-pitched yapping. A feisty Jack Russell Terrier pup barrelled at a high rate of speed into the middle of the group and lunged at the German Shepherds. A fifty-something man ran awkwardly behind, yelling at his dog.

To Harrison's astonishment, one word from Mike and both of his search dogs sat quietly and obediently, staring at the crazy, hyper dog. The dog's owner arrived out of breath, apologizing profusely. "Come here, Cassie. That's a bad girl. What were you thinking?" The owner scooped the agitated dog into his arms. "I'm really sorry. I should have had her on a leash, but we just arrived in our canoe and she leapt out before I could stop her."

"You give your dog canoe rides?" Jason quirked an eyebrow.

The man nodded. "She loves being on the water."

A thought crashed into Harrison's brain as he half-listened to Mike assure the man that no harm had been done. Harrison pulled Brent aside and shared his idea. Brent nodded.

The policeman extended a hand to the dog's owner. "I'm Officer Brent Nichols from the Grand Beach OPP detachment. Are you aware of the Amber Alert?"

"Gordon Parsons, but everyone calls me Gordy. I'd shake your hand, but I need both to restrain this crazy pup. And yes, I'm aware of the alert. Is that what this is about?" He glanced at the dogs and around the group of men.

"Yes. How long have you been on the river?"

Gordy shrugged and pointed. "About fifteen minutes, I think. I just set out from the opposite bank over there."

"Have you seen a man and woman in a battered brown canoe with duct tape?"

The man shook his head. "No, can't say that I have."

"That's good news." Mike wrapped the leash around one hand. "It's possible he didn't make it this far. That might narrow down our search."

Gordy shook his head. "If he was fast, he could have gotten down the cut and out of sight before Cassie and I hit the water." The affectionate puppy licked Gordy's face at the mention of her name.

Harrison couldn't help himself. "We have a favour to ask of you, Gordy. Can we borrow your canoe for the next hour or so? We'd like to get to the other side of the riverbank."

"I'll do anything to help find the poor woman and her daughter. But you didn't mention the little girl. Is she okay?"

Brent pointed with his thumb in the general direction of the area they'd found Jasmine. "We found her safe and sound."

"That's good to hear." The man let out a breath.

"We'll need to make a couple of trips," Harrison informed him. "I'll take Mike and the dogs across first. It's imperative that they pick up the scent."

"You do whatever you need to do." Gordy waved a hand through the air. "My canoe is just around the bend there on a small section of beach."

A few minutes later, Harrison climbed into the canoe with Mike and the dogs. Within fifteen minutes he was across and back, and ready for Jason and Brent. After he paddled them across, he came back one last time to pick up Gordy, so the man could take him to the other side to join the searchers.

Harrison thanked the man for his help, disembarked, and hurried to catch up with the group. He hobbled behind the other men as they painstakingly made their way along the overgrown riverbank. It was obvious not many people had travelled this section at all. It was even worse than the other side they had just pushed their way through.

Within forty-five minutes, they had made it back to the makeshift log bridge over the mucky Placid River, near where they had found Jasmine. The dogs had not picked up the scent again.

It was now two o'clock in the afternoon. The sun was scorching. And Harrison was getting low on water. His shoulders sagged. Where was Lily? The longer time went on, the bleaker things appeared. Had the kidnapper managed to get Lily into Port Hanks after all?

Only God knew.

CHAPTER FORTY-THREE

Lily stared through the small kitchen window as her captor paced the decrepit outdoor deck. The top of his head appeared and disappeared in a precise rhythmic pattern; judging by the sound of muffled words, he was conversing with his imaginary accomplice again. How long had it been since she was hauled from the canoe to begrudgingly help him hide the old brown watercraft under the deck of the cottage on the lake, before being painfully bound to the kitchen chair?

At least he'd been humane enough to allow her a drink of water.

Lily's eyes roamed the inside of the meagre dwelling. Judging by the sparse furnishings, dangling cobwebs, and blanket of dust, it had been vacant for a long time. How had her abductor obtained access? Was this where the mentally ill man had been holed up since losing his job? If so, his house-cleaning skills were sorely lacking.

How stable was he? What were his plans for her now? Lily's stomach churned with worry. How was her sweet daughter faring? Would anyone find Jasmine?

A tear slipped down her cheek as she recalled Jasmine's pitiful wails when Brad Pit hauled Lily away from the cage. It had been a torment of the worst kind, leaving Jasmine behind.

A rumbling sound broke the silence. Lily's eyes widened. The sound grew louder by the second. Was that the engine of a Coast Guard Helicopter?

The back door crashed open, catapulting her heart into an erratic stampede. Brad Pit was panicking. He paced the kitchen floor, raking a hand through his hair. "What do I do now, Frank? I didn't anticipate they'd be on to me this quick. I thought we'd at least have until darkness to carry out our final plans."

When her kidnapper picked up a kitchen chair and hurled it violently against the wall, Lily screamed. Her body trembled as she stared at a gaping jagged hole in the wall and the chair on the floor on its side with one splintered off, broken leg.

"That's good advice, Frank, to stay put and not panic. They can search all they want, but they won't find her here."

Lily listened to her captor's conversation with his imaginary accomplice. She didn't know how authorities would ever find her, but the fact that a helicopter was searching the Port Hanks area was promising.

"Don't make a sound," he barked at her suddenly.

Lily looked at him oddly. She hadn't said a word. And she didn't plan on speaking to him either. Ruffling his fragile nerves might cause him to react violently again. She didn't want to end up like the chair ... or worse.

Nothing is impossible with God.

The words flitted through her mind.

Hope flickered.

Was God speaking to her? She repeated the words. Over and over. And the more she said them, the more her hope grew.

Perhaps she'd be rescued after all.

CHAPTER FORTY-FOUR

Contrary to the OPP's wishes, Harrison charged out alone, heading back toward the cut. He didn't know why, but deep inside he felt compelled to search the Port Hanks area. He recognized the feeling as the same one that had driven him to the Sandy Dunes Beach in the middle of a tornado warning. Was God directing him as he had before?

Officers Brent and Mike had been ordered to await further instructions from their supervisor, so their hands were tied, and they were unable to accompany him. The officers pleaded with him to wait, but when they realized their demands were falling on deaf ears, they warned him to be careful and not do anything foolish.

Jason received a call to report immediately to the group camping area to settle a brawl that had erupted among drunken and disorderly college students. He apologized to Harrison and hurried off.

When Harrison heard the unmistakable rumble of the Coast Guard helicopter as he limped along the overgrown trail, he was encouraged. *Please God, let them locate her alive and well. Don't let him hurt her in any way.*

Once he arrived at the Placid River Cut, he scratched his head as he studied the water. *Now what?* He didn't have any way to cross except to swim. That was possible since he was a strong swimmer.

But should he cross?

He ambled along the north side of the shoreline heading towards Lake Huron before stopping and rubbing a hand down his face in frustration. Completely exhausted, he dropped to a sandy section. He stared up at the bright sky, his eyes squinting in the brilliant sunshine.

Dear God, I don't know what to do or where to look. Please lead me and please keep Lily safe. I foolishly made a promise to Jasmine. For the child's sake, don't let anything happen to her mother.

A niggle of guilt settled in his chest. He hadn't been completely honest with God. Yes, it was true that he wanted to spare Jasmine heartache, but he had another, more selfish, reason for his request.

Closing his eyes, he fought the raging conflict inside him. Terrified because of his past hurts, he finally came clean, allowing himself to be completely vulnerable for once. *Yes God, I think I'm in love with Lily. Please keep her safe for me too.*

He scrambled awkwardly to his feet. Without conscious thought, he limped along the cut, toward the lake.

A robin hopped a few feet ahead of him. A turkey vulture soared overhead. Three mallards squawked loudly and waddled along the shoreline. Nature went about its daily routine as if nothing was amiss. He was aware of it all yet saw it through a fog. He couldn't keep his thoughts from Lily. When had he fallen so desperately, head-over-heels in love with her?

I'll tell her as soon as I find her. I'll tell her what I love the most about her ... that's she beautiful inside and out. That she's kind, gentle, compassionate, and a wonderful mother. Not to mention that her dazzling dimple almost knocks me over with desire. She's everything I've been looking for all my life. Thank you for the journey that has led me to you, God. And to Lily and Jasmine.

Praying was beginning to become as natural as breathing.

For the next few minutes, it was just him, God, and nature.

He approached several homes built along the top of the small but steep rise running adjacent to the Placid River Cut. Directly ahead he could see the sparkling, tranquil waters of the lake.

Maybe I should go door to door and ask residents if they've seen Lily and her abductor. His calf complained as he climbed the rise and approached the first cottage.

No luck. It was vacant. He even peered through the large window that faced the river. He was not a Peeping Tom, but desperate times called for desperate measures. Didn't they?

Starry Lake

The next place, large and stately, was nestled among tall white birches. Party balloons and decorations adorned the yard and deck.

A sophisticated-looking blonde woman in her late thirties, dressed as if she'd just been photographed for the cover of a fashion magazine, was unloading her SUV. With arms full of beautifully-wrapped gifts, she glared in his direction. "Can I help you?"

The look of disdain on her face spoke volumes. If he could read her mind it would probably say, *I don't know who you are but you're disgusting; get off my property now.*

If he looked as terrible as he felt, she was correct in her assessment. Bedraggled, exhausted, and muddy, he wiped his perspiring brow with the back of his hand. "I'm sorry to bother you. Are you aware of the Amber Alert? I work for Piney Campground and I'm helping in the search for Lily Martin. I wondered if you happened to see a man and woman paddle by your place in a beat-up brown canoe within the last hour? Or perhaps walk past?"

"Yes, I'm aware of the Amber Alert. I just arrived for my parents' twenty-fifth wedding anniversary and no, I haven't seen anyone fitting that description. As you can see, I'm very busy." The lady turned away from him.

Harrison didn't have the time or energy to deal with the woman's uncaring attitude. "Thank you for your time." He whirled around, a little bit annoyed, and took a step down the steep, sandy slope toward the cut.

"Wait a minute, Mister."

Harrison turned to see a tall, skinny, pre-teen boy with white-blond hair barrelling across the yard towards him, carrying a basketball.

"I saw those people in the canoe."

Still clutching her packages, the woman stepped closer to them. "Caleb, get back here now. There's a kidnapper on the loose. It could be him for all we know."

"Mom, are you blind? He obviously works for the campground. Look at the logo on his shirt and cap." Although Harrison didn't condone disrespect, he was, in a satisfying-sort-of-way, pleased with the kid's response.

The boy's mother stomped her foot. "Come up here immediately and don't you dare speak to me like that." She placed the gifts back in her vehicle and took several large angry strides toward them.

"Oh Mom, don't get your pantyhose in a knot. I'm coming. I just want to tell this man that I saw those people he asked about in the canoe."

"How could you? We just arrived," she snapped.

"Remember when we got stuck on the bridge over the cut because of the construction?"

The boy's mother stopped in front of them, her arms folded across her chest. "Yes."

"I spotted a great blue heron, so I pulled out the binoculars that Dad keeps under the seat. I followed the bird to see where it landed. A canoe with a man and woman in it came into my vision."

The woman snorted. "That's not unusual. People canoe all the time on that river."

The kid looked as if someone had deflated the air on his bicycle tires. "I was trying to be helpful. The canoe was brown and in rough shape." He looked at Harrison and his face brightened. "Could that be the kidnapper and the woman? If so, where is the little girl?"

A surge of hope filled Harrison's chest. He was tempted to hug the young guy but figured his mother would object.

"We found the child, safe and sound. And your information has been extremely helpful. This may be the tip we've been waiting for."

The boy smiled widely. "I wish I could help you search, but ..." He kicked at a pinecone on the ground and looked up at his mother. "One day, I'm going to be a detective."

"In your dreams, Caleb. Go back up to the house." His mother pointed toward the building.

"Thank you for your help, Caleb." Harrison extended a hand toward the young boy.

Harrison couldn't help but compare this woman's parenting skills to the way Lily treated Jasmine. This cranky blonde fell far short ... at least in his estimation. To be fair, maybe she was having a bad day.

The youth returned a hearty handshake. "Good luck, I hope you find her."

With urgency in his step, Harrison slipped a few times and almost tumbled down the sandy slope. At the bottom, he pulled out his cell phone and placed a call to Brent, relaying the teen's information.

Although Brent was encouraged and promised to pass on the tip, he warned Harrison to wait for the police, who were being mobilized to Port Hanks as they spoke.

Harrison half-ran, half-jogged toward the lake. Lily was nearby. He knew it.

The lake waters shimmered in front of him. He was so over-heated, he felt unwell. And he was out of water. Sweat dripped down his face and stung his eyes. His shirt stuck to his back. He didn't want to waste precious time, but ...

He let his backpack slip off his shoulders to the ground. Then he whipped off his shirt, sandals, and cap and immersed himself in the refreshing lake water. Oops. Probably not a good idea. He wasn't supposed to get his stitches wet. Oh well. It was imperative that he cool down or he'd suffer heat stroke.

He breast-stroked into deeper water for a minute. *What now, God?* Treading water, he studied the shoreline. To the south, handsome cottages dotted the landscape as far as the eye could see. To the north, there were only a few dilapidated cabins. Since the old Scout Camp shared the shoreline, and Piney Campground owned the next several kilometres, there wasn't much land allotted for private residential properties to the north of the cut.

Could Lily's kidnapper have taken her to one of those cottages?

Harrison front-crawled back to shore. He blinked as he clambered out of the water. A robin was perched on his backpack. Was this the same crazy bird that had hopped ahead of him as he'd hiked alongside the cut? Wildlife did unusual things sometimes. It was almost as if the bird had become a friend.

"What do you want, pretty little robin?" Harrison shook his head as he slipped his shirt on and buttoned it up. The stress of the day was really getting to him. Now he was talking to a bird as if it could answer him.

When the robin cocked its head sideways at him as if contemplating his words, jumped from his bag onto the sand, and hopped down the beach, Harrison couldn't tear his eyes away. He stared after the bird as he plunked his cap on his head. The robin turned back and looked at him as if to say, *are you coming?*

He must be losing his mind. Since he didn't have any better options, Harrison followed the bird. What did he have to lose? He had no clue where to look anyway. This direction was as good as any in his estimation, even though it was away from the town of Port Hanks where the police were headed.

Which meant that, if he did manage to find Brad Pit and Lily, he was on his own.

It wasn't long before the robin flew off, leaving Harrison to fend for himself. He shook his head at the hare-brained notion that perhaps God had sent the bird to lead him to Lily.

Loud quacking emanated from behind some shrubbery to his right just before three male mallards wandered in his direction. When they stopped at his feet, craned their necks upwards, and stared directly at him, Harrison was dumbfounded. Was this the same trio he had seen a few minutes ago as he walked alongside the Placid River Cut?

Stymied, Harrison rubbed his chin. *What is all this about?* Abruptly, the mallards took off running down the beach, again in a northerly direction. Harrison limped after them, hard-pressed to keep up.

Five minutes later, all three ducks took a ninety-degree turn, splashed headlong into the lake, and swam away, leaving him to stare at several webbed imprints in the wet sand. Harrison looked heavenward at a brilliant sapphire sky and lifted both hands. *What do I do now?*

The thought was still fresh in his brain when he caught a glimpse of a large, dark object from the corner of his eye. He watched the soaring turkey vulture until it appeared to stall its flight, making circles above a rundown-looking cottage a few hundred feet down the shoreline.

And he knew in his heart that Lily was inside.

CHAPTER FORTY-FIVE

The sound of the helicopter's rotors was now a distant memory. Her hopes dashed, Lily struggled to stay positive. Harrison and many others had to be out searching for them by now.

Her stomach rumbled loudly. No surprise there since the last thing she'd eaten was a brownie in the restaurant in London. Was that only yesterday? So much had happened over the last twenty-four hours. Over the last week, in fact.

There was the incredible miracle of the storm dissipating in front of their eyes and Harrison's decision to follow Jesus. Lily's heart warmed at the thought of not only that life-altering scene but the man himself. Her mind wandered to his warm embrace at the campfire. He was a man who made her laugh—something she hadn't done in a very long time. He was a man who understood her daughter when not many did. When she remembered his unselfish acts of replacing both tires on her bike, her sweatshirt, and Jasmine's stuffed animal, her heart felt as though it would literally burst. She loved this man. How and when had that happened?

But then a frosty chill settled over her as reality came charging back.

Breaking free from the horrifying situation and returning to her daughter was her first priority.

Lily listened carefully. Where was her abductor? After his volatile chair-against-the-wall incident, he had waited until the Coast Guard copter left then disappeared outside again.

Maybe he had gone to meet his friend Frank and get some advice. She could always hope and pray that Frank urged him to let her go. An idea popped into her brain. She sat up a little straighter in her chair.

Perhaps she'd have a talk with Frank herself.

❖

"It wasn't my fault, you know."

Lily cringed. Goosebumps prickled her spine as her abductor's fingers crawled through her hair, twisting strands back and forth.

"What wasn't your fault?" Her voice cracked.

"I did it for her. She over-reacted, reported me to the authorities and wham, I lost my job. The headless bird was meant to show how serious I was—that I would go to any length to please her. You see, that bird had been nesting on her front porch, waking her up at four o'clock every morning and making a mess. She complained about it incessantly. So, I did her a favour."

Lily could feel his stress rising as his fingers, inter-twined in her wavy locks, pulled tightly. "Ouch!"

His hold relaxed a bit. "I'm sorry. I didn't mean to hurt you. I promise I'll never hurt you. I love you. I'll do anything to make you happy. Do you remember when we first met?"

Lily nodded. *Best to play along.*

A hoarse chuckle escaped his throat. "I knew it would eventually come to you. That's okay, I like a woman who plays hard to get." His finger traced a path along her chin. "As soon as it's dark, we're leaving."

"I don't think so." Was her voice as shaky as she felt?

"What? Who died and made you commander-in-chief? We're meeting Frank at the dock in Port Hanks. Then we'll be whisked away in his boat to our honeymoon paradise along the lake, where we'll live happily ever after."

His demented sideways grin filled her with dread. She couldn't let that happen. *Wait a minute.* If Frank was imaginary, she wouldn't be leaving the cabin. Would she?

Lily's mind whirled with possibilities. It would take quick thinking and improvisation. Would it work? At all costs she had to stall Brad Pit, in case there really was a man named Frank coming. If she left the cabin, she had a sinking feeling she would never be found.

"I met Frank when you were outside a few minutes ago."

Her tormentor spun. In a flash, he was squatting in front of her, his face inches from hers, eyes bulging with excitement. "Really? Frank spoke to you? Everyone keeps telling me that he doesn't exist—that he's all in my mind. I knew it." He slapped his knees. "What did he say?"

Putrid breath stung her nostrils as she stared into wild eyes, a large angry gash over his left eyebrow, and bucked, plaque-encrusted teeth. In front of her was a man that needed physical and mental care.

"Frank is a really nice guy." Lily summoned up the courage to smile, not easy, considering her circumstances. "He came in to tell me that before we leave, we'll need to eat. He's planning a barbecue."

Brad frowned. "What? He changed our plans? There was no mention of a barbecue. He isn't even supposed to arrive until ten o'clock tonight."

"Apparently, he got an early start this morning and took the chance that you'd be okay with the change. He figured you'd be hungry since you've been hiding out in the bush and running from the authorities."

The kidnapper jumped to his feet, cackling hysterically, and threw his hands on his hips. "That Frank. What a great guy. Smart too. He's as close to me as the brother I ..."

His eyes darkened. Did his body just shake? "He'll never take his place, but he's a good guy."

Had this man endured a traumatic childhood event, possibly explaining the conflicted soul that stood before her today? Lily's mind whirled again. Where could she go with this act, now that she had her kidnapper convinced she'd spoken to Frank?

"Wait a minute. Are you trying to pull a fast one?" His fingers wound tightly around her hair again.

"No. Why would you say that?" Lily winced as her neck was pulled at an odd angle.

"If what you say is true, why didn't Frank tell me this? And where is he now?"

"He couldn't find you." Lily bit back a groan at the writhing pain.

"Oh." Brad released his grip and Lily's neck snapped back into position. Without warning he did a farmer's blow with his nose, sending a wad of snot onto the aged, ripped-up linoleum. Lily's stomach whirled in revolt as he wiped his face on his sleeve.

Please, God, get me out of here.

Her kidnapper paced back and forth in front of her, rubbing his chin. "I was under the deck retrieving something I left in the canoe. That could have been when I missed him. And there is an old barbecue on the back deck we could use. I do hope he thought to buy charcoal and lighter fluid."

"He's stopping at the grocery store in Port Hanks to buy wieners and buns. He'll be back in a few minutes." Lily blurted, glancing out the living room window at the lake.

What she saw made her heart race.

The unmistakable form of Harrison Somerville loomed a few hundred feet down the beach, heading in her direction. Hope charged through her. The man she loved was searching for her.

But the play must go on. "In fact, there he is right now." Lily pointed.

The strange man squinted out the window. "Are you sure that's him? I'm a little near-sighted, but he appears taller than I remember. My sunglasses, the ones your pain-in-the-butt kid destroyed, were prescription."

"That's him for sure. I recognize his black backpack and cream-coloured ball cap." Lily hoped beyond all hope that her abductor's altered mind would perceive just what she had told him she could see.

An excited yip left the kidnapper's mouth. Her eyes widened as the wiry man threw his cap in the air then performed a strange and un-coordinated happy dance around the meagre dwelling. "I didn't realize how hungry I was. I don't even remember the last time I ate. How did Frank know just what I needed?"

The kidnapper retrieved his knife from the kitchen counter. When he approached, her mouth went dry. He reached behind her and cut the ropes holding her ankles to the lower rungs of the chairs, then freed the restraints that bound her arms behind her back. She breathed a small sigh of relief as she massaged her chafed wrists.

Before she knew what was happening, he had yanked her to her feet and pulled her body up against his stinky, unkempt one. "Come on, sweetheart, let's go help Frank. The thought of food after so long has my taste buds salivating."

CHAPTER FORTY-SIX

Harrison's eyes shot wide open. As the turkey vulture soared overhead, Lily and her abductor walked along the side of the broken-down cottage, cementing the miracle in his mind. Harrison knew, without a doubt, that God had led him to Lily. Miraculous as it was, there was very little time to concoct a plan.

Had the kidnapper spotted him? What should he do? Race for cover behind some trees? What could he use for a weapon? Did he have time to call the police? Harrison searched his shirt pocket for his cell. He slapped his chest with his palm. Where was his phone?

A sick feeling charged through him as the kidnapper's arm encircled Lily's waist, holding her tightly against him as they approached. Harrison reached inside the pocket of his pants. He checked the other. Panic escalated.

"Over here, Frank," Lily yelled, waving a hand at him. "I hope you brought the hotdogs because we're starved."

Harrison stomach churned. Had Lily been drugged? She didn't appear to know who he was, and what she said didn't make any sense. Hotdogs? Who was Frank? A thought ran through his brain and he remembered something Jasmine had told him—that the kidnapper talked to an imaginary friend. Had Jasmine mentioned his name? Was it Frank? His gut told him to play along.

"Yep, I've got the food right here in my backpack." Harrison held up the bag. Frantic for his cell phone, he reached inside the outer pocket. Bingo. His hand clasped the small device. But to his horror, it slipped from his grasp and fell into the tall dune grasses nearby.

"Did you remember the charcoal and lighter fluid?" her abductor yelled.

Charcoal and lighter fluid? Harrison panicked. A quick scan below him did not reveal his phone. "Sorry, Brad. I knew I'd forget something. But no matter. We can eat them raw. I'm hungry enough and I bet you are too."

"True." The kidnapper chortled as he dragged Lily towards Harrison. Then he stopped abruptly, eyes bulging. "Wait one minute. You're not Frank."

Harrison froze. Now what should he do?

The demented man gave Lily a shove, sending her sprawling onto the sand. "You lied to me, you little witch. That's not Frank. That's that stupid park employee and he's come to take you away from me."

On her hands and knees, Lily tried to crawl away. Harrison charged toward the kidnapper. Gripping the backpack in both hands, he swung it at Brad Pit with all the force he could muster. But the vile man was quick and jumped out of the way in time.

A large, shiny blade flashed dangerously close to Harrison's face. As he backed up, the knife sliced the air. Another wild swing and it slashed his bag, spilling several granola bars onto the sand. Again, and again, the sick man charged him. The next blow was so violent it sent the bag hurtling from his hands. Staggering backwards, Harrison fell awkwardly onto the beach, near the water's edge.

The possessed man stared down at him, spit drooling from one corner of his mouth. "You married that evil woman and then she killed him. She killed my baby brother. Why, Dad? Tell me why."

Harrison blinked. What in the world was the man talking about?

Behind the kidnapper, Lily staggered to her feet and lunged at her abductor. Harrison rolled out of the way as the pair hit the beach, landing hard beside him.

A scuffle ensued. There was no way Lily could defend herself for very long against the strength and adrenaline-filled madness of the man. As Harrison scrambled to get up, her screech stopped his heart. Her body grew limp and rage filled him. "No!"

In a flash, Harrison was on his feet; he yanked the kidnapper off Lily's chest and knocked the knife into the sand. But again, the demented man took him by surprise and squirmed from his grasp. As he turned to run, Harrison threw his weight into him and the pair tumbled to the sand, half-in and half-out of the water.

They wrestled together and somehow Harrison found himself under water with the wiry, agile man on his chest. His injured leg was twisted awkwardly beneath him, the writhing pain hindering his ability to fight. Harrison pushed Pit away and broke the surface of the water, gasping hungrily for air. Pit jumped on him and Harrison went under again. In a stalled pattern of submerging and resurfacing, Harrison knew he was losing the battle.

Just as reality began to blur, the weight lifted from his chest and he shot up coughing, choking, and spitting out tepid lake water.

Relief filled him at the scene before his eyes. Jillian and Gentry, the police dogs, had managed to efficiently subdue the attacker. One sat on the mentally ill man's chest, growling viciously at his face, while the other had its teeth clamped tightly around his shirt sleeve.

Brad Pit wailed loudly, "Get them off me."

Footsteps and loud commands echoed behind him. Mike and Brent ran full-speed toward the downed abductor, weapons raised, issuing threats as they advanced.

Harrison scrambled to his feet and sloshed toward Lily's prone form where he dropped to his knees. Her crimson-soaked T-shirt tightened up his chest until he could barely breathe. "Lily. Oh God. No." Her eyes were closed and her pallor ghastly-white. "Please hang on, Lily. I made a promise to Jasmine," Harrison rambled, as he pressed her wrist for a pulse.

He could not detect one.

"Jasmine. Is she safe?" The incredible words were so soft, Harrison strained to hear them above the commotion behind him.

Harrison choked back his emotions as tears of relief blurred his vision. "Yes, Jasmine is safe and sound. The police dogs found her. She's with your parents now."

Lily's chest rose and fell ever so slightly.

"Oh, Lily. I couldn't find your pulse. I thought ..." he paused to collect himself. "Where do you hurt?"

"My neck and shoulder."

Harrison pulled back her tattered, bloody T-shirt. A large gaping gash at the base of her neck oozed blood. He ripped off his shirt, sending the buttons airborne, then scrunched it into a ball and pressed it tightly against the wound. Lily moaned and appeared to slip in and out of consciousness.

"I need an ambulance. I wish I had my cell." Harrison glanced helplessly toward the tall dune grasses in the distance.

A comforting hand rested on his shoulder. "It's okay, I've already called for an ambulance." Brent stared down at him, his eyes warm and compassionate. "Seriously, Harrison, we don't know how you found Lily and her kidnapper. You were one step ahead of us all the way. If you ever want a job in law enforcement ..." He waved a hand in the direction of Brad Pit.

Harrison followed the movement to the handcuffed perpetrator, now being led away by two husky officers, flanked by Mike and the dogs.

Harrison shook his head and gazed down at Lily. "Thanks, man, but I don't think I have the stomach for it. I'll stick with my calling. It's a lot less dangerous." The events of the last few hours and the murders that had happened at No Trace Campground while he was employed there flitted through his mind. Was his last statement actually valid?

"It looks like you paid attention in First Aid Class, judging by the way you knew to put pressure on that wound. But I do have to say that your pulse-taking skills are sorely lacking." Brent squeezed his shoulder before letting him go.

"Huh?" Harrison's brow wrinkled as he looked up into Brent's grin.

"The last I heard, driftwood doesn't have a pulse. But then, you would be the expert at this sort of thing, being a park naturalist and all."

Perplexed, Harrison glanced down. A long, slim piece of smooth white driftwood lay adjacent to Lily's arm. In his panic, he must have grabbed it. No wonder he couldn't feel a pulse.

Was that a hint of a smile on Lily's face? Had she just heard? Either way, it was the most beautiful thing he'd ever seen. Even if it was at his expense.

"What can I say? I was distraught." He kept pressure on the wound with one hand and stroked Lily's cheek with the other.

"I hear an odd sound coming from the vegetation over there. I'm going to check it out. The ambulance is here now. Seriously, man, I hope she pulls through." Brent strode toward the bushes.

"Lily?"

"Yes?"

"I want to tell you something, because if you don't ..." His throat tightened in unison with the pressure in his chest. He couldn't bring himself to voice the thought he dreaded. "I want you to know how I feel." Lake water dripped from Harrison's hair onto Lily's shirt.

Her eyelids fluttered open briefly then closed again. Her lips moved, and he strained to hear what she was saying. "I love you too."

Harrison was suddenly aware of a ruckus behind him. No time to process those four amazing words, or to tell her how he felt. The paramedics were now at his side, shoving him out of the way. He clambered to his feet and, as if in a swirling, surreal fog, stared at the mayhem below him.

"Is this yours?" Brent's voice distracted him momentarily and he tore his eyes away.

Harrison reached for the cell resting on Brent's palm with trembling fingers. "Yes. How did you find it?"

"It's not every day that you hear the theme song to Hawaii Five-O coming from the bushes. I had to check it out."

Frantic with worry, Harrison fumbled to tuck the phone into his shirt pocket. The device slipped down his bare chest and hit the top of his hiking boot. Oh right. His shirt was scrunched into a bloody ball beside Lily. In one swift motion, he bent down, retrieved his phone, and slipped it into the pocket of his pants. "Thanks for finding it. I dropped it when I saw the kidnapper with Lily and tried to call 911." Harrison couldn't look away from the life and death scene before him.

The paramedics lifted the stretcher and hurried across the shoreline. Harrison hobbled behind, ignoring the fiery burning in his calf.

But he couldn't care less about himself. *Please God, let her live. Please don't let it be too late.* Had Lily just told him she loved him? Was she in her right mind? Was he? Or had he imagined the words in his state of shock. The last few minutes blurred together in his mind.

At this moment, all that mattered was that she lived. He'd made a little girl a promise that really wasn't his to make. Life and death were in God's hands. Not his.

Jasmine needed her.

But he did too.

CHAPTER FORTY-SEVEN

Harrison tossed the empty coffee cup in the trash can and rubbed a hand over his irritated stomach. He'd had way too much coffee and no food, always a recipe for indigestion. But until he knew that Lily was out of danger, he wouldn't be able to eat.

A quick check of his cell phone revealed that it was six o'clock in the evening. He continued to pace the small room. It had been two hours since they'd rushed Lily in for emergency surgery in the large London, Ontario hospital. Surely, there would be news soon. He found himself repeating the same prayer over and over—pleading with the God of the universe to spare Lily's life and bring her out of surgery alive and well.

The elevator in the hallway dinged and before he knew what was happening, a whirlwind of energy jumped into his arms. "Mr. Somerville. How's my mommy?"

A couple in their fifties followed their granddaughter, the woman spewing forth apologies. "Please, Jasmine. Get down."

Harrison smiled. "It's okay. She's fine right where she is." He rubbed the back of Jasmine's head. "It's so good to see you, sweetie." Turning to the couple, he extended a hand. "I'm Harrison Somerville, a park naturalist with Piney Campground and a friend of Lily and Jasmine's."

"Nice to meet you." Despite his salt and pepper hair, Lily's father seemed young and vibrant. His handshake was firm and vigorous. "I'm Sam Reinhardt and this is my wife, Stephanie."

"Have you heard any news yet?" The petite, attractive woman was almost identical in looks to Lily; the family resemblance was remarkable.

"Not yet. She's been in surgery for a few hours. I'm anticipating an update anytime now."

"You're a hero." Jasmine touched the side of his face with one hand while snuggling her stuffed monkey under the other arm. "It's all over the news. You helped save my mommy's life."

Harrison choked back his emotions. "I can't take any credit, Jasmine. I had lots of help from some very smart dogs in the Canine Unit, the OPP, and nature."

"Nature?" Jasmine's eyes were gigantic.

The curious stares of Jasmine's grandparents almost bore a hole through him.

"It's a miraculous story. Sit down and I'll tell you all about it while we wait for the doctor."

All three listened intently while he rambled on nervously.

"You found Mommy because you were led by a robin, three mallards, and a turkey vulture?" Jasmine jumped to her feet from the couch in the waiting room and faced him. Her monkey toppled to the floor.

"That's exactly right." Harrison nodded, still awed by the experience.

Jasmine picked up her monkey and threw it in the air, caught it and twirled in a circle. "Inconceivable."

That word transported him back in time to the miraculous night when Jasmine's sweet and powerful words had knocked him to his knees. When she started singing the chorus in the waiting room again, his eyes misted.

Jasmine's grandmother reached in her purse, pulled out a tissue, and blew her nose. He wasn't the only one that song affected.

Another elevator ding and a man in green scrubs and a cap on his head entered the waiting room. "I'm Dr. Reynolds. Are you the family of Lily Martin?"

Harrison jumped to his feet.

"We are." Sam Reinhardt also stood. "How is she?"

A broad smile crossed the young doctor's face. To Harrison the man didn't look old enough to be a doctor. But as long as he was bringing good news, that fact was inconsequential. "She's doing extremely well. The knife wound did not result in any muscle or nerve damage that we can detect at this time. The gash wasn't as deep as it appeared. If the blade had nicked the carotid artery, it would have been a different story. She received two units of blood and fifteen stitches. You should be able to see her soon. I expect a full recovery."

A whoosh of gratitude escaped Harrison. "Thank you so much."

"You're welcome. A nurse will come by shortly to take you to see her."

When the doctor walked away, Stephanie faced Harrison. "Maybe this isn't the best time to ask, but you seem, um, how can I put this, to be taking this very personally. Are you and my daughter involved?"

Harrison froze. Just how did he answer that question?

A high-pitched tinkling sound filled the room. "Oh Grandma, you have such a funny way of putting things. Involved." Jasmine held up her hand. "I can answer that question, since Mr. Somerville appears to be tongue-tied."

Heat rushed to Harrison's cheeks. It usually took a lot to embarrass him. Just what would the youngster say?

"Mom and Mr. Somerville are sickening. Their eyes do wacky things when they look at each other. And they almost kissed at the picnic table. Yuck!" Jasmine jabbed a finger in her mouth in a throwing-up gesture.

Harrison shifted his weight from one foot to the other. *Really wish I could hide in some tall dune grasses right now, like my cell phone had.* Was his growing attraction to Lily that obvious? Kids were more intuitive than he thought, and this one more than most.

"In the animal kingdom, he's doing what's called the mating dance. If you've ever seen the woodcock's performance ... well, let's just say that it pales in comparison to Mr. Somerville's."

Seriously aghast, Harrison fought to keep his jaw from dropping open. As he recalled the antics of the male timberdoodle in courtship, he pictured himself twirling and dancing high in the air, then diving full-speed toward Lily on the ground. Once, he'd observed a woodcock break his leg in the process. His calf ached in unison with his thoughts. Perhaps there were some similarities after all.

Stephanie Reinhardt pressed her lips together and reached for her granddaughter's hand. "Okay, Jasmine, that's quite enough. We get the picture. Let's go for a snack. We passed a coffee shop in the lobby. How would you like a doughnut?"

"Yippee! Can we get one for Homicide Detective Harry too?"

"You can get as many as you like." Stephanie grinned at Harrison as she passed.

He blew out a breath as Jasmine and her grandma disappeared behind the closed elevator doors. A wry smile crossed his face. That child sure had a way with words. His smile faded when he turned around. Mr. Reinhardt levelled a stony gaze his direction. Harrison's throat went dry.

Sam's face softened, and he punched Harrison lightly in the upper arm. "Thank you for saving my daughter's life. If she has set her fancy on you, then you must be worth her affections. After all she's been through, I never thought she'd have eyes for another man. You must be very special."

Harrison sighed and wiped his damp palms against his jeans. Having Lily's father's blessing was wonderful, but maybe a bit premature. He still wasn't exactly sure where things stood with Lily and him.

Fifteen minutes later, Jasmine and her grandmother appeared with doughnuts and sandwiches. Harrison couldn't believe how hungry he was. His turkey sandwich tasted as good as a prime rib dinner.

A young nurse with long, curly, blonde hair in a ponytail stepped off the elevator and approached as he tossed his sandwich wrapper into the garbage pail. "Are you the family of Lily Martin?"

"We are," Sam responded.

"Come with me." She led the way to the elevators.

"You don't have to tell us twice." Jasmine skipped ahead and practically danced in front of the elevator doors. Everyone piled in and the doors closed. The young girl held up her pointer finger beside the panel. "Number please?"

"Oh, right." The nurse smiled. "Just press that large red number six, sweetie. Do you know your numbers?"

Harrison coughed to cover the escaping cackle. If only the nurse knew how intelligent this child was. He dropped his hand as a thought struck him. How would Jasmine respond—being the vocal child she was?

Jasmine pressed the button and reached for Harrison's hand. Then she reached up on her tiptoes. He really didn't have to stoop to hear her emphatic whisper. "I was going to ask her to tell me the square root of 1,024. That would surely put her in her place. But I'm trying to be kind." She cupped a hand over her mouth and snorted.

Harrison's eyes shot toward the young nurse, who no doubt had overheard Jasmine's comment—impossible not to, in the small confined space. The nurse quirked an eyebrow but didn't respond. Instead she fixed her gaze on the digital number display. Was she trying to figure out the answer? Harrison knew without a doubt that he couldn't figure that one out without a calculator.

Harrison's lips twitched in amusement as the elevator doors slid open. Jasmine was learning how to curtail her outbursts ... sort of.

What a long and stressful day it had been. Hopefully the worst was now behind them. His leg throbbed like an abscessed tooth. But Brad Pit had been apprehended. And Lily was going to pull through. Had her semi-conscious words truly meant something?

Only time would tell.

CHAPTER FORTY-EIGHT

Despite the ordeal she had just experienced, Lily felt no pain, just extreme exhaustion. It was an effort to keep her eyes open, but she pushed herself. Her family needed to know she was okay.

Her heart leapt with joy as Jasmine bounded into the room. The thrill of seeing her daughter alive and well superseded any injuries she suffered from. She listened raptly as Jasmine explained the order of events that had occurred, from Homicide Detective Harry's wonderful job at alerting the authorities, to the Canine Unit discovering her whereabouts in the wire cage.

But when she told the story of God leading Harrison to find Lily by using wildlife, her eyes grew large. Was Jasmine exaggerating? Could that really be true?

A quick glance revealed Harrison hanging at the back of the room, hands stuffed in his pockets, staring out the window. Perhaps he felt awkward, since her parents were very emotional.

The same blonde nurse poked her head in the room, reminding them that their visiting time was up. Her parents and Jasmine hugged Lily goodbye and started for the door, promising to be back first thing in the morning. Harrison lingered by the window.

"Are you coming, Mr. Somerville?" Jasmine skipped to his side and pulled at his arm.

"I'll be along shortly."

Was that a tremor Lily detected in his voice?

"Come, Jasmine. Let's give Mr. Somerville a few minutes with your mother." Stephanie took her granddaughter's hand and led her to the door.

"Okay, I understand."

Did her daughter just wink at Harrison?

Harrison hobbled to the side of Lily's bed and stared down at her. His eyes were large and ... worried?

"A robin, three mallards, and a turkey vulture?" Lily blinked and blinked again, fighting against the meds flying through her body.

Harrison nodded. "I know it's hard to believe, but that's exactly what happened."

Lily reached for the fingers wrapped tightly around the metal bed rail. They felt cold and clammy. "I want to thank you for finding me. You saved my life. That man was going to take me away to some remote cabin to be his wife." She closed her eyes at the memory.

"He was?" Harrison blanched. "I can't take any credit. God led me to you." He tightened his grip on her hand. "By the way, who is Frank?"

"His imaginary friend. Brad is mentally ill. He talked with Frank a lot." Lily heard the tremble in her own voice as scenes from that horrifying nightmare flashed through her mind. "Was he apprehended? My memory is really fuzzy."

"The authorities have him. Don't worry, you're safe."

Lily swallowed. Her mouth was so dry. "Could I have some water, please?"

Harrison slid his hand behind her head to lift her slightly and held the glass for her as she sipped from a straw. Then he gently placed her back down on the pillow and set the glass on the tray.

"Lily ... I ... um ..." Harrison reached for her hand and stroked a thumb across it.

"Yes?"

"Do you remember our conversation on the beach just before the paramedics came?"

Were those beads of perspiration on his brow? It wasn't that warm in here. In fact, she was cold. Terribly cold. "I remember someone teasing you about your first aid skills." Lily's eyes grew heavy. She fought to stay awake. The medications they had given her must be strong. "I'm sorry. I'm so tired. Was there something else?"

"Um..."

That same blonde head poked itself around the doorway again. "I'm sorry, sir. You really need to leave now. Ms. Martin needs her rest."

Harrison let go of her hand. "I'll let you get some sleep. See you in the morning, Lily."

Lily closed her eyes and drifted into sweet oblivion.

CHAPTER FORTY-NINE

Harrison dragged himself out of bed. It had been a long restless night, but finally, toward dawn, he'd come to a decision. Until he brought the matter front and centre he'd never have any peace. So that was exactly what he would do today.

After a quick shower and a stop at his favourite coffee shop's drive-through for his morning brew, he drove to London. He parked and made his way to the locked door of the Critical Care wing. Pressing the buzzer, he waited.

"Hello? Can I help you?" a male voice responded.

"I'm here to see Lily Martin."

"May I ask who's inquiring?"

"A friend, Harrison Somerville."

"One moment please." A clicking sound came over the intercom. Must be looking her up on the computer. "Oh, she's no longer with us."

Harrison's heart puttered, skipped several beats, and threatened to stall. "What happened? When I left her last night, she was doing well."

"Oh no sir," the man sounded horrified. "You misunderstand. Ms. Martin has been moved to the surgical floor. Let me check. She's in Room 317, eighth floor, East Wing."

Harrison blew out a shaky breath. That nurse could have answered a little more delicately, considering the serious medical condition of patients on this wing. His nerves had really taken a beating lately. He hurried toward the elevator, stabbed at the button, and studied the posted hospital floor plans as he waited. A few minutes later, he again found himself up against a locked wing. He pressed the buzzer and waited.

"Hello, can I help you?"

"I'm here to see Lily Martin."

"The doctor is with her right now. Can you come back in half an hour?"

"Okay, thank you." Harrison blew out a frustrated sigh as he studied his watch. Perhaps he would locate the hospital cafeteria and eat something substantial. He pressed a hand to his stomach, which growled its agreement. After breakfast, he would find the gift shop and purchase something for Lily.

Harrison made his way through the crowded cafeteria with a tray full of bacon and eggs, hash browns and toast, and of course another large coffee. As far as he could tell, there weren't any seats available. Now what should he do? When he heard a high-pitched shriek, his hands jerked so badly, his breakfast almost hit the floor.

"Mr. Somerville. Over here." A little hand waving in the air caught his attention.

Harrison willed his nerves to settle as he made his way toward the Reinhardt table. Was Jasmine's screech wreaking havoc? Or were his nerves taking a nosedive after the adrenalin spike of the traumatic events yesterday? "I'm so glad you saw me. There isn't a vacant table in the place." Harrison set his tray down and settled himself on a hard, plastic chair.

As he took his first bite of toast, Jasmine spewed forth information about an article she was reading in National Geographic on the effect of the moon on the ocean's tides. "Did you know that some of the world's highest tides occur in the Bay of Fundy and can reach fifty feet high?"

Harrison's mood lightened as he again marvelled at the child's thirst for knowledge.

"How would you like to take a trip there to experience the tide firsthand?" the child's grandfather asked.

"For real?" Jasmine jumped to her feet.

"It just so happens that your grandma and I are in the process of planning a trip to the east coast. The Hopewell Rocks and Bay of Fundy are on our list. Perhaps Mommy can take some time and join us too."

Jasmine clapped her hands. "And Mr. Somerville? Can he come?"

Warmth flooded Harrison's chest. Did Jasmine really want him along on a family vacation? He shot a look at her grandparents. Maybe they wouldn't be thrilled at the idea of a stranger tagging along.

"If Harrison would like to join us, he is most certainly welcome, but I think we need to speak to Mommy first."

The mouthful of scrambled eggs he'd just swallowed scrambled up his insides. The state of his and Lily's relationship was still in limbo in his mind. And he needed resolution one way or the other. Half an hour passed quickly. Harrison thoroughly enjoyed getting to know Lily's family. They were people that he would like even if they weren't Lily's parents.

As they all stood and carried their trays to the garbage pails, cleared them of any leftovers, and set them on top, Jasmine entwined her tiny fingers with his. "Are you coming with us to see Mommy?"

"I certainly am, but I have a stop to make first. I'll meet you up there." He smiled at Jasmine.

The child giggled and skipped to join her grandparents.

The first thing that caught Harrison's eyes in the gift shop sent a shock wave through him. What were the odds that there would be something so appropriate for their situation? He made the quick purchase and, with as much pep as he could muster in his awkward painful steps, approached Lily's room.

It was difficult waiting, but he hung back and allowed Jasmine and Lily's parents time with her. He listened as they enthusiastically shared their plans for the Maritimes with Lily.

"Do you think you'll be joining us for our trip to the east coast?" Stephanie asked her daughter. "If not, do we have your permission to take Jasmine along with us?"

"Please say yes, Mommy, I really want you to come. And Mr. Somerville is coming too." Jasmine skittered another wink in his direction.

Again, Harrison's heart felt three sizes too big. He loved this little girl so much. How that was possible in a few short weeks was beyond his ability to understand. But it had happened. And he was glad. If things didn't work out with Lily, he didn't know what he'd do if he couldn't see Jasmine again.

All eyes landed on him and he cleared his throat. "I'm flattered that I'm invited, but I'm not sure I could get the time off work, or if you'd even want me along. This is family time and I'm only ..."

"What a great idea, Mom and Dad. I would love to go. It will give me a chance to rest and recuperate before I go back to work." Lily's eyes locked on his. "And don't be silly, Harrison. Of course, we want you along." When she smiled, exposing that dazzling dimple, Harrison's extra-large heart felt like it would burst from his chest. That was all he needed to hear. Did it mean what he thought it could?

"Then give me the dates and I'll harass my boss for vacation until he gives in." Harrison's firm answer elicited another ear-piercing screech from Jasmine.

"Remember, Jasmine, I asked you to stop doing that," Harrison scolded gently. "There are a lot of sick patients here who need their rest. You don't want to get us kicked out now, do you?"

"Oh no. I hadn't thought of that." Jasmine pressed her lips together and made a zippering motion with a finger across her mouth. "I'm sorry. I will absolutely attempt to amend my outbursts."

"I'm in agreement." Mr. Reinhardt pressed a hand to his chest. "Whenever you screech like that Jasmine, your grandpa just about needs CPR."

"I'm really sorry, Grandpa. I don't want anything to happen to you. Do you forgive me?" Jasmine hugged him around the waist.

"That's okay, darling. All is forgiven. Just work at that, okay?" Sam wrapped his arms around her.

A soft tap and the door to Lily's room opened. A kitchen employee carried in her lunch tray.

"I think it's time we left and let your mommy eat." Stephanie reached for Jasmine's hand.

"We'll be back to see you tomorrow, sweetie." Sam kissed Lily's forehead and headed for the door.

"We're praying for you, honey. Get well soon." Stephanie brushed her daughter's hair back from her forehead and Lily smiled up at her.

"I'm so happy you're feeling better, Mommy. I'll be back tomorrow to tell you more about the moon and its effect on the tides."

Lily grinned and hugged her daughter. "I can't wait. How did you know I've always wondered about the science behind that amazing phenomenon?" Her eyes followed her daughter as the little girl skipped from the room.

Suddenly, the room was silent. Too silent. Again, Harrison found himself at a loss for words. Why was it so hard to talk about the issue that had kept him awake all night and tormented him every minute?

"Is that for me?" Lily pointed at the gift bag.

"Oh yes." Harrison winced as he limped forward and plopped it on her bed. His calf had a persistently annoying heartbeat. But his wound paled in comparison to hers. The pain relievers would kick in shortly and he'd been fine.

Lily removed the gift from the bag and held it up. Her eyes widened. A tear escaped and rolled down to her chin. She swiped at it with a hand. "How in the world did you ever find this?"

Harrison fought his own emotions as he stared at the piece of driftwood with three intricately carved, wooden mallards perched on top. It was such an incredible reminder of how God had not only used nature to help him find Lily but had obviously been in control of every detail of the rescue. The appropriateness of the gift was the confirmation that sealed God's involvement in Harrison's mind.

"It makes me want to laugh and cry at the same time," Lily whispered. "Harrison, what you did for me yesterday was ..." Her voice broke. "You didn't wait for the police but, despite the dangers and risks, charged ahead to find me. Some might call that foolish, but I call it..."

Harrison reached for her hand and stroked it with his thumb as the traumatic events of yesterday charged through him.

Lily drew in a shuddering breath. "Well, just the most wonderful thing anyone's ever done for me. Every time I gaze at this gift, I'll remember how you saved my life."

Her words came with a look that sent a charge of heat radiating through Harrison's hand, up his arm, across his shoulders and into his chest. *I love this woman.* And it had happened so quickly. When he least expected it. It blew his mind to think he didn't even know Lily a few weeks ago. He felt as though he'd known her his whole life.

But did she feel the same?

"What is it that you wanted to tell me yesterday before that nurse made you leave?" Lily's eyes probed his.

"Did you mean it?"

"Mean what?

"The words you said just before the paramedics arrived."

Lily's brow furrowed. "Things are kind of fuzzy. I do recall some teasing about a missing pulse and soft driftwood." She tapped a finger to her cheek.

Harrison's shoulders sagged. "You heard that, did you? I was kind of hoping you didn't. What can I say? I was panicking and thought I'd lose ..." Now his voice was cracking.

Lily pulled herself up a little straighter on the bed. "I also remember you saying that you were worried because you made a promise to Jasmine that you would find me, and you were afraid you wouldn't be able to keep that vow."

A drop of sweat trickled down the side of his face. With a quick swipe of the back of his sleeve, it was gone. Why were hospital rooms so incredibly warm? "You whispered something to me too."

"I did? What did I say?" Lily's eyes twinkled, and her cheek dimpled. The message she sent was playful and sent his heart rate sprinting.

Harrison's lips twitched. "Oh, I think you remember all right. I'm going to ask you again. Did you mean it?"

A sly smile graced her face, but she didn't say a word.

"So, that's how we're going to play the game. We've come full circle here. I understand your strategy."

But he didn't like it one little bit. She was throwing the ball back in his court. Making him take the shot. His heart pounded, and his breath hitched in his throat. He let go of her hand and raked a hand through his hair. His nerves skittered to and fro throughout his entire body. He shoved his hands in his pockets and walked back to the window.

Could he tell her how he truly felt? It meant risking everything. If he took the throw, hit the backboard, and missed the net, he'd never try again. But this time things were different. Weren't they? He'd never felt such a deep attraction that went beyond the surface. But would she take a chance with him considering her failed, still painful, past marriage?

"Harrison?" He turned back to her. Lily's smile was tight now, the twinkle and dimple gone. He was worrying her. Time to lay it all on the line.

He stepped to the side of her bed, grabbed the metal bed rungs with both hands to squelch the trembling, and held on for dear life. "Lily, over the last few weeks, my life has been literally flipped upside down and inside out. It all started the day I found Jasmine dangling from that tree for dear life. Then you barrelled full speed into the back of my truck and it didn't take long for you to barrel into my heart too."

A bright crimson flush crept up her neck and into her cheeks.

"Several months ago, I'd come to Piney Campground just about at the end of my rope. I'd been searching for meaning for almost a year. Deep inside I knew there was more to life than what I had experienced. In fact, there was an incredible void. To be honest, I didn't even know what was missing. I was about to give up when ... well, I have to say that God works in mysterious ways."

"Looking back over the last few weeks, God not only revealed his truth during that powerful storm, but he allowed me to meet two very special people. I think you know how I feel about Jasmine."

Lily covered one of the hands gripping the railing with hers. Her bottom lip quivered.

He couldn't help himself; he covered her hand with his other one. "I'm in love with you, Lily. Deeply. I want to protect you with every ounce of breath in me. For the rest of my life. If you will let me."

Lily closed her eyes as tears trailed down her flushed cheeks. A basketball-sized lump lodged itself in his throat. His heart pounded against his ribcage. What would she say? Would she tell him to take a hike? The silence was killing him.

"I know how you feel." Her words were shaky, but she met his gaze and held it. "To be honest, the last thing I was looking for was a relationship. It's only been a year since the divorce and the wounds I sustained during my marriage still run deep."

Harrison clenched his teeth as he remembered her ex-husband's cowardly flight from the coffee shop.

"But from that first day, when I totally humiliated myself and rammed into the back of your truck, I could barely look you in the eyes because the attraction was so strong. It shocked me. I thought you were the most incredibly handsome man on the planet and I didn't know what to do with those feelings. But I know a physical attraction, although important, is not what will make a good relationship. Ross was a handsome man but ..."

Lily licked her lips and continued. "And Jasmine was right. God kept dropping you in our paths and it was getting harder and harder for me to ignore the attraction. My head denied it, but my heart was telling me something else. There is definitely something happening between us and I believe it's good, but I'm a little scared."

"To be honest, I'm scared too. I haven't had a great track record with women. But, I was up most of the night thinking and praying and this is what I arrived at just before dawn. Why don't we take it slow? Spend time together, you, me, Jasmine and, occasionally, your parents. We can take it one step at a time and see how things go."

He had to work to force the words out. Take it slow? That wasn't what he really wanted to do. But it was the right thing for their situation, since they were both skittish.

Full of emotion, her moist, hazel eyes grew large. "I'm touched that you have prayed about us and are willing to wait."

Harrison squeezed her hand tightly. "Time spent with you and Jasmine will not be arduous."

"And you love Jasmine. You don't know how special that is to me. To be honest, she is a hard child to know and understand, let alone love. But you've managed to do that, and very, very quickly."

Harrison's throat tightened. He couldn't speak for fear he'd blubber some unintelligible sentence and reveal the sap that lived inside. It was true. Somehow God had given him a deep affection for the spunky, gifted child.

When Lily touched his cheek with her other hand, he thought he'd come unglued. He couldn't take his eyes from her lips. An intense desire to lean down and kiss her almost won out, but he'd just told her that they should take it slow. Bummer! Restrained by his own advice, he brought her hand to his lips and planted a soft kiss on her palm.

"Have a good rest, Lily. I'll come by tomorrow." Why was it so hard to go?

The next second, Lily's eyelids drifted shut. Clutching her hand tightly, he stayed a few more minutes, until her breathing became regular. He gazed down at her adoringly. *I hope I don't have to wait too long.* But then, the best things in life were worth waiting for. With reluctance, he gently placed her delicate, soft hand on the hospital bedding and slipped quietly from the room.

Life was incredibly good. God loved him. And Lily just might too.

CHAPTER FIFTY

Harrison listened intently as Allison, the Bay of Fundy's National Park tour guide, led the group of about thirty enthusiastic nature lovers along the bottom of the bay at Alma Beach. "At low tide, one can walk more than a kilometre from the high tide line across the tidal flats to the water's edge."

This was Harrison's first visit to the area and he was enjoying every minute of it. Anything nature-related fascinated him.

Jasmine, clad in rubber boots, held her pail for collecting. In her eagerness to learn, she was only steps behind the nature guide. The guide had informed the group that they were only allowed to gather stones or sea glass, not sea life.

Harrison hoped Jasmine would allow the guide to lead. Lily had warned her daughter to offer information with respect and courtesy. The guide held up a sand dollar that she had picked up from the ocean floor. Jasmine's eyes grew large.

Lily, who was holding his left hand, tugged him down until her lips were level with his ear. "Jasmine is behaving herself."

"Yes, she is." He smiled as he straightened up.

A surge of joy flooded Harrison as he thought back over the last few months. Everything that had happened seemed almost surreal. To think that, not very long ago, he was lost in his journey to find the meaning of life. All those lonely despondent nights staring at the moon for answers.

But all of that had changed. It began with Jasmine and Lily. What if he hadn't taken that far loop of the camp road while on patrol? And what if he'd been blaring his truck radio and never heard the screech from the precious child dangling from a tree branch? Even worse, what if he'd lost Lily and Jasmine to the mentally unstable kidnapper?

It was crazy to think like that now. Instead, he would count his blessings. He squeezed Lily's hand. "Lily?"

She looked up at him with furrowed brow. "Is something wrong?"

"Wrong? Heavens no." He bit back the words that he really wanted to say. Words that went something like, *I'm deeply, head-over-heels in love with you. And I really don't want to take it slow anymore.*

Lily's shy smile made her full lips extremely enticing. His eyes locked onto them like a missile on its target. If it was up to him, he'd steal a kiss. He wouldn't care if the entire village of Alma saw. But that sort of public display of affection would embarrass Lily so he restrained himself.

Suddenly Jasmine was in front of them, talking a mile a minute as the tour ended and their group headed back to the shoreline.

"Did you enjoy yourself?" Harrison patted the young child's head.

"You bet I did." Jasmine clomped alongside them in her muddy boots. "Allison is super. Not at all like 'Old Cranky Pants' at the campground." Her words, followed by an obnoxious snort, had to have been caught by most of the group, including the guide.

"I'm glad to know that." Allison laughed.

Harrison fired a gaze at Lily who was shaking her head and biting her lower lip.

"It's my fault. I asked Jasmine to forget about that inappropriate nickname, but I guess she didn't." He shrugged as the tourists in the crowd began to go their separate ways.

"Kids have long memories." Lily's dimpled smirk sent his heart rate thundering loudly in his chest. Yep, he had it bad and he knew it.

Jasmine wandered away from them, sidetracked by twin boys about her age who had apparently discovered something interesting in the mud.

"I'm a little warm." Harrison removed his jacket.

"You are?" Lily wrapped her arms around herself, hugging the navy sweatshirt that Harrison had bought her to her body. "That breeze is cool. Of course, it is late September."

He slung his jacket over his arm, stepped in front of her, and turned his back. His heart flipped and flopped while he waited. He had no idea how she was going to react. When he heard laughter, he relaxed ... slightly.

"I can't believe you got a Captain Addlepated T-shirt made. I love the park ranger figure wearing a cape and blowing on a large campfire."

Slowly he turned. His heart was about to climb out of his throat. Just how would she respond?

Still laughing, Lily read the words aloud from the front of his shirt. "Captain Addlepated requests the hand of his ... Lily ... flower ... in marriage." Lily gasped. Her hand flew up and covered her mouth while her hazel eyes grew enormous. Then moist.

Oh boy. He'd made her cry. Were those happy tears that women sometimes got? If not, he was in deep trouble.

Lily fingered the diamond ring on the chain looped around his neck. "It's so pretty. It's in the shape of a star."

"I chose that shape, so we'll never forget that starry night on the beach when God performed three miracles." Harrison's gut clenched as he watched her. What was she thinking?

"Three?" Lily's voice squawked. She swiped one hand across her wet cheek and studied the ring in her open palm.

"He dissipated the storm. He saved my confused heart. And he gave me you."

Lily fell against his T-shirt—her tears soaking his proposal.

"I know we said we'd take it slow. But ..." He spoke into her hair as his hands encircled her waist.

Lily tipped her head up to look at him, a sassy grin on her face. "Slow is for turtles."

Did her dimple just wink at him? He must be delirious with emotion. Harrison's heart was acting insanely crazy, as if it was doing a funky dance inside him. "Does that mean your answer is yes?"

"You really do fit your name, Captain Addlepated. Yes, of course I'll marry you."

Barely able to contain himself, he let out a whoop, picked her up by the waist, and twirled her in a circle. After setting her down gently, he claimed those delicious lips that had mesmerized him all day. And he didn't care how many people were watching.

At that moment, Harrison Somerville was higher than any ocean tides in the world would ever be. And with Lily at his side, he knew he always would be.

ABOUT THE AUTHOR

The desire of L. D. Stauth's heart is to encourage readers through the written word. An avid camper, she continually marvels at God's creation revealed in nature. Her husband of forty-two years, four children, and eight grandchildren bring her much joy, and sometimes fodder for her stories. A medical lab technologist by profession, L. D. has been writing for many years. She has had both poetry and articles published. The three novels in her *Campground Series* are filled with laughter, romance, suspense and, most importantly, the love and truth about Jesus Christ.

Also by the Author

Stormy Lake
A Campground Mystery, Book One

A camping trip with creepy spiders and menacing thunderstorms? Seriously? Little did Maya realize those fears would be the least of her worries.

Maya Montgomery is in desperate need of a vacation. When her best friend, Karly Foster, convinces her that a camping trip in Northern Ontario will be the remedy she needs, Maya is skeptical. After all, she has never camped a day in her life.

The moment Kerrick Kendall, park superintendent at Lake Williwaw Campground, lays eyes on the novice camper with the dancing freckles and large coffee-coloured eyes, he feels compelled to tell her his story.

But is opening up old wounds worth the risk?

From frightening encounters with nature, to non-stop—often humourous—bickering between her friend Karly and an irritating park employee, the trip is filled with conflict.

But when Maya suspects she is being stalked, everything else that has happened pales in comparison.

As danger escalates will Kerrick be able to protect the life of the woman who has captured his heart?

**Lake of the Cross
A Campground Mystery, Book Two**

Tumbling waterfalls, white pelicans, and sweet serenity were just a few of the reasons Karly Foster became a park naturalist. But when rumours of an unsolved murder surface and a friend mysteriously disappears, Karly's world becomes anything but peaceful. Then, as if she needed her tranquility shattered further, her ex-boyfriend, Blake, literally flies back into her life.

Blake Fenton, the owner of Wilderness Bush Adventures, can't believe it. Was that really Karly Foster he'd just flown to the Aspen Ridge Emergency, suffering from heat stroke? After three years, she has gotten even more beautiful ... if that were possible. It quickly becomes apparent, however, that flying sparks between him and his feisty former flame could leave nasty burns. Again.

Then Blake makes a horrifying discovery, and strange and terrifying events begin to unfold. As Blake wrestles with fear for Karly's safety and confusion over his feelings for her, his wilderness-guide friend, Henry, implores him to seek God for answers. For centuries, God has been revealing Himself to the locals in Henry's remote community—in a very unusual way.

When Blake and Karly join forces to compete in the No Trace Canoe Race, they find themselves fighting, not just to win, but to stay alive. Because someone has committed murder in the campground, and the killer's sights have turned on them.

Do Blake and Karly have a future together? Or will this moment, when they have finally found each other again, be the last one they ever share?